Also by La'Von Gittens

The Divine Apocalypse Series

Book 1: *The Beginning of the End*
Book 2: *Addiction and Clearing*
Book 3: *Attis*
Book 4: *Coming soon...*

Nonfiction

Chicken Caesar Salad For the Gay Soul

DIVINE APOCALYPSE

The Beginning Of The End

La'Von Gittens

First published by NoV'al Publishing in 2010

Republished by NoV'al Publishing in 2021

Copyright ©2010

This book is a work of fiction. Names, characters, places, and incidents are either the product of the author's imagination or are used fictitiously, and any resemblance to actual persons, living or dead, business establishments, events, or locales is entirely coincidental.

First paperback published in 2010 Reprinted in 2021.

All rights reserved. No part of this book may be reproduced or used in any manner without written permission of the copyright owner except for the use of quotations in a book review.

ISBN: 978-0-9843466-0-8 (paperback)

Published by NoV'al Publishing

www.novalpublishing.com

Thank you to all my family and friends who helped me along this journey

> "Religion comprises a system of wishful illusions together with a disavowal of reality, such as we find in an isolated form nowhere else but in amentia, in a state of blissful hallucinatory confusion."
> **Sigmund Freud**

Every New Yorker knows the cautionary warnings of the midday street preacher. We hear these apocalyptic predictions every day but often dismiss them as the nonsense of a maniac or conspiracy theorist. Their speeches are intense but filled with conviction, passion and often revolve around similar themes and details—not everyone is as crazy as you think.

Since the beginning of time, religion and mental illness have been intertwined. As divine intervention has been linked to bipolar disorder and schizophrenia to demonic possession, understanding these truths is left for interpretation. In some religions, the mentally ill are the chosen—as they claim they can see into an invisible world, while other prophets are locked away as lunatics.

Science calls the ability to pass memories down throughout generations "collective memory," while religion names it "reincarnation." Regardless of how you define it, buried in our subconscious are pivotal celestial events, spiritual lessons we are all born with. There is more to instinct, emotion, memory, and feeling than can be explained.

In a world governed by the unseen and unexplainable you cannot always trust your mind.

All myths have a seed of truth.

Prologue

"If one wishes to form a true estimate of the full grandeur of religion, one must keep in mind what it undertakes to do for men. It gives them information about the source and origin of the universe, it assures them of protection and final happiness amid the changing vicissitudes of life, and it guides their thoughts and emotions by means of precepts which are backed by the whole force of its authority.... Religion is an illusion, and it derives its strength from the fact that it falls in with our instinctual desires."

Sigmund Freud, New Introductory Lectures on Psychoanalysis

"'Who has seen a beautiful lady, being led by the dead?'" the frail man sang to himself as he inspected every nook of the cafe with a long black cane. Fresh and earthy, the scent of coffee grounds rustled his long white nose hairs and filled his weak lungs twice their dried size. Wearily he sang as though he were gasping for air, "'Did you hear, my Constantine, what the little birds have said? They are little birds; let them sing. There are little birds, prayers on wing.'"

He could smell it; something was under the sugary notes of cakes and cookies. It was beneath the bouquet of perfumes and shampoos, then beyond the whiff of salted skin and spiced blood—this coffee shop was alive.

"'And a little further on their way, other birds called and said,'" he serenaded whimsically as he tipped his large black Amish hat to a passing pedestrian. The Mermaid Cafe was built on the ground with a heartbeat. It surged with consuming energy that kept the tiny eatery filled with many frequenters.

"'Isn't pity and unfair, very strange, the alive to walk along with the dead?'"

Industrial sized cappuccino machines steamed hot milk under the massive green mermaid logo. He was sure his acolytes were here—hidden among the decorative ceramic mugs, stuffed animals, and designer hot chocolate bags. He could sense an invisible audience on this living ground—the demonic spectators to a private baptism.

"'Did you hear, my Constantine, what the little birds have said? That the alive walk along...with the dead...'"

With purpose, the wrinkled man buried his cane into the green carpet and pronounced through rotten teeth, "Come now, don't be shy! You have summoned me here, and I have prepared the ritual."

As all the attention fell onto him, he adjusted his dusty black suit and continued in a husky spill, "Tired? Alone? Weighted down by humanity? You will never be cleansed! You will never be purified, never! You know you don't belong here. That is why you summoned me; that is why you need me!"

Collectively the crowd rolled their eyes and continued about their day. In New York, street preaching was more frequent than the A train. Irritation shook through his bones fingers as he protested, "This is a test; you know what is required! Stand up, have faith in me! You know why I'm here."

In a nearby booth, a patron's palms nervously sweated. The younger man's heart pounded so slowly in his chest that he thought he would faint. He threw his shoulder-length dark locks behind his tiny pale ear then wiped grease and soil from his cheeks. All his life, he knew the words of this Amish preacher to be real: There was nothing in his heart but hatred—

raw and robust—but sedated by society and social order. He did not belong… but when his recurring nightmares and lucid dreams led him to make specific promises to bodiless voices… Could this all be real? Did he call this spirit?

His skin was hot with anticipation. He wanted to believe so severely, and blindly he followed through. With this creature before him in living flesh, he was happier than he had ever been. Remorselessly, he looked over to his wife, who had been nervously watching the scene.

"Show yourself!" The older man was getting impatient.

It was now or never. With a toss of oily hair, he grabbed his wife from behind her neck and dragged her into the Mermaid Cafe center.

"What are you doing? Get off me!" she screamed, but his heartbeat drowned out her voice in his head.

Breathlessly, he struggled to hold her as she yelped and failed to escape his grasp. Her shouts drew all the attention of the other patrons. But he could not stop—he was too deep in. He approached the Amish man dressed in black and announced, "I am the White Horseman of the North. I bring my wife as an offering…"

"Now, what the Hell is going on here!" the manager of the cafe interrupted. "Leave now, or we're calling the police!"

As soon as the manager had spoken, he dropped dead. Almost instantly, New Yorkers fearfully disbursed through a cafe in shrieks of terror as, one by one, half of the group fell lifelessly. Prisoners, the surviving members, attempted to escape, but the doors were mystically locked, trapping the mob inside.

"Ascend my child," the crippled spirit welcomed the oily couple.

A blue-eyed spectator advanced from the shadows and threw her glossy blonde hair backward. With eyes like enchanted diamonds, rosy cheeks, and perfectly painted lips, the woman wore a pink undershirt beneath a white blouse, under a blue cardigan tied around her shoulders.

He recognized her immediately. They'd met before… at club Solace. He stepped out of his marriage for this woman… not too many nights ago.

Lilith shined a flawless grin and daintily crossed the floor. It wasn't until she was closer did he realize she was pregnant. She opened his hand, placed an upright golden cross in it, and then slowly turned it upside down to invert it.

Leaning over, she whispered, "Don't make this awkward…"

He blinked in confusion, but as his wife struggled beneath him, he had to focus. Holding his breath, he spoke, "Over this death, I prophesy that mothers shall but smile as they run nails under their infant's eyes. Each heart on earth will understand my pain..."

The White Horsemen shoved the cross into his wife's neck.

As the crowd shouted in fear, the street preacher opened his arms as if waiting for a second person from the group to speak out. There was a scream from the center of the mob. A man fell to the ground as his brother dragged him before the Amish man.

"You understand me making you wait," his voice rang with a wild and uncontrollable dominance. His straight red hair was pulled back into a stringy ponytail, and his thin lips curled with a perverted pleasure as he continued, "Tactical move and all... Had to let you make the first move to make sure it was you."

He crippled his brother with a blow to the knee and took him by the throat. Covered in piercings, he had found excitement in pain but never experienced a more mind-blowing high than when he inflicted it on others. "Got me, brother, here—big thing, ain't he? I am War the Horseman of the West, and I'm here to start a war, simple as that, amen."

Lilith handed him the cross, and without hesitation, the Red Horseman slaughtered his brother.

The Amish preacher watched as the man bled out until a particular weeping caught his attention. "Come now, let us reveal ourselves..."

From the crowd waddled a seven-foot-tall man. He weighed just shy of six-hundred pounds and carried a crying six-year-old in his arms. The overweight man was bald and sweated profusely. He, too, sobbed with an emotion somewhere between regret and fulfillment.

"Why are you crying?" the Amish man asked.

"This is my little sister..." the heavyset man blubbered. The small girl grabbed at his neck and snuck her face into his pasty flesh in pure fright.

"And?"

It took him a moment. "I want to eat her," he woefully admitted.

"Go right ahead," the preacher smiled.

"No!" the girl shouted, "I want to go home!"

"A quart of wheat for a day's wages, and three quarts of barley for a day's wages, and do not damage the oil and the wine! I am the Black Horseman of the East," he sobbed, "and I... I'm so hungry! I'm sorry little sister; I can't help it, you look delicious..."

When the Black Horseman started to bite off his sister's fingers, the crowd cried in horror, but the preacher cooed with satisfaction, "Embrace who you are..."

"I brought one too." A stylish blonde man walked out of the crowd and rolled an infant on the consecrated floor like a bowling ball. "Damn, thought I would be the only one smart enough to bring a kid."

He cleared a wheeze in his throat and ornately lit a cigarette. This man was an albino and was more dapper than anyone in the room. Smugly he announced, "I am the Yellow Horseman of the South. I brought a baby because I figured the whole circle of life things…" He took a deep inhale of his cigarette and released a confident huff of smoke, "What most people don't realize is that no one is owed life. Not even this child… So there you go… poetry."

The polished albino stomped on the child below his feet. The infant's scream was like a piglet's, and the entire room shuddered helplessly at the gooey display of new organs.

"The positions you have just taken should not be engaged frivolously…"

One by one, all remaining humans in the room dropped dead, sacrifices to the unholy audience. Finally, everything was silent. The Amish man raised his hands in victory. "I am your Hallowed One," he introduced himself. "This vow extends your physical existence and destruction. Your jobs must be completed…There will always be the Four Horsemen of the Apocalypse. As they shall be ensured by my blessings and the celestial exalt of my touch."

A stir of whispers swept into the room as the invisible chorus celebrated. In the order of which they presented, the Horsemen disappeared in a clap of thunder as the remaining humans slowly died.

"Come!" they yelled in unison as they departed.

Bursting ashes from the blaze brushed across the White Horsemen's pale cheek like fiery dandelion seeds. It was only a few hours later, but the scene was incredible. He could feel the death dissolve into the atmosphere as the cracking flames engulfed Manhattan Bridge.

It was beautiful.

Thirty-foot long, red and orange tongues of fire danced across the bridge and crisped everything in its path, leaving the air filled with the smell of burning metal and gasoline. Within minutes, the 6,000-foot pathway became burning genocide. He didn't know these people, but he wanted them all dead.

This was a revolution; he was their leader. Ever since he was a human child, the White Horseman always knew he was capable of this destruction, although he never believed he would see it. Now, he was so much more than human, blessed with the touch of Hades; he felt invincible.

"Magnificent," he muttered as his fingers tightened around his ivory bow. The long-range weapon vibrated with an unquenchable power. He was a different person now; everything was different. Pestilence was the demon he had invited into his human body. He willingly shared his flesh so long as it could assuage the hatred in his soul.

Burning down Manhattan Bridge was an excellent start.

As both exits were sealed, many plebeians left their vehicles and tried to escape on foot. However, the Hallowed One had designed this trap as a murderous playground for his children and perfectly crafted to keep the victims there.

Snuggly, the White Horseman beheld his gift from the Hallowed One. Invisible to the crowd, he fired round after round of flaming arrows into the fleeing mass.

With a small pointed sword, War lopped off the heads of anyone he could catch. He was violent and wild—as if he was continually fighting the urge not to fight. Usually unstable, the Red Horseman was now focused when in his element.

The Horseman of Hunger and Disease embodied his namesake with open cysts on his pasty pale skin and enlarged stomach. His odd shape reminded the White Horseman of a rotting boiled egg with toothpicks for limbs—but much more terrifying. With his gray human teeth, the Black Horseman ripped at the humans who had fallen, unable to resist the tasty smell of their spilled blood. He was given a set of ivory scales, which helped him manipulate gravity and balance.

Last in line was a thinner man, the Yellow Horseman—Death gathered the recently departed souls. Like a ghost, he floated over the burning victims and, with a mysterious scythe, guided them into a world unknown.

This was only the beginning.

Bright and festive, the streets were swarmed with hundreds of people eager for the New Year. Jackie Adams had fought for weeks to cover the station's midnight bash. The night was a news correspondent's dream, as pedestrians flocked the streets hoping to get a glimpse of the traditional ball-dropping in Times Square. Fanatics dressed in colorful glasses and hats expressed both excitement and fears for the new year.

Puck, the cameraman, ignored the cold and the cheering crowd as he rapped along with the song playing on his cordless headphones,

"'The name's Anansi, I got coin, and I fancy,

Pretty girls, short skirts, no panty,

Uh, and against all odds,

Fuck the Twilight of the Gods

Fear not, I'm the king of the block

Bitch, now suck my Ragnarok!'"

The entire audience shuddered, and reporters alerted their cameramen as electronic numbers appeared on the large screen and counted down. Just as the ball dropped, a nervous wave shook the audience as Jackie Adams received a report live on air. Her jaw dropped as she snapped at Puck with his camera.

Manhattan Bridge was burning down.

Chapter 1: Enter Neil Qin

> "The Son of Man will send his angels, and they will collect out of his kingdom all who cause others to sin and all evildoers."
> **Matthew 13:41**

    Bitter murmurs fogged the outside with apocalyptic rumors, but Neil's windows trapped the dry heat in his apartment. The entire room smelled like salted sex. Luminous fingertips gently flowed from the fireplace and warmed the small collection of football trophies and academic achievements that hung around the living room. Shadows from the fire crawled across the mundane brick walls and shaded patterns on his journalism degree and three award-winning articles on political injustice.

    Though Christmas had passed weeks ago, the room remained unchanged, and the aging decor appeared bare and joyless. A small voice whispered through his lifeless condominium; its dull sound echoed across the kitchen's minimally decorated living room. An overused, dirty coffee machine sat atop the counter beside the flat-screen television that was always on.

    A news reporter's ornate speech seeped into the vintage apartment from the t.v. But Neil Qin ignored it and continued to watch the ants crawl across the stained oak countertop. It had been a few weeks, but the media was still looking for someone to blame for the terrorist attack on Manhattan Bridge.

"Neil?" her voice was like a horn. "Is that my voice I hear out there?"

He had almost forgotten she was still in his bed. Jackie Adams of Channel 7 News was a blonde-haired, hazel-eyed bombshell who Neil had met earlier that year at a journalist holiday celebration. She was just his type, 5'11, with a small waist and a pushy attitude.

"Don't flatter yourself. The t.v. is on," Neil corrected as he watched a prerecorded taping of a report Jackie made earlier that day. The terrorist attack on Manhattan Bridge was still making headlines—the public begged for an answer. You write it t.v. above but T.V here. I would stick with t.v.

"Do I sense a hint of jealousy? Keep working, and maybe you'll get on t.v. someday," Jackie giggled. "Come back to bed."

"I don't want to be on t.v., and I'm eating," Neil huffed.

He was hunched over a flat plate of piping hot microwaved lasagna and stared at the empty chair beside him. He took a deep inhalation of the rancid aroma and pushed a wave of his chestnut hair from his dark eyes and dust-colored face. A massive stone sat in Neil's stomach and left no room for food. He poked at his t.v. dinner several times with his fork, flirting with the long white tendrils of steam that slithered in the air like dancing snakes.

Unnerved, he was unsure of the source of this depression, and it was impossible to ignore. Yet here he sat, feeling the same way he had for years now—uninspired and hopeless.

Underfed and unsatisfied, he walked into the living room and sank into his tattered brown leather couch, and gazed at his accomplishments with displeasure. Neil wrote for Pluck A Feather Magazine and quickly outshined his mentors. He was young and deservingly successful but felt his life was a worthless puzzle with too many missing pieces.

Black-brown and heavy, Neil's dynamic eyebrows demanded respect for the struggle they exhibited. Success was critical to Neil though he never really enjoyed the attention. But as competitive as he was, there was just no other option.

Middle-class parents raised Neil with strong religious morals and a faith that they pressed upon their loving child. When he was fourteen, he caught chickenpox and had to stay home from their weekly church visits. That Sunday, his church burned down, trapping and killing both his parents. He hadn't touched a bible since. He always questioned if there was more to life than what he saw before him.

When he aged out of the orphanage, he lived alone and scraped by on earnings he made as a cashier at a local grocery store. Eventually, he worked his way through college, earned a master's in Journalism, and then secured himself a job with Pluck A Feather Magazine. Often admired for his testimony, he remained indifferent. There was nothing in life but routine, work, and death.

Neil took a sip of wine and grabbed a pen and pad of paper. He ran his fingers across the brown scruff above his lip, the neat, hardly-there beard on his chin, and gazed at his notebook. Neil had to interview an actor at a rooftop party the next day, but his fear and big-mouthed but sexy bedroom blonde kept him distracted. Unable to think of a single question for the actor, he filled his barrel chest with dead air and tried to relax. He knew he could write a great article regardless, but he always preferred to be prepared.

"Neil! Get your ass down here!"

He followed the voice to the window and paused in awe of the red moon that appeared strangely bigger than usual. Neil recognized the sound and long blonde hair. His ex-girlfriend stuck her head out of her car window and slammed her fist on the car horn.

"It's the time!"

"Shit," Neil gasped.

"Everything okay out there?" Jackie called naked beneath the tattered bedspread.

"I gotta go," Neil said, shut the window. "Make sure the door is locked when you leave."

It seemed like Victoria Harvey, Neil's college girlfriend, was pregnant forever. He often wondered why they broke up, but it turned out the love between a college football player and cheerleader was not always a happy fate written in stone. Victoria complained that Neil was too focused on his studies, and he knew she was right. Once they graduated, he was deeply involved in his work that Victoria was left bitter, resentful, and pregnant. The two soon split with nothing but an unborn child between them.

She slid over into the passenger's seat as Neil jumped into the car. A thick black brow rose when he asked, "How did you do this by yourself?"

Victoria's blue eyes were arrows as she spat, "None of your damn business! Now, drive the damn car!"

He grunted then confidently drove over the speed limit toward the hospital. A bead of sweat trickled down Neil's face when his concentration began to wane. His skin felt warmer, and a headache entered his mind, accompanied by a distant static sound—Victoria's voice.

"God, the baby is coming now! I wish Neil would hurry up!"

Victoria was in labor, he knew, but his patience for her had run slim. He gave her another evil glance and looked back to the road before announcing, "I'm going as fast as I can. It would help if you were quiet!"

"I didn't say anything to you!" Victoria panted while sweat melted on her cheeks. Her hands grabbed the sides of her stomach, and her powder blue eyes met his in aggravation.

"I heard you," Neil retorted, turning a sharp corner.

"What the hell is wrong with him?" Victoria thought.

"Nothing is wrong with me," he grunted. "I just wanna concentrate on the road."

"Then concentrate!" Victoria shouted.

"I'm talking about me doing the best I can!" his voice dropped an octave as they entered the hospital parking lot.

Lungs full of hot air, he whipped out of the car and guided Victoria into the hospital lobby.

Victoria was lifted onto a bed when a young nurse pressed a hand on Neil's chest and stopped him from following his unborn child. "Sir, she's in good hands. The doctors will take it from here. Wait... are you the father? Because we're going to need some information..."

Beads of perspiration collected on Neil's face, "Y-yes..."

The nurse curled a string of red hair around her finger. *"Okay, a little greasy... but still kinda cute..."*

"I'm going to need you to fill out some paperwork. You can see your girlfriend soon..." she said with a wink.

He tried to focus his thoughts, but his temples pounded too heavily around a rising fever. Through his delirium, he nodded and grabbed the clipboard. Neil fell solidly into his seat, exhaled a hot breath of exhaustion, and tried to steady his dizziness.

Just as the light dimmed around him, his heart rate dramatically increased, and the fine chestnut hairs on his arms pointed. Something was about to happen. The room shook. Instantly he was alert, but it was as though no one else in the room noticed the quake.

A roar rattled paint-chips off the walls and ruptured Neil's eardrum like a railroad spike. Illustrious and with esoteric wisdom, a hungry lion was erected at the hospital's entryway. His dirty blonde mane was soaked in blood. It stared directly into Neil's eyes as if they were alone. No one seemed to notice the 250-pound beast as it began a bloody trot toward Neil. Bold but ghoulish, the creature left massive grisly footprints as he shuffled over the white and blue tile.

Rotten scents invaded his nostrils as the smell of sulfur and brimstone coiled in his stomach. Neil struggled to make sense of the scene; his heart was in his throat, and his mind fell blank. The mighty feline, engulfed with flames, approached. Invisible and silent to the rest of the room, the creature's voice shook the very floor beneath Neil's feet. Once he was face to face with the monster, Neil shut his eyes.

"Why don't you just hurry up and die, you old bastard, I'm sorry, Dad, but I just can't afford these weekly visits to the hospital. I have too many bills! Bills that your life insurance money could help fix! Boy, I'd be on easy street... Wow, that guy doesn't look so good."

What was that? Neil struggled to hold the clipboard between his hands. The lion was gone, and the room appeared normal. He shifted his gaze to the young man who pushed his father, who used a wheelchair, to the front desk.

"You okay, buddy?" he asked.

Neil nodded.

"Please," he said to the nurse as he smiled painfully and lied through his teeth, "I want my father to live. Do everything you can."

What was going on? Neil swallowed hard. What are these voices in my head? Why am I feeling so sick all of a sudden? Bursts of electricity exploded in his mind as he struggled to read the pages before him.

"Dumbass! Pay attention when I talk to you before I kick you in the nuts!"

Neil looked up to the small blonde girl who stood before him, holding a box of chocolates. She smiled, then tilted her head and repeated. "I said... 'Hi sir, would you like to buy a candy bar?'"

Quickly, Neil fought through his queasiness, fished a dollar from his shorts, and hesitantly bought a chocolate bar. As fast as he was able, Neil scribbled answers onto the clipboard and entered the labor room.

Victoria gave a loud, parched scream, her eyes narrowed into a complete line, and her mouth exposed all of her teeth. Neil grasped her hand and let her squeeze as tightly as she needed while Dr. Devanne worked.

"Everything will be okay. Just breathe..." Neil muttered.

"I am!" Victoria screamed.

Neil's fever grew more robust, and his headache pounded more intensely. "Just breathe..." he murmured as the room began to blur, and consciousness lifted from him like a puff of smoke.

Neil's brown eyes blinked in the fluorescent light above him as he awoke several moments later, realizing he was still in the hospital.

"I hope Alex remembered to get milk."

Sounds entered Neil's ears like water through a bursting dam.

"What?" he asked.

"Nothing..." the nurse spoke, entering the room, and pulling earphones from her ears. "You're up...?"

Neil shook his head slowly, "No, I heard you," he said, "something about milk."

The nurse backed up, then smiled. "Did I say that out loud? I guess you would like to see your baby now?" she asked. "Don't worry, lots of fathers faint at the sight of birth. It's nothing to be ashamed of."

"Hmph," Neil huffed, leaning over toward the glass of water, embarrassed of his shortcoming. "Yeah, right," he muttered as the nurse left the room.

"It's a boy," the nurse said as she returned and rested the child in Neil's arms. The baby had a head full of brown-black hair, like his father, and his pinkish face glowed. His hands and feet were so tiny. Neil had never been around a child so young—the size made it look so innocent... delicate...ignorant... and helpless. It had no idea what the world was like or the horrors that enviably waited for him.

Could I be a good father? Neil wondered. What can I offer a child when life is senseless? When we have no reason to continue... when all our actions are meaningless? Is there more to life than this?

The next day, Neil abruptly woke up to a shrieking alarm clock. He overslept but was still exhausted. The rooftop party was in a few hours. He sat on the side of his bed for a few seconds and recapped the night before. He realized he had forgotten to prepare questions for the actor, but forced the panic away with confidence and indifference. This interview was pivotal for the magazine, but he figured he'd do fine. He always did.

Again Neil drove over the speed limit. Like every other day, he stopped at a fast-food restaurant. He threw an old coffee-stained paper cup into the graveyard of empty wrappers at the bottom of his blue jeep. A shapely teenager was there to greet him when he drove up to the window. She fidgeted with her nose ring and licked some bright red lipstick off her teeth. "Good morning or whatever, my name is Clara, may I take your order, sir?"

He sighed, "Just a medium coffee."

"That's a dollar ninety-eight, sir," the youth said. Her voice broke with puberty and attitude.

Neil snagged a dollar and a handful of change from his pocket. The teenager brought over a paper cup filled to the top with the steaming hot brew. Slowly, trying to keep her balance, she reached the window and leaned out, holding the coffee far away from her body.

"Ay, Dios Mio!" she shouted as she tripped.

Before Neil could grab the beverage, it spilled. Steaming liquid burnt Neil's knees and stained the passenger seat.

"This is Versace!" Neil bellowed. An intense feeling erupted within him—a sense that pulled at every part of his body at the same time—a feeling that pounded loudly in his head—a feeling that telekinetically sent the yellow crowbar in the passenger's seat through the passenger window.

Chapter 2: I'm Aurora

"But of that day or hour, no one knows, neither the angels in heaven, nor the Son, but only the Father."
Mark 13:32

Her slender yet curvy body squirmed uncomfortably beneath the designer bedspread as her cellphone blared again. Aggravated and fatigued, she was careful not to smudge her guacamole facial mask, ignoring her phone until the caller left a voicemail. After the call ended, regretfully, she played it on speaker.

"Aurora! This is your mother calling *again*!" She didn't know why she listened to it. The voice boomed from the machine, "I know *you* left on bad terms, but I am still your mother, and you need to return my phone calls! After all that your father and I gave to you, how dare you still disrespect us? If you think you're an adult and have control over your own life, you're *completely* and utterly wrong! There are certain responsibilities that you will hold up to because you are part of this family! Aurora, you will call me back, you will move back home with your husband, and you will continue the Haith family line! End of story!" The message ended and filled the phone's memory.

Behind her floral green cake mask Aurora burned in wrath.

"How did you get my number again? Go to bed, you old crabby bitch!" she screamed.

Aurora squirmed uneasily and reminded herself that tonight's rest was essential for work the next night. In celebration of the new Sands' movie, a rooftop party was to be held at the city's most lucrative landmark, the Eugene Martinez Museum—and she was invited! The company was known for its lavish parties, and no celebrity, photographer, fashion editor, or socialite in Manhattan would miss it. It was crucial for her modeling career that she be flawless. Aurora growled as she accidentally smeared her guacamole face mask across her fingers and her white four-hundred count bed sheets.

"Damn it to hell!" she screamed. The model ripped off her eye mask and stomped into her bathroom. Her full lips thinned in anger while she swung open the cabinet door and reapplied her face mask.

Even with her face caked in green sludge, Aurora was stunning. Her skin was deep ebony, her dark hair spilled to her mid-back, and her eyes were a piercing copper brown—her left, bejeweled with a small black beauty mark. As a retired rugby player and pageant queen, she was admired for her beauty but feared her aggression and strength. Dragooned by her parents to marry at a young age, Aurora proved she could not be tamed, and once she had saved enough money, she moved to Manhattan to chase a career in modeling.

Her dainty feet flitted across her fluffy white carpet and the white kitchen tiles. Aurora's apartment was small, but her modern style expressed her flamboyance and poise. Elegance made her drool, and she would spend her last penny on anything designer. With a clean, crisp white color scheme, the living room was decorated with bold African art, immaculate glass tables, and pictures from her wedding with the groom's face sliced out.

A towering photograph of Aurora wrapped in nothing but her arms hung vainly in the center of the room. It drew in the eyes of anyone who entered and left them feeling belittled under her larger-than-life stare. Most of what was in her apartment, she stole from her affluent parents and loveless husband. Distant from her family and too ambitious for friends, she lived alone but never felt lonely.

Aurora searched through a refrigerator full of organic health foods and grabbed a bottle of distilled water as a cold, tight tremor ran down her spine. At first, she ignored the slight shiver. Then it hit her more intensely. Lightheaded,

Aurora placed the bottle on the marble counter as the feeling beat again.

She took a moment to compose herself, but a horn cut through the silence. Aurora's jaw dropped, and she knocked the bottle of water off the counter. Behind her stood a 1,500-pound white ox. The massive horned beast bellowed as its flesh crisped, and blood poured from it like molasses off a cotton ball.

"What the?" Aurora started, but before she could scream, the bloody ox exploded. A river of blood rushed through her living room like a lake bursting from a water balloon.

As if struck by lightning, she straightened out her back. Her arms slapped to her sides, and her fingers arched until they hurt. Her head jerked upward, and her mouth yanked open. Painfully stunned, she was in an ocean of needles washing over her.

First, there were screams. They sounded like squealing animals, and it made her stomach curdle.

Visions trampled through Aurora's mind.

The streets were on fire. Civilians trampled over the half-eaten rotted bodies of their neighbors. Broken glass and debris scattered among the red puddles while burning buildings blew dry ash into the already foul air.

Aurora begged to breathe as she witnessed Manhattan in an impossible transformation.

A familiar Fifth Avenue shoe store was utterly ransacked. Fresh brains smeared the cash register, and claw marks branded broken pieces of furniture. Walls graffitied with Chi-Rho symbols and upside-down crosses read: "God is dead! For he lives again! They are the Alpha, and they are the Omega! Save yourselves and die."

People rioted and fought each other in senseless and violent primordial war. Families were caged and burned alive like pork roasts in the open streets. Tanks and police cars shot down citizens as quickly as they would swat mosquitoes.

Images chaotically flashed before Aurora's eyes, and her very veins tighten as if to pull energy from her blood.

White lightning detonated in the dark sky. Skyscrapers were torn down and replaced with massive Egyptian pyramids. Winged leather beasts swarmed from the heavens, crawled out of the earth, and emerged from the waters. Like starved hyenas, they feasted on anyone they could catch—the horned creatures pounced on men and women in the roads and defiled them with an alien curiosity.

Unnatural sex ripped open soft human bodies as quickly as a child would tear apart pink paper. The lucky died instantly, while others were left with enough life to watch their mutilated remains crush under the rushing riot. With an undiscriminating glee, the monsters took them apart and played with their innards. People of all races genders and were served as edible sex toys to the rampaging monsters.

A sour taste entered Aurora's mouth while vision after vision hit her brain. Her eyes remained open in shock while the terrible movie played inside her. Aurora's fingers arched till her hands hurt. There was more coming, she could feel it, and this time she could scream as blood ran down her face in tears.

She saw a different time now... Closer to the present day...

A tall man dressed in a white cape fired an arrow between the eyes of a brown-haired stranger. He fell lifelessly in the Manhattan streets. Then she saw herself standing not too far from the dead man. A second man, pierced and wearing red leather, decapitated her with a small sword. A third man, young with curly black hair, fell quickly to the third man's scythe in a yellow fur coat. And finally, a blonde woman was chased down and turned to ash, disintegrated by an unbalanced pearl scale.

Exhausted from her vision, Aurora fainted and, while falling, bashed her head into the countertop. The foggy edges of the omen faded as blood mixed with her guacamole mask.

Several hours later, consciousness entered Aurora's body like an earthquake. She glared around and breathed heavily. The microwave read 5:39 pm, and she had to be out of the house in three hours. It was barely enough time for her to get ready. Aurora pressed play on her laptop and walked to the bathroom. She listened to her voice boom through the apartment as she recited the recording every morning.

"Hello, Aurora!" her voice echoed through the room, "today is going to be a great day because you're here to live it! Now it's time to dazzle everyone with your charisma, grace, and charm! Everyone is attracted to your good looks and positive energy! Those who aren't are just jealous! Aurora can if she believes she can!"

Her new diet pills. That was the only explanation for her strange dream. Aurora cleared her throat; she had to start getting ready. The model stared into her bathroom mirror, looking back at herself, covered in green and red. Aurora wiped the blood and guacamole from her face—nothing was going to stop her from attending this party, especially not some sleepwalking, crazy nightmare. Aurora pulled her hair from her face and smiled. She spoke in unison with her laptop, "Aurora, you are beautiful!"

Although she always thought it was beneath her, she couldn't afford a cab and had to take the subway. Her black designer dress hugged her hips and chest so tightly that she had to concentrate on not falling out of her outfit. Gold heels with sparkling chandelier earrings matched her jacket and oversized Italian leather purse.

A disheveled man entered the almost empty train car as she pulled out a fashion magazine. As she flipped through the pages, she studied the women in them when a nauseating smell flew up to her nostrils. "Can I have a dollar?"

Her heart pounded. She looked back down into her magazine and scowled, "'Can I have a dollar?' Wow. I wish it were that easy, but apparently, I have to work for a living. Why don't you learn to do the same?"

The man turned up his nose, but before he could react, someone shouted behind him.

"Aurora!" Rebecca Haith choked with astonishment. The middle-aged woman placed her slender white glove on her wrinkled cheek. "Oh honey, the subway… really? Why did you have to make me come here? Have we fallen so low?"

"Argh!" Aurora screeched. "Mother, what are you doing here?"

"I followed you from your apartment," Rebecca admitted.

Aurora spat with disdain, "I thought I told you to go to Hell!"

Rebecca's expression fell somber as her eyes cut with sharp vexation, "Luckily, your father and I don't listen to you. Now, what are you so angry about? You're not still upset about that World Miss University Pageant, are you?"

"Mother, I won that beauty pageant in all fairness," she spat, recoiling like a viper, "but you voted for the other girl."

"The other girl deserved it more than you!" Rebecca defended herself and beat a fist on her chest. "I told you to lose the extra weight, and did you listen? No. You never listen, and that's the problem! Now you have me crawling in the filthy subway like a pedestrian!"

"You didn't have to tell the judges that while I was receiving my crown," Aurora retorted, then forced away the memory. She folded her arms neatly under her breasts and huffed. "This is all beside the point. How did you find me?"

"Your father and I have connections, dear," the older woman said and adjusted the cufflinks on her ruby sweater.

"Private agents and such. So, you see that there is no use! Wherever you go, we will eventually find you. You're coming home with me!"

Aurora clenched her fists and closed her magazine. She turned away and disregarded the older woman in hopes she would disappear. Under her breath, she murmured, "Eat dirt and die."

Rebecca growled, then grabbed the purse from Aurora's tight hold. She wrestled for her handbag and started toward the connecting train car, but before she had a chance to open the door, Rebecca slammed her up against the wall.

"Stop!" Aurora struggled and could feel all her energy rush to her eyes—as if they were filling with boiling water. Her pupils slowly turned a fiery copper. She felt a heavy burden lifting as energy rippled from her body.

The air became thick and static-like jello filled with electricity.

Rebecca stood there, motionless. Aurora cocked a flawless arched eyebrow and took a breath of static air. Rebecca was immobilized, covered in white light that rose off her like steam. She turned to the homeless man, and he too was frozen in this misty light. Aurora bit her full red top lip, squeezed past her mother, and hurried to the other side of the train.

As the acidic flavor of fear entered her mouth, she glanced around the frozen space. Just as she thought she was losing her mind, Aurora regained the energy that rushed from her body, and the train returned to normal.

"Where did she?" Rebecca gasped, no longer in her smoky white encasement. She fell into a fetal position and whispered things to herself. Aurora didn't care to know. The train doors wheeled open, and without hesitation, she ducked out. It must have been a tunnel, she told herself. Aurora took a bus to the museum.

She was late and rushed the glass and iron doors with anticipation. The model completely ignored the flashing lights, the guards that protected the entrance, and the desperate crowd that hoped to get into the party.

"Get yourself together, girl," she whispered to herself. Aurora stomped her feet as the elevator continued to the top floor and coached herself, "Now."

She pulled out her blush and reapplied her makeup before bathing her cocoa butter scented skin in her watered-down, discount Chanel perfume. The elevator doors opened to an enormous, fully lit rooftop decorated with the most exceptional modern art and filled with New York's most lucrative socialites. The smell of salty and expensive hors d'oeuvres filled her nostrils while gigantic elephant ice sculptures poured champagne from their trunks. Aurora smiled, adjusted her jacket, and shielded herself from the cold winds. She was among the giants she stalked since she was little. She couldn't worry about her mother now; her new life was just beginning. Things finally were changing for the better.

"Excuse me, Miss."

Aurora turned to see a young man standing before her. She recognized him immediately from her dream last night as the white rider impaled the victim. Her chestnut eyes looked Neil up and down as her hand slipped over her mouth and stumbled a few steps.

"Have you seen Michael Byrant?" Neil's voice waned in confusion. "I... have an interview."

Strokes of fear ran through her body, and her heart convulsed as she asked, "Do I look like I know where he is?" Aurora paused for a moment. She turned her head and tucked a piece of raven hair behind her ear. "I said I don't know where he is! You're standing here. Why?"

Neil frowned. "Okay, if you don't know where he is."

"I said I don't!" she snarled before turning away from him altogether. "Damn it; I can't deal with dead people tonight. I still haven't met anyone important yet!"

"Whoa, what?" he gave a nervous smile, and his adrenaline pumped vigorously as the smell of shea butter and coconut filled his nostrils. "I have no idea what you're talking about. Dead people?"

"Lies," she disagreed. Aurora's eyes thinned as she stared him down. Neil shuddered nervously, telekinetically blasting a small marble vase from its wooden showcase.

"That looked very expensive!" Aurora declared before she started toward the staircase.

It was the second object Neil had moved that day. Flabbergasted, he followed and grabbed her shoulder. Hesitantly he commanded, "Wait!"

Swiftly, Aurora turned to smack him in the face before she spun on her heel and launched to the staircase.

"Nice!" someone shouted.

"Stop!" Neil screamed as Aurora rushed off.

Immense brown irises coated themselves in crimson. It was happening again. Aurora exhaled as energy rippled from her, and the air became thick. Everyone that stood on the rooftop froze, bathed in a smoky white light. She pushed herself against the wall of the staircase door and slid to the ground. With tears in her eyes, she cried, "Why does this keep happening to me?"

"Something tells me," Neil whispered, stood before her, and remarked, "it's not all about you."

Aurora shook and sniffled, "You're not frozen? W-why does this keep happening?"

"Weird things... all day... you too, huh?" Neil searched for words as he examined the frozen bodies covered in glowing mist. "I think you actually froze time. How long does this last?" He sat down beside her.

"I-I don't know." Aurora wiped her eyes with her leather jacket and continued, "Why does this keep happening? I can't stop it…"

"If you're really the one that did it, you should be able to stop it," Neil concluded. He put his hand on her shoulder and stopped her from shaking. "Relax, breathe, and just do what you did before." Neil took hold of her hand.

Aurora placed a shivering hand on her forehead. She took a deep breath, and her eyes returned to a dark hazel while the room slowly commenced movement.

"See, everything's okay," Neil reassured her.

"Is that why I saw you die last night?"

Chapter 3: Cross the Threshold, Ezekiel Wallace

> "And behold, there was a great earthquake; for an angel of the Lord descended from heaven, approached, rolled back the stone, and sat upon it."
> **Matthew 28:2**

Ezekiel David Wallace stood wearily before his front door, as he often did, and traced the cruelly bent metal 4E nailed there with his eyes. He just finished working a late shift at the Pizza Palace and was exhausted. Ezekiel placed the key in the stained door and drowsily walked into the tiny kitchen. Instantly, he inhaled the thick, foul layer of grime that discolored the apartment.

The kitchen was cramped, and the brown tiles grew filthier each day under his father's bare feet. Flies circled the sink full of dirty dishes, and though the family had no pets, the scent of cat urine resonated off the chipping walls. Half-empty cans of stale beer and dead roaches were left about carelessly. The small kitchen table was full of used plates and crumbs. Ezekiel sighed as he had just cleaned the apartment earlier that day—but within hours, this is what happened.

Fred Wallace sat at the small plastic blue table in a wooden chair. He was forty pounds overweight and wore a tight stained wife beater. The balding man looked over at Ezekiel with a grimace and a beer in his hand.

"You're two hours late!" he screamed.

Ezekiel's eyes fell to the floor as he routinely apologized, "I'm so sorry. I thought I told y-you that I was going to work a late shift."

"Well, you didn't tell me!" Fred frowned. "Liar! Where's this month's rent?"

Ezekiel shook his head. "Dad, I p-p-paid you already." His voice was almost a whisper, "Remember, on the first."

"'P-P-Paid' me already? 'P-P-Paid' me already?" Fred bellowed mockingly at the top of his lungs. "If you p-p-paid me, then why don't I remember it? The next time you pay rent, you better make sure that I remember it, or I'm gonna kick your ass and start charging you double!"

"I'm s-sorry," Ezekiel shivered and shamefully lowered his head. "I-I think that's fair…"

"Are you talking back to your father?" Lauren asked as she entered the room. Her hair was messy, and clothes loosely clung to her weak, sick body.

"No," Ezekiel confessed as he turned to her. "Mom, could you please go lie down before you get dizzy?"

"Listen," Fred warned, "I don't need help raising my own damn son from a woman! He needs to learn how to be a man!"

Ezekiel's eyes enlarged as he turned back to his father and muttered, "You don't have to speak to her like that..."

"I swear if I have to get up out of this fucking chair!" Fred yelled and threw his open beer bottle at Ezekiel, hitting him in the face.

For a moment, he felt like he was unconscious. As the bottle hit him and the pain receptors in his face lit up—it was almost as if time had slowed. His body felt out of his control. Ezekiel closed his eyes and heard the squawks of birds. When he reopened them, dozens of eagles swarmed his kitchen. Each bird was drenched in gore and screeched like starving kittens.

Ezekiel ran his fingers beneath his sleeves and bit his lower lip. One by one, the fowl disintegrated into pillars of salt. A sudden fever rushed his brain. He shook his head in disgusted alarm, but when he reopened his eyes, the room was ordinary.

Ezekiel fought the tears that crept to the sides of his eyes and fought the urge to vomit, "Okay."

Habitually defeated, he walked into his room and gently closed his door. He sat on the same bed he had all his life and gazed into his childhood bureau mirror. Ezekiel was always a shrimp with a small frame and youthful sadness. Tears rushed down his cappuccino cheeks. His eyes were nearly black, round, and wet while his hair grew in thick black curls and flopped over his cinnamon-colored face.

Ezekiel always wore hand-me-down long-sleeved shirts, mostly in dark earth-tone colors. His money all went to either rent or to help pay for the treatments for his mother's unknown illness. It didn't matter to him what outfit he was wearing.

He had accepted the dynamic of his home and never fought or caused trouble. Ezekiel understood that his father was bitter and angry because his wife was sick, and his mother suffered for that anger. He had to be pleasant. He had to stay. If he didn't take care of his mother, who would?

Ezekiel pulled his recycled sweater's sleeves over his fingers and then started to clean his room frantically. Everything needed to be in its place, or he got very uncomfortable. Ezekiel's bedroom was covered in his drawings of desolate fields, sketches of dismal birds, and paintings of open skies and melancholy oceans.

As he carefully organized his artwork, he came across a picture of violets he had drawn earlier that week. His mother loved violets, and he had forgotten to give her the gift. He ripped the image from his pad and slumped it to his mother's room.

Lauren was awake in bed, pulling her dense hair back into a bun when he knocked. "Yes," she said restlessly.

"Oh, um, I j-just remembered. I-" Ezekiel stuttered as he held up the sketch. "I drew you a picture the other day. I saw some violets and I-I know you like them. I couldn't buy them, so I did the next best thing."

Lauren continued to wrap her hair and responded carelessly, "Thank you, could you leave it on the dresser?"

Ezekiel nodded and did as told.

"I'm," he paused awkwardly before he continued, "I'm going to start on the dishes…"

He then rolled up his sleeves and did so. The young man looked toward the refrigerator and smiled at an invitation he had won on the radio last week. He didn't care much for parties, but the lead singer of his favorite band, R.I.P., would be at Eugene Martinez rooftop extravaganza tomorrow night in Downtown Manhattan! He had to see them. He finished off the dishes, got into bed, lay awake for hours, then drifted asleep.

A cold and bitter chill pressed Ezekiel's cheek as he slept. Above his face hovered a white cloud with two gray circles, like eyes, on a tadpole body. Ezekiel awoke and leaped out of his bed. Several figures floated around his room and faded within seconds. Tart liquid filled his mouth, and he ran out of his room and slammed the door behind him.

A cloud faded into the living room and pushed the small outdated television off its stand. Then it parted into the darkness. Ezekiel screamed as his parents rushed in.

"Is everything alright?" Lauren asked.

Ezekiel relaxed and managed to utter, "I-I d-don't know. Mom, I t-think I see g-ghosts or something."

"Looks like he finally lost it," his father added.

"I don't know, maybe, I guess?" Ezekiel admitted, narrowed his eyes at his father, and sauntered to the fridge. "I'm getting a glass of water," he muttered. D-does anyone want anything to d-drink?"

"I'd rather go to bed," his mother groaned and walked back into her room.

"Again, with the stupidity. I better see a new television here tomorrow," Fred said, following his wife.

He refused to return to his room, and instead, Ezekiel remained on the couch, awake all night. His eyes remained open in constant but necessary surveillance.

At the bus stop the next day, clad in a long-sleeved white sweater and black jeans, Ezekiel fished into his pockets for change as he fought down the excitement of meeting a celebrity.

He checked the street for an oncoming bus but only saw a crowded block full of cars and people. Reminded of his hatred for the city, Ezekiel noticed a shadowy bus-like mass rise above the street lamp's horizon.

A bubbling sensation erupted in his chest as he struggled to see.

Ezekiel instantly found himself standing down the block, watching the number thirty-eight bus pass him. He was a little lighter... and his body felt empty, hollow, and—was floating? How did he get down here? Before he could form a thought, the bus zoomed down the block and pulled up in front of him. He found himself standing right where he was before.

"Fred was right. I am losing my mind," he thought before the bus drove away.

The museum was a gigantic building made of blue glass and steel. It gave off a clean smell that soothed him. The front desk was guarded by a bulky man dressed in a black suit and dark shades. Relaxation melted away as Ezekiel took a deep breath and pulled his sleeves over his hands.

"Invitation..." the man said in a deep intimidating voice.

With a burst of excitement, he handed over his invitation that he had won on DJ Puck's radio show and ran to the elevator. He pressed the top button and waited for one of the many doors to open.

"Hold it!" interrupted a blonde in pigtails holding plastic bags full of food ran up to the elevator. "Top floor, please," she beamed while they entered.

Ezekiel shyly pressed the button and asked, "Hi, yeah, a-are you going to the p- party too?"

"Absolutely positively! Thirteenth floor!" she announced before she put down her bags, "You know, the number thirteen gets a bad rep, but I don't think it's so awful. I mean, it's only one more than twelve, and good things come in twelves. And have you ever heard of a baker's dozen? That's like thirteen cookies! What sick individual would have a problem with thirteen cookies? Unless you're on a diet... or have diabetes... I guess... but there are always sugarless cookies! But I'm just going off again, huh...?"

"Okay."

"Oh, I'm Amanda! I run a vegan enchilada and ceviche food truck. I'm part of the catering." Without taking a breath, she rambled on, "If you never had ceviche before, you won't get it from my truck. Everything is all-natural and sort of yummy. Lucky, huh?"

"Sure..." Ezekiel agreed and nodded hesitantly.

"And I got such a good deal on all this food! Would you believe that all this stuff is sugar-free? All that sugar—for free! Ah, I love the farmer's market! I don't know if they were feeling generous or if there was some type of promotion... but I'm feeling really great about how this batch turned out! These enchiladas are much less liquidy than the last ones. I tell you, there was a time I couldn't tell the difference between the enchiladas or the ceviche... before or after they were inside of you..." Amanda giggled. She pointed to the bags on the ground and continued, "Make sure you stop by and try a little!"

He watched through the slits of his eyelids while she failed to pull out a wedgie from her overalls discreetly. When the elevator stopped, she hurried out.

"See you later, you cutie!" she cheered. A vast, almost frightening smile crossed her face that exposed all of her white teeth. "Stop by! Free food. Everybody loves free food!"

The lavish party was crowded, and Ezekiel felt underdressed. Like asteroid dust among a supernova, he roamed aimlessly, unable to make eye contact with anyone. He watched as an attractive woman slapped a guy.

"Nice," he commented awkwardly as the crowd continued to move along without him. Nothing seemed abnormal today until Ezekiel suddenly felt lightheaded. A bubbling feeling erupted from his stomach to his chest.

The bathroom.

His senses benumbed—sight and sound were all that remained. Without smell, and he couldn't feel his skin or taste the adrenaline in his mouth. He felt like he was floating and possibly... high?

There he spotted Neil.

The journalist searched for the bathroom. Once inside, he crouched up against the door of a stall. Water slowly floated from the sink in a long levitating stream and splashed against the wall. Neil looked up at his feet Ezekiel as the free flow of water fell to the ground.

"Oh m-my god," Ezekiel muttered, shaken.

Neil rushed over to Ezekiel. "What does this all mean?" he spat as he tried to get a hold of Ezekiel but phased through his incorporeal body. Ezekiel fell through the bathroom wall and rushed through the party and to the elevator. Frantically, he tried to press the button, but his fingers slid through the wall.

Chapter 4: Welcome, Mandy Randall

"And he will send out his angels with a trumpet blast, and they will gather his elect from the four winds, from one end of the heavens to the other."
Matthew 24:3

Amanda smiled her trademark toothy, overly ecstatic grin. She shrugged nervously in her undersized baby blue gown and inched to the edge of her chair. She gazed over Henry Dunham with huge eyes, the color that matched her dress. Her blonde hair was pulled up in a tight bun with a large white flower hair clip, and she wore her boyfriend's favorite lipstick. Amanda's makeup was immaculate and correlated with her blue nails and dress that tightly covered her slightly plump body.

She tried not to blush too hard and gaped at her boyfriend of two years while the dim lights shaded the traditional restaurant in a romantic blanket. She always appreciated the elegance of the strategically placed candles and ferns. This was absolutely her favorite eatery because they made the best vegan double-decker cheeseburgers.

Henry boasted, "So, I said to him, 'Sir, I know I'm just the lieutenant, but I ain't scrubbing another man's ass with my toothbrush! That's not my job, gosh-darn it!' He just walked away without a single word."

She exclaimed with the joyful cheer of a child opening Christmas presents, "Finally! He was a creep, anyway! You should have been ruder. You should have just done as I told you."

"What?" Henry's voice was saturated in his Southern accent. "Call his momma?"

Amanda laughed, "I mean, it would have worked. I'm sure if his mom knew how to mean he was, she would have to say something... But I'm glad that you stood up to him. I'm so proud!"

He looked at her for a while and smirked, "Hell, I'm proud of you too, gorgeous."

"What did I do?" she asked with a blink of her big eyes.

Henry shook his head and admitted, "You ain't gotta do nothing."

"I mean, I do your laundry, make your lunches, cut your hair and your toenails...even when they're yellow-green." Amanda continued to blush. "We do everything together. It's almost like we're already..." She giggled, "You know... made one in the eyes of the lord...? Or something like that, no pressure!"

"On that note, I got you something," he announced.

Amanda's heart dropped into her stomach as Henry reached into his pocket. Had he finally noticed the more than apparent hints she dropped? Was he finally going to ask her to marry him? Her body tensed, and she suffocated with excitement. Her blue nails tapped the white tablecloth as Henry pulled a rectangular box from his pocket.

It was a colossal box for a ring, Amanda thought, as she shamelessly brought the package closer. Her heart beat loudly in her chest as she flipped open the box. Her jaw dropped and tears bundled at the corners of her eyes. Inside sat a massive diamond ring on creased white paper. She was breathless. It was so perfect her body trembled. Her lips pinched themselves together as she tried to keep her composure.

"Oh, my Gosh…this is the same one I wanted all my life ever since I saw it in a magazine last week!" Amanda screeched, "Yes!"

Henry smiled.

"Yes. Yes! YES!" Amanda repeated as she cried. "Yes, I'll marry you!" With those words, she leaped from her seat and threw her arms around Henry. She forced kisses onto his lips, and he gently pulled away.

"Mandy...what has gotten into you, girl? I just gave you a necklace," he said, discouragingly.

She was breathless again, but disagreed, "No. No, you gave me a wedding ring." Amanda reached for the box and exposed the diamond ring. "That's an engagement band, Henry," Amanda's voice suddenly cracked then became stern.

"But... I bought you a necklace," he gasped. Henry was clueless. He struggled to speak as Amanda's face turned red with anger.

"No, you bought me a wedding ring!" the blonde demanded. Amanda slammed the box on the table as she stood from his lap. "Do you think that's funny?"

"Mandy..." he tried to get his words out.

"So, what are you trying to say? You don't want to marry me?" She shook in doubt, and her voice got louder as other restaurant patrons took notice of her tears.

Her skin became hot. A migraine trampled her mind like a monster truck would a bicycle. Amanda grabbed her pumping heart and beheld the restaurant guests around her—no one had any faces.

Featureless with blemishes that dripped gore as slop fell from a pig's mouth. Everyone was watching her, but no one had any eyes. The room said nothing but judged as she shouted.

Amanda paused and swallowed a rock in her throat. Suddenly, it was as if nothing had changed. The hot flash was gone, and the room was back to normal. She rolled her eyes and shook off the delirium. Henry gazed up at her with confused brown eyes. She felt queasy, but she was still angry. Relentlessly she continued, "So, you buy me a wedding ring, but you don't want to marry me? Let me ask you a question: I think you are sick, just sick!"

"Mandy," he repeated, "the jeweler must have made a mistake and put the ring in there!"

"No," she shook her head and threw her baby blue pocketbook over her shoulders. "I think you made a mistake... Or maybe I made a mistake... I mean, somebody here made a mistake, and it wasn't the jeweler! This whole thing is a big mistake!"

Without another word, Amanda exited the restaurant and marched home.

Amanda's fingers arched as she screamed at the top of her lungs and entered her living room. She slammed the door, which rattled the Barbie dolls and stuffed magical ponies on the shelves of the purple dorm room-like apartment.

Cat-shaped clocks chimed meows, and dying cacti cluttered the windowsills. The old art class papier-mâché sculptures housed spider webs, and unorganized crate bookshelves made the room resemble a garage sale in the center of a trash obstacle course.

Home.

A short redhead in a perfectly ironed suit walked out into the living room and stood before the plastic-covered green couch, gazed into a small silver Victorian hand mirror with flowers and the name Giselle, engraved on the back. Frowning she asked, "Mandy... my, are we unusually doleful?"

Olive comforted Amanda while she cried on the couch, "Oh, my goodness, Olive, Henry just did something really mean!"

"Men. I should have deduced. The pseudo backbone to every society! Especially your man. He *is* in the military. What'd that egotistical, chauvinistic, condescending, thinks-he's-all-that-because-he- has-a-flap-of-skin-between-his-legs do now? And baby, where is your coat?" Olive asked.

Amanda's face fell blank, as though she had just become suddenly aware. She parted her pink lips, her expression unchanged. "I must have left my jacket in the restaurant. I thought it was a little cold outside."

"Aw," Olive cooed and rubbed Amanda's shoulders. "What happened?"

"Stupid, Henry!" Amanda sobbed. "He makes this whole really big super cute deal and gives me a freaking wedding ring! So, I start screaming like a psychopath. 'Yes! Yes! Yes, I'll marry the fudge out of you!'" Amanda paused and smiled in remembrance, "He's such a sweet and handsome guy, and the ring was really pretty and sparkly. He treats me so well..." Amanda fisted her hands in anger, "Except for when he acts like a complete jerk! The fat-head goes, 'Um, what are you talking about? I didn't give you a ring; I gave you a necklace. Are you crazy? Blah blah blah.' Is that supposed to be funny, Olive? Because it's not!" Amanda hyperventilated and struggled to control her breathing.

"No, sweetie, it's not," Olive frowned.

"See, we're not the crazy ones here!" Amanda conceded and threw up her arms, "You know it's not funny. I know it's not funny. The American people know it's not funny!" Crushed, she ripped the flower clip from her hair and released the long blonde locks that curved around her shoulders. "He's such a caring guy. I just," Amanda paused,

"I just wish sometimes I knew what he was thinking, you know? We can't get a divorce before we're even married...I just wish I could get inside of his head and shake things up a bit and be like, 'You want me. I know you do!' Gosh, I could just... I mean, if I was him, I would want me, you know? I'm good! I mean, I just wanna, I wish I could just..."

As the words left her mouth, Amanda could feel the energy rise within her. Her flesh crawled and felt like tiny fingers pushed beneath her skin. Olive watched wide-eyed as Amanda began to shift. Heat rose from her body, and steam simmered off like hot food. Her skin, hair, and features gracefully changed color and shape as though an artist were smoothly repainting her.

Moments later, Amanda sat in the same chair; only now she was a little taller, a little darker, and a little stronger. Hair and muscles burst the seams of Amanda's blue dress as Olive screamed, falling off the green couch. Amanda looked over to Olive and spoke in her boyfriend's voice, "What?"

"Oh, my God!" Olive spat and charged out the front door.

Amanda stood up to follow Olive, but the seams of her dress tore utterly. She looked over her body, now hairy, taller, and manly. The former blonde ran to the bathroom, but the face in the mirror was not her own. She started to hyperventilate. Milliseconds felt like hours. She could not think and could hardly breathe. Slowly, her form sizzled, and she melted back into normal shape.

Amanda fell onto the bathroom floor's cold yellow tiles with her fingers in her wild blonde hair and her dress torn in several places. There was a reason for everything, but why had this happened to her? She donated to charity, gave up her seat on the train, and even returned lost money. Why did karma betray her?

Surrounded by a white picket fence in Staten Island, Amanda was raised by strict Christian parents. Her family's beliefs followed her all her life. God must have temporarily changed her for her sins. It must have been God teaching her a lesson for acting up in the restaurant. What else could it have been?

After hours of sitting on the bathroom floor, Amanda repeatedly and unsuccessfully called Olive. She desperately needed to speak to someone. Was she on the verge of a psychological breakdown? She needed to make a phone call to him.

"Hello?" he was cool and calm.

"Sorry for being crazy," she apologized immediately.

Henry paused for a moment, "I'm sorry, too. The jeweler must have switched the jewelry by mistake. Ya can keep the ring if you want."

"No," Amanda answered quickly. "You should return it."

"Are ya sure?" Henry asked.

Amanda watched her cat, Purrson, jump from the couch, and it scurried across the room before she answered, "Yes, I'm sure, but there is something I have to ask you before we move on from this. I'm really scared. It's something that I've been wondering for the past few hours, and it's really been bothering me..."

"What?" Henry sighed.

"Do you have my coat?" she inquired.

Henry laughed loudly, and Amanda joined, "Yes, darling, I have your coat."

"Good! It's just that it's my favorite one, and I got it while I was in Boston, and I don't see myself going back there anytime soon!" she said with a laugh.

Amanda awoke in the afternoon the next day just in time for work. She rushed over to Olive's bedroom. The door was wide open, but the room was still empty. Feeling down, she got dressed. She wore a baby-blue shirt with a huge smiling cartoon kitten on the front, fitting overalls with flowers in the stitching and a butterfly necklace covered with rhinestones and fake gems. With her long blonde hair tied into pigtails, she hopped into Randall's Boneless Vegan Delights food truck and left for the museum.

"Em!" she squealed as she rushed to the elevator of the museum party. "Hold it!" Inside was a man with curly black hair. "Thirteen, please," she said and placed her bags on the floor.

He pressed the button. "Hi, hey, are you going to the p-party?" the skinny boy asked, then pulled his long white sleeves over his fingers.

"Yeah!" she charged. As he turned his direction to the glowing numbers above them, Amanda speedily fished out a wedgie.

When she got to the rooftop, she bid him departure and set up her stand. She picked an area in a corner where a table was already prepared with a white tablecloth. The caterer opened her materials and placed a black plastic tray of vegan sushi and soupy enchiladas onto the surface. Amanda opened a pack of napkins, folded them, and put them about the table. Her job was done.

"Good enough," she groaned as the scrawny man from the elevator walked past her.

"Hey!" she yelled. He looked a bit preoccupied, but she continued. With an over-excited squeal, she walked straight up to him and tapped him on the shoulder. He plummeted onto her table of food. The crowd gasped. Amanda knelt next to him and tried to wake him. Failed attempt after failed attempt, she settled on calling 911. She pushed past the wealthy huddling crowd to an empty and clear space where she could get a cellphone service. Just as she started to dial her huge pink phone, she saw the boy standing before the elevator fading in and out of transparency like a hologram.

"Th-this is im-impossible," his voice was garbled. He attempted to touch the elevator, but his fingers slid right through the button.

Amanda's mouth gaped. She shook her head and tried to say something—anything—but before anything could escape her lips, a rush of energy blew onto the building top from an unknown direction.

Ezekiel's physical body lit up. From his chest, a brilliant white light burst and temporarily blinded Amanda. All the air left the rooftop. Discombobulated, it felt like her heart was slowing.

Everyone around her was immobile, frozen in time. Ezekiel's body levitated off the floor. As Amanda realized her skin shone, she began to float. A white light surged from her chest, then Aurora and Neil's.

Across the rooftop, they wafted in the air as though guided by magnets. Neil hovered in the southern corner of the roof, Aurora in the Western, Amanda in the Eastern, and Ezekiel in the Northern. Amanda reached out to Ezekiel for support as he looked back in horror.

Two rays of red and gold lightning shot from Ezekiel's back like sky beams. The flashes were attached to his shoulder blades and crackled like mighty wings made from electricity. Bits of rock, clay, and other earthly minerals twisted around him like dandelion seeds in the breeze.

Then white and copper currents blasted from Aurora's posterior as her eyes filled with crimson. A tiny stream of white water spun around her feet with such choreography that not a single drop was lost.

Neil was next. As he floated, the electric wings on his back popped so loudly that the dark blue color illuminated the rooftop. A blue fire arose at his feet but grew no taller than a small bush or a tiny tree.

Finally, Amanda's shoulders lit up with emerald green voltaic bolts that flapped around her like wings. Wind twisted around Amanda's toes and carried faint hues of jade.

When the flash faded, Ezekiel, Amanda, Aurora, and Neil stood alone and wingless at the now empty party. Aurora rushed to the edge of the rooftop. The vacant building was void of light, save the stars' luminosity, red moon, dawn sun, and lights that the city cast. It was apparent several hours had passed, and the party was long over.

Amanda approached the others and, for a moment, did not know what to think or say. Confused, she tilted her head and remarked, her voice cracking, "This is the most interesting and life-like daydream I ever had..."

Ezekiel lowered his head and nervously pulled his sleeves over his fingertips before he muttered, "I-I don't think you're dreaming unless this is some sort of group nightmare! I-I feel sick!"

"Wait, no, that doesn't make any sense," Aurora swallowed hard. "I started a new diet pill. This must be one of the side effects... and... and I just dyed my own eyelashes so that I might be seeing things..."

"Glowing eyes and levitation? Get real," Neil corrected her and narrowed his brow. "I don't know what to tell you except that whatever happened, it's obvious we're all a part of it."

Aurora tried toward the elevator again before dismissing them, "Screw you, I'm not a part of any..." but Neil interjected.

"Yes, you are," Neil confirmed. "Didn't you say you had a vision where you saw me, and you get mutilated and ripped apart by monsters?"

Shivering, she answered, "All of us actually..."

"What!?" Panic boiled out of Amanda's throat, and her watery blue eyes grew twice their size. "You saw us get 'mutilated by monsters'? 'Ripped apart'... Does that mean...." Amanda's lower lip quivered with such trepidation she could barely speak, "D- did we all get...?"

Aurora folded her arms neatly under her breasts. Her shoulders sunk as she recalled her horrifying vision into memory. She exhaled slowly as her heart started to race, and tears crept at the corner of her eyes. Aurora lowered her head and woefully admitted, "Yeah... every single last one of us..."

"Well, hallelujah, isn't that a relief?" Amanda giggled with reprieve.

"W-what do you mean?" Ezekiel dreadfully gasped and covered his mouth in dismay. "How can you say that?"

"We were all *killed,* you idiot!" Aurora snapped.

"Oh," the blonde took a few steps back in retreat, "Sorry, I was gonna ask, 'Did we all get out okay?'"

A thunderous neigh echoed across the empty rooftop. Before the astronomical full moon, a man appeared standing in an opulent white cape that draped over his shoulders and moved like a squid dancing in water. The White Horseman wore a spiked-milky crown made of gold and silver. He had a set of ivory arrows to his back and held a longbow across his hairy chest. He pushed back his black oily hair as the second Horseman shimmered in from the shadows.

The Red Horseman wore a red suit of leather armor that looked more like bondage material. The outfit showcased his dozens of body and facial piercings and tribal tattoos. His hot fingers trembled as though he could grab any one of the knives he secretly held within tight leather pockets, but the bottle-dyed redhead settled on drawing his short pointed sword, given to him by the Hallowed One.

Next to emerge was the Black Horseman. Out of thin air, the massive man materialized. He was shirtless and had rolls busting out of his black slacks. He drooled, and his skin was so thick with sweat that it made him sparkle. His mouth twisted with an incurable hunger as he proudly showcased a pair of tiny weighing scales.

Last to surface was the Horseman of Death. Lavishly dressed as if he were going to an expensive funeral, the long-haired blonde wore an excessive lion mane coat that dripped to the floor. The cumbersome yellow fleece covered his tiny body like a finely fashioned broomstick as he entered. Casually he sauntured in with a lit cigarette as if he was happy to be the last one to arrive at the party.

"Oh my God," Aurora gasped.

"W-what is happening?" Ezekiel followed in horror.

Poised, like a magnetic moth, the one in white finally spoke, "So you are the Cherubim of the Throne? Oh, sacred angels descended to Earth to serve as God's hand to caress and strike as needed." The White Horseman scoffed as if he wanted to laugh—but stopped caring halfway through, "I sense no real power here."

"Trust me, we have no idea what you're talking about," Neil quipped, taking a step forward. "Who are you? Do you know what just happened to us?"

He spread his arms open, his white cloak still covering his hands and feet. Slowly he spoke, "We are seeds to be planted in what must come to pass."

"Tone down the drama, you're scaring them," the slickly dressed horseman took a drag of his cigarette and announced, "I'm Death, the Yellow Horseman. That's

Hunger in Black, War in Red, and the great and long-winded Pestilence in White. The Horseman of the Apocalypse—maybe you've heard of us."

"This can't be real," Neil muttered in disbelief.

"My stomach is killing me," Hunger wrapped his arms around his continental waistline and groaned, "I just want a little taste…"

"Gotta say, I'm with tubs here," War rolled his eyes and agreed, "They're never going to abide voluntarily."

Pestilence's stoneface stewed in silence but suddenly boiled over, "God damn it, you know how I hate it when you interrupt me! I will have tranquility one way or another..."

Under the tutelage of his leader, Death folded his arms, shrugged then took a step back into formation.

"What do you want?" Aurora asked from behind Neil's shoulders.

"To breathe in this world, every fiber, molecule, and piece of dust. This world is the devil's oyster. It always was and always will be filled with the forsaken and the sinful. The darkness that is in all blood can never be cleansed! Walk with us and have a chance at true freedom…. or you may die where you stand." Pestilence opened his arms while the other Horsemen stood behind him like soldiers.

Neil looked to Aurora, who cowered behind him, then to Ezekiel, who trembled behind her and finally to Amanda, who ducked behind her overturned concession table. The Horsemen turned and extended their open hands.

Neil's eyes enlarged with confusion and fear, his skin soaked with sweat. He reached his hand forward but retracted when chirping pierced the still air. A small gray bird with a black beak and cotton underbelly fluttered around repeating, "'Anxiety in the heart of man causes depression, but a good word makes it glad.'"

The screeching was continual and deliberate and grew louder with every caw. Pestilence lowered his hooded head and turned to the owl. "What annoyance is this?"

The animal screeched and hooted, then landed before Neil. He pecked at a small rolled-up sheet of paper attached to his leg until it dropped.

Small yellow eyes glared up at Neil. Before it fluttered away, the bird opened its beak, "Who?"

Quickly, Neil unfolded the paper and read it. He dropped his arms and took a few steps back.

"Well?" Aurora whispered impatiently, her fingers clenched at his arm.

"It it-t says that," Neil swallowed a rock in his throat and put the note in his pocket, "we shouldn't trust them, that we should get out of here as fast as we can. Then it leaves a name and an address."

Pestilence took a step forward and laughed, "Foolish woman, she's seen so much light she is blind!" He reached into his robes and pulled out his ivory bow and arrow as he uttered, "Now it is too late."

"No!" Neil yelled and instinctually directed a hand toward Pestilence. Telekinetically the demon was hurled off the roof. As the White Horseman crashed through the air like a broken dove, Neil opened his palm and gazed in awe of the unusual abilities that he had yet to understand or control fully.

The Horsemen readied their weapons—a broadsword, an unbalanced golden scale, and a thin scythe. War dashed toward Aurora with his massive bloodthirsty sword. Paralyzing fear ran through her, and she felt her eyes warm-up, and her pupils turn red. As War inched closer, he froze, covered in a glowing mist.

Neil looked over toward Death, and with a twist of his wrist, the Horseman was thrown over the rooftop. Hunger held his shining unbalanced scale before him, and the roof shook.

Apprehensively, Ezekiel turned to run, but there Hunger stood behind him in his heavy black slacks.

"Ahh!" Ezekiel wet himself as his spirit literally rose from his flesh and jettisoned fifteen feet into the air before falling back into its host.

Stunned by Ezekiel's display, Amanda fell to the ground. And her unintentional disguise melted off her as quickly as a chameleon would change color. She shook her head apologetically as Ezekiel shook off the disorientation and the embarrassment of public urination.

Swiftly, Neil threw his arm at the real Black Horseman and telekinetically hurled the massive mound of flesh over the roof's edge as well. Neil's heart rate sped even more rapidly than before. He was scared to death, but the pumping adrenaline felt natural to him. Again, he looked at his hand, impressed by his own power, "Who else...?"

"Duh, anyone in Salvation Army Fashion..." Aurora gulped and glared toward Ezekiel and Amanda, "Besides them!" She rushed toward the staircase as Neil and the others chased behind her. "Screw this..."

The lobby was on fire, and this was no hallucination. As the furniture burned around them, Neil flung his hand at the iron and glass doors that prevented escape. Not even rattle. Again, he focused and failed at mentally bursting the doors. Then once more with two hands.

"I can't," Neil bashfully began to panic, "it isn't working..."

"I have to get out of here!" Ezekiel desperately launched a wooden chair through the large glass windows. Frantically, they leaped over the broken glass and into the street. The streets looked normal as Amanda guided them into her food truck and whizzed down the street as the fire department started to arrive. Aurora scanned the streets then slightly relaxed. Manhattan roads were bare for once, and she wasn't sure how she should respond to it.

"Do you see anything?" a deep voice startled her as she turned to Neil.

"No," Aurora answered, "but how would I know? I can hardly think right now."

"There is some cold water, vegan ceviche, and other refreshments in the cooler if anyone is hungry..." Amanda muttered through tears as she struggled to drive the van. "Everything should be fresh, but the cooler is always warm, so sometimes the water is hot, and I can never tell when it's on... Here, let me just get it for y—"

"Just watch the road!" Neil instructed.

Ezekiel pulled his sweater sleeves over his fingers and asked, "W-why were those men trying to k-kill us? Who were they?"

"I also didn't get out a notebook and conduct a full interview." Aurora frowned.

"They said they were the 'Horsemen of the Apocalypse,'" Neil answered. "That's... biblical, right? If you believe in that sort of thing."

Amanda shouted from her seat, "You betcha, it's biblical! Is anyone going to mention the fact that we all sprouted wings made of light and lost a couple of hours of our lives because I'm pretty sure that's looking biblical too—I think. What's there not to believe? We all saw it!"

"W-we should call the police!" Ezekiel shouted while everyone irately turned to him. He timidly continued, "Or a p-priest... I-I guess if what we all saw was real. Or we should at least stay here together, you know, in case someone scary needs to get thrown off a roof..."

"Last night," Aurora interjected slowly, "I saw in my head, like a movie... those four horse guys killing us. At first, I thought I was just hungry... or on this bad diet pill or something, I don't know...like a bad dream. There was even a big cow... in my living room... and a river of blood... Then, I was in the subway, and I did that mist thing to my own mom."

"Oh, my goodness, is she…?" Amanda paused then lifted a palm commandingly, "Let me finish!" She hesitantly continued, "Is she okay?"

"Ugh," Aurora hissed, "I don't care!"

"Something's going on with all of us, but no one here has the answer," Neil declared as he retrieved the crumpled note from his pocket. "Maybe the person at this address does. Three-nineteen Rector. 'Lyssah Rhamiel.'"

"We're supposed just to trust some random note you get from a dirty bird?" Aurora spat.

"The dirty bird that saved our lives?" Neil shot back, then lifted an eyebrow as she folded her arms in defeat.

"Okay!" Amanda announced, "We trust in what that very cute and adorable little birdie had to say. We go to that address." She continued, "I just realized: if we're going to be driving around in my family's food truck, we should all get to know each other a little better. Hi, my name is Mandy Randall."

Chapter 5: Destiny Awakened

"After this, I saw four angels standing at the four corners of the earth, holding back the four winds of the earth so that no wind could blow on land or sea or against any tree. Then I saw another angel come up from the East, holding the seal of the living God. He cried out in a loud voice to the four angels who were given the power to damage the land and the sea."

Revelations 7:1-2

319 Rector, Church of Alpha and Omega Church, was built like a small castle. Massive brown bricks took up the entire block and overlooked rose bushes, desolate statues, and tombstones; they were all enclosed by a tall black gate. Stained glass with images of saints covered each window under large daunting arches and pointed bartizan rooftops. Neil rechecked the address written on the crumpled note, and cautiously they crawled out of the food truck.

"Told you it was biblical!" Amanda released a cold cloud of air into early dawn morning.

"What do you think is inside?" Aurora asked and threw a lock of her shiny raven hair behind her substantial chandelier earrings.

"When you wake up with superpowers one morning, and a cute birdie saves your life that night, you don't know what to expect," Amanda retorted. "But my guess... is church-like stuff." Amanda advanced toward the staircase. "Let's go in."

Ezekiel leered at the church's fearsome gargoyles and slipped his fingers under his sleeves. He struggled to pull his shirt over the spreading urine stain on his jeans. Ezekiel frowned and asked, "Do we have a plan, or are we just going to go in like crazy people?"

"Either we get into the church and find out more about what's going on, church-like men of the Apocalypse show up again and nail us to a wall on fire and naked. I would say fifty-fifty." Amanda smiled as she inched closer to him.

"Maybe you should lie to me," he shivered.

Unlike Amanda, who had gone to church quite often, Neil hadn't been to church in years. His heart throbbed in his throat as he walked up the staircase. Engraved with the pious yet terrifying images of angels, the magnificent oak entry caused Neil to shiver. The doors screeched as he opened them below a mammoth circular stained glass window.

"That's not funny," Neil said softly.

Amanda shook her head as she continued up the stairs and replied, "It's a little funny."

"No. It's not." Aurora glared. "When I moved here, I knew I should have bought a gun..."

The immense, dark oak portals revealed a vast inside with wooden floors and pews leading to the altar. At the front of the church knelt a man with shaggy brown hair, dressed in black. He stood when he heard the door and turned. His eyes peered toward the visitors beneath a pair of thin horn-rimmed glasses.

"Good morning," the priest said with a straight white smile. "You're a little early. Service starts in a few hours."

"We're not here for service," Neil continued as the priest looked at him with complexity. "We're here to see Lyssah Rhamiel. Is she here?"

"Oh..." the priest scrunched his eyebrows and laughed a bit. "Is she here? She owns the place. She's always here. Yet, I've never seen her out past the garden since I've been here, but she never gets visitors. Are you friends of hers?"

"I'm a reporter. Pluck A Feather Magazine. I was doing a piece on the church." Neil nodded as the priest led them down the hall.

"C-Can you t-tell us more about her? This p-person…" Ezekiel reluctantly asked and followed behind the others. "You know before we go off and meet someone we've never met before on this very normal and average night?"

"Well, you know," the priest shrugged and led the four into the castle-like hallway, "she's an eccentric." Through stained glass, dappled dawn light illuminated the enchanting archways and kissed the stone walls' history. "All the great people are, though, right? I know she's been here longer than anyone else. She used to be a nun here or Great Schema, but now she's retired and mostly just stays alone in the rectory. The rectory is attached to the church, and we're all supposed to have access, but she keeps the entire house to herself. Most of the church's donations come from her, and we have more than enough room so no one really complains or asks questions, not that she would answer them."

"You know," the priest laughed and continued, "some call her 'the Ghost that haunts the church,' but that's just because we never see her." They came to the end of the hallway to a large white door, and the man rang the doorbell. He announced, "Sister Lyssah Rhamiel d'Youville, you have guests!"

"That will be all, Father Matthew," the answer was quick, as though the voice was waiting to say those words forever.

"Oh!" the priest remembered, "Clara said she's going to be a little late this week with her grocery delivery. They ran out of the canned veggies you like. She said that she's going to have to wait until the supermarket gets more cans in."

"That will be all, Father Matthew," the voice repeated.

Father Matthew shrugged and turned. "Nice to meet you all," he said before he retreated down the hallway.

The door swung open and spilled the stench of old food and musk. A tattered middle-aged brunette woman answered with unkempt hair full of frazzled grays. A broken pair of dirty gold-framed glasses covered her faded blue eyes. Her pink lips quivered, and her gaze shook suspiciously with tension and anxiety.

"Fear not; it's just a vile stench."

A smelly unknown substance dangled from the ceiling in tiny brown sacks with red string. Worried piles of open books, anciently marked up newspapers, and empty cans of rotten food were haphazardly strewn about. Eerie photographs clashed with the archaic symbols that painted the walls. Hanging gargoyles and threatening amulets overfilled the chaotic room and almost covered the large birdcage and olive trees near the boarded-up window.

"Your home is very artistic," Amanda gulped a gust of foul air and slowly closed the door behind her, "I like your… little bags and creepy dudes and stuff.."

"'Anxiety in the heart of man causes depression, but a good word makes it glad.' The Horsemen of the Apocalypse are degenerates. Most inhospitable," the woman remarked almost whimsically. She stammered to her frayed brown couch covered in loose papers and perched herself on the cushion sunken in with her imprint. She sat with her legs to her chest and held her knees. Her back arched, and her bare feet grasped at the cloth on the couch. Like a gargoyle looking over a city, the woman gazed at the four and addressed, "Insights, to dimensions undiscovered! Reality's walls melt around us—the touched are the chosen as they understand things in ways others do not. This is not the first time the world has ended…"

Amanda walked to the smaller couch adjacent to Sister Lyssah Rhamiel, made room for herself to sit, and pushed some papers aside.

"Don't touch anything!" Sister Lyssah Rhamiel screamed. Amanda awkwardly fixed the articles just as she had found them. "Oh! You're making me nervous! Sit on the papers if you must sit down, but be careful not to confuse them. They're in a particular order."

Neil nodded ineptly while Aurora walked over to the birdcage. The gray owl they saw the night before perched proudly inside. She frowned, "There's the pigeon that dropped that note."

"He is an owl, and his name is Stolas...Maniae..." Lyssah Rhamiel shouted as though she were a teapot of boiling emotions, "The process! Nowadays, no one cares about the process! You impatient children think they can get wine without planting grape seeds. I can tell you have questions. Just another department is totally handling the investigation.""

Neil frowned. "We got this note from you."

"Sit, and I will begin our first session. What I am about to reveal to you is of the utmost severity and dire truth." Stone-faced, Sister Lyssah Rhamiel's steel voice sounded like a knife dragging against metal, "Change is hard-uncomfortable, but it is a necessary part of growth. You may find this hard to believe, but this is not the first time you were here. As Cherubim of the Throne, you've painted Yahweh's design for millennia. It is only now when you four are together do you form the Alpha Omega."

"Anomalies," the dull skin beneath her eyes flattened out their wrinkles as she tightened with an air of repulsion and commenced, "art, abominations."

Her fingers clawed into the soiled fabric of the couch beneath as she struggled to stay still. She hissed, "Angels reborn as humans, souls that bound you to this plane. You are God's chosen to represent his love, his glory, and vengeance. Eons built your supernatural flesh, and you are the strongest, the fastest stars. Born to this region, you must protect it: all four of you. Or we will all suffer eternal torment."

Lyssah Rhamiel's pale blue eyes darted between the four, almost as if she were scanning them. Ultimately, her inappropriate ogling settled on Neil. Speaking directly to him, she uttered, "Michael, most powerful of the army and leader, the Angel of the Existential, with sway over the preternatural psyche."

Her eyes then launched toward Amanda and announced, "Raphael, the Angel of Balance and Alchemy, manipulator of universal highs and lows of extreme transformation."

She turned to Aurora and identified, "Gabriel, the Angel of Destiny, with authority over all hours before Judgment Day." Finally, Lyssah Rhamiel pointed to Ezekiel and called, "Uriel, the Angel of Death with the power of the life hereafter. Totems of God, together you form the Alpha Omega. If it is not meant to be—stop the Apocalypse."

"Apocalypse?" Ezekiel asked, his voice breaking. "Like e-end of the w- world, apocalypse?"

Lyssah Rhamiel crookedly confirmed with an awkward nod, "The Apocalypse is a string of harbingers leading to Armageddon. Seals have already been broken; gates have been opened, and the walls that separate reality is starting to melt. All dimensions are becoming one, and things are getting through."

Aurora's eyebrow arched, and her lips curved at their edges with a churlish rile. "This is the most ridiculous thing I've ever heard!" She spat relentlessly, "You don't know us; you don't know me! For one thing, you didn't even call us by the right names! This crone must have drugged us! You're not getting a red cent from me! Aurora Haith will not be scammed by some cracked-out hag in dire need of a hot comb! I'm leaving town."

Aurora stomped to the door, but Lyssah Rhamiel blocked her exit, "You cannot deny the will of God! I saved your lives tonight, and if I wanted to kill you, I'd have left you there! Your paths are already chosen."

Aurora propped her hands on her hips, and Neil lowered his head shamefully as she continued, "Now you listen to me, bitch. You're talking about all these Apocalypses and God's fists; *if* this was all true. Cracked-out ridiculous isn't in the Bible, is it?"

"No, you listen to me, harlot!" Lyssah channeled Aurora's misguided but relentless anger and raised her voice to the top of her lungs. Lyssah Rhamiel slowly peeled the sleeve from her arm. "Your scripture is shrouded in mystery but written on the bodies of your acolyte." As the woman continued to pull up her sleeve, the soft gray fabric revealed several scars protruding from her skin in neatly carved mystifying and otherworldly symbols. An unknown language ran itself in tiny white rows spiraling around Lyssah Rhamiel's pale arm and seemed to have no end.

"Feel connected to the text? It is Enochian, an angelic language. I am your last acolyte and your high priest. I know that you had a vision last night, and I know what you saw. I know it because it is cut into my body! It is the will of God that you fight this war, and trust me; no matter what you do, you cannot deny God's will. You must rise above your psychological limitations! Demons, like the ones you've witnessed this very night, will be coming for you, and if you want to survive them, you will sit on the couch and listen to me!"

Aurora locked gazes with Lyssah Rhamiel, but an unblinking stare defeated her stern glance. Her eyes dropped to the floor, and she irately retreated to the couch. Unable to completely accept humiliation, however, she rolled her eyes and folded her arms in disgust.

Lyssah perched herself in the same position she had been in before. "This is not a joke! We all felt you were coming! So, we must prepare and get you ready for what must come to pass. The preservation of all that you know literally relies on you."

"Stop!" Ezekiel swallowed hard, "This is too m-much pressure! I can't handle this!"

"Don't be afraid," Lyssah Rhamiel warned and inhaled. "A gruesome death will always threaten you, but each of you is blessed with gifts that will grow and strengthen. Given time, you will vanquish the Four Horsemen of the Apocalypse from this plane. Many demons will come, but greatness begins with overcoming daily battles. You can't allow them to break your circle. It is your destiny to beat back the forces of Hell!"

Neil shook his head slowly and tried to comprehend, "So, we...are just tools? We have no choice in the matter?"

"Lyssah Rhamiel..." Amanda's bottom lip quivered, "can I call you, Lyssah?"

"It doesn't matter," the retired nun snorted.

"I've never fought anyone in my life," Amanda persisted. "You guys are the only strangers I know, but I have to tell you: I'm a bit of a pacifist. Sure, that doesn't include political marches or family reunions, but do you really expect me, or us, to kill those four scary guys? We barely got away with our lives the last time we saw them, and you're telling us that other demons will be coming after us? Shouldn't we alert the professionals?"

"Does everyone finally realize what she's asking us to d-do?" Ezekiel muttered as he slapped his hands on his legs in frustration. Bewildered, he proceeded, "F-facing demons for the p-preservation of our daily l-lives...? L-literally fighting monsters... Call me psychotic, but I don't think I can handle it!"

Lowering her head, Amanda bit her bottom lip. Overcome by the ominous sour taste of fear that entered her mouth, it was as if reality had just hit her. All her life, she had never been a fighter.

"But I'm just a girl..." Amanda whispered.

"We're all going to be killed by the Four Horsemen of the Apocalypse!" Ezekiel cried as he buried his face in his hands.

"Yeah, leaving town," Aurora confirmed, folded her hands beneath her bosom. "Alone! You're all crazy!"

"No!" Lyssah Rhamiel jerked about like an angry bird and objected. "This is your destiny; there is no time for

Earthly human disorders! I've no patience for the petrified or mentally weak."

Neil studied Aurora as she scowled beautifully beside him. He could feel furious flames flux from her body. As the smell of cocoa entered his nostrils, he placed a hand on her knee. "Aurora, are you okay?"

She slapped his hand aside and eased away, uncomfortably, "Neil, are you blind? I'm shaking in my stilettos..."

The Alpha Omega are the Cherubim of the Throne are the four strangers in the room.

The Four Horsemen of the Apocalypse are the end of the world are the four murderous attackers that tried to kill them only a few hours before.

He shook his head slowly and still could not satisfy his existentialism. If he was an angel—what did that make his son? What would that make of his life? Is this world even worth saving? Neil ran miles in his mind. There were too many questions that were still left unanswered.

Neil's heart fell to his gut as he tried to think. His Christian roots dried up after his parents' deaths. How could he fight for something he stopped believing in so long ago? Is there more to life than violence, responsibility, and death?

Ezekiel's eyes welled with water as he pulled his sleeves over his fists. His stomach ran up in knots, and he wanted to vomit. In one day, his life was ruined. Every second alone that was once filled with tranquility would now be filled with paranoia. He was a danger to everyone in his life... and they were a danger to him. A swarm of tears poured down his face, and he prayed to wake up from this dream.

Amanda sunk into the worn-out couch as the thought of being the Angel of Amends began to thrill her. She often wished her own life had been more interesting or exciting in a new way. With thoughts of glee and magical powers, she giggled and cracked the awkward silence.

Lyssah arched her back as she placed her hands on her cold bare feet. Positioned like a frog, she growled, "I have prepared a room. Every second from now to the Apocalypse is vital. Tomorrow you will wear loose, comfortable clothes and meet me here. Get ready for your second session."

Chapter 6: Renewal of the Vow

> "Then the angel of the Lord said to Elijah, 'Go down with him; you need not be afraid of him.'"
> **Kings 1:15**

Neil parked in the darkest corner of the baroque church's parking lot. He shoved his uneasy fingers into the pockets of his brown leather jacket and gazed into the night sky. Was this for real or had work, and Victoria finally sent him off the deep end? Was... he crazy? The entire concept of it shattered his soul. Yet here he sat, the very next night in the parking lot wearing what he was instructed to.

After a moment, Neil left his car and walked up to the front of the church, where he found the other angels waiting. Ezekiel and Amanda wore sneakers and gym clothes; however, Aurora covered her tiny feet in silver high heels and her slender thighs in skinny jeans. Her chandelier earrings blew in the breeze like wind chimes, and her makeup was as thick as clay. Amused by her rebellion, Neil snickered, "I can't believe you actually showed up like that."

"You're welcome." Aurora sighed.

"Well," Neil cleared his throat and complimented her, "you look nice today."

"Was there something wrong with the way I looked yesterday?" Aurora snapped and wrinkled her brow. "Didn't we say we were going to meet up early?"

"But Aurora, you were late, too," Amanda reminded her.

"That wasn't my fault," Aurora shook her head and confessed, "because my girlfriend got evicted, then her grandmother died, and she got bit by a stray dog with rabies or something all in one day… The way she goes on and on, you'd think no one else had any problems…"

"Well, I always try to arrive early, even if that means I have to wait two or three hours," Amanda beamed. "So, did anyone go to work today?"

"Work?" Ezekiel grumbled. "Are you kidding? After what happened to us? I could barely drag myself out of bed this morning."

The blonde let out a hysterical laugh as they entered the church, "Me too. Today was def an order-in kinda day. It's just crazy because we have like a really huge secret! And there are some pretty weird things going on, and we're not allowed to tell anyone. So everyone else just walks on by thinking everything is normal, not knowing that the whole entire world will end soon or not…"

Neil placed a solid knock on Lyssah Rhamiel's door while Aurora snarled to herself, "I still don't trust her."

"Ugh," Lyssah Rhamiel recoiled. "Your emotions hang off you like engorged leeches. I felt them as you made your way down the path." She swung the door open, and the stale smell of old tuna cans rushed into the hallway. Owl at hand, Lyssah examined them for a moment. She fixed her dirty glasses as if to check her vision, then swiftly tottered away.

"Are you referring to me?" Aurora's nostrils flared as she asked with an offense, "There's nothing leech-like about us. You invited us here, okay?"

"I-I don't think she meant anything by it…" Ezekiel interjected.

"Are we really going to do this right now?" Neil cut in and rolled his eyes.

"Madam, if you wish to speak, split your lips!" the older woman answered. Lyssah's fingers rolled into fists as she fired back, "I am *abhorred!*"

"Oh no!" Amanda cooed and reached out a hand sympathetically, but Lyssah pushed back. She shrugged away the rejection but still wanted to console the older woman. "You shouldn't say those things about yourself, especially when there are others in the room who are wearing much bolder and more *promiscuous outfits* than you..."

"Seriously?" Aurora seethed and placed her hand on her hip, "We almost got killed together, and you're on her side?"

"I'm sorry," Amanda quickly apologized. "Your outfit really isn't that bold...or ab-*whorish*"

"Aggressive and wild; nervous and afraid; slimy and defensive. You're like eels trapped in my mouth!" Lyssah screeched before she rested her owl on a potted olive tree in the living room. "It's been so long since I've been this close to humans...You're a sickly batch. Follow me, as I have prepared the basement for your arrival..."

Equipped like a supernatural gymnastics' room, the basement was chilly and spacious. Like the rest of the house, its walls were covered in archaic texts. Overtly expensive exercise machines, punching bags, stunt dummies, twisted knives, and ancient weapons filled the room. Lyssah Rhamiel awkwardly led the four to the hollow center of the basement and frantically paced.

"Why don't you tell me a little about why you're here?" Lyssah Rhamiel asked flatly.

Amanda raised her hand with excitement and exclaimed, "Because you said to meet you here at seven for training!"

Stolas the Maniae fluttered from his olive tree and cawed atop Lyssah Rhamiel's silent shoulder. She kept a stone face and ignored Amanda as she repeated, "Why are you here?"

"To save the world?" Neil hesitantly answered the strange woman.

"Deep down, you know it is your responsibility," Lyssah declared. "Each and every one of you knows it is your duty and his undeniable will. Remember your sacred duty. Stopping the Apocalypse is the only thing that matters. Only through therapy will you understand your powers." She pointed an arched finger to Neil and alluded, "You first."

The older woman guided Neil over to the room's southern corner, cluttered with bench-presses and barbells. She lifted two of the larger dumbbells and dropped them in front of him. Neil was impressed by her strength, but at this point, he was used to surprises. She surrounded him with heavyweights of various sizes.

"Do you need any help?" Neil inquired.

"I don't need help from anyone!" Lyssah defended, then lugged the heavy equipment and cursed as she did so,

"Most of my life, I've been alone! I've had to work for every damn thing I've had! None of this matters anyway; I don't even care about you people. I've never needed help, and I don't want to start now. I had to work! Work harder than anyone before! You don't know what I've been through, and it doesn't matter! In summary, I can carry these weights myself."

Neil curled an eyebrow but decided it was best to shut his mouth.

Lyssah Rhamiel fixed her tattered outfit, "Mighty Archangel Michael, Like Unto God," she cooed, then her voice grew into a scream. "Your radiance blesses me, bathes me... and reminds me. Impressive. I want you to work harder than ever before! Shake this Earth down to the core!"

"But it isn't my radiance," Neil huffed uncomfortably, "The way you make it seem, I'm just a tool in all of this. That my choices are irrelevant and who I am doesn't matter because I'm just a puppet playing out a scene. I do have a newborn son to think about, you know."

"No one chooses their existence," she said and crouched. "You just accept your responsibilities and move on. Mentally lift these weights at the same time, then orbit them around you. The more strain you can take, the more power you will endure. Free will is yours, but you can't quiver at its price. Your son has his path but will not survive the coming days if you don't stop the Apocalypse."

Could she be right? Neil had never lifted two objects at once before. He tensed his brain and focused on the barbells to little result. Lyssah Rhamiel stepped away from him. She walked to Amanda, who anxiously twiddled her thumbs. The older woman grabbed the angel's hand and led her to the east corner of the basement.

This space was designed explicitly for Amanda. Scientific posters of tigers, wolves, fish, and birds displayed their anatomies. Each sign dissected the animal into its unique parts and biology. The walls hung huge mirrors and several Petri dishes with strange samples of rocks, leaves, medals, crystals, liquids, and various unnamed materials. Amanda ogled the walls quizzically until she came to a large bulletin that showcased the Periodic Table of Elements. She moped and miserably turned her attention to Lyssah Rhamiel and sheepishly asked, "This isn't going to be like college, is it?"

"On second thought," the nun reconsidered, "I am in the mood for a break… perhaps a vegan burrito of some sort… I haven't seen a featured film in eons."

"I was thinking the same thing!" Amanda cheered.

"Precisely," Lyssah said with a nod. Then the nun shook out the desires she absorbed from Amanda and continued, "It isn't as though an understanding of the otherworldly or the sharpening of our most effective skills could ever help us in a life-threatening situation."

"Or we could do your thing first..." Amanda smirked and tucked a long blonde lock behind her ear.

"God Heals, Archangel Raphael, ruler of the East Winds. You are the Sacred Angel of Amends, Alchemy, and Healing. Stabilizing your condition will take a great deal of treatment and perhaps the rest of your life. Randomly bouncing between the extreme highs and lows of your morphing episodes will further unbalance your chemical state unless you can learn to alter your behavior accurately."

"What?" Amanda blinked. "I think I only understand like half of what you just said, but my mom says as long as I have a super positive attitude and a friendly smile, I can handle anything. So what exactly do you want me to do?"

"Study," Lyssah Rhamiel groaned. "Remember that energy cannot be created or destroyed, only transferred. The shape of objects and even the composition of the elements can be manipulated if you have proper knowledge and training. To successfully balance and rearrange your chemical state, you must understand biological makeup." She pointed to the giant poster of a scorpion on the wall and instructed, "Focus on this creature. Its appropriate and individual behaviors. Analyze every hair, tooth, every fiber. Then transfix into it."

"Scorpions always remind me of land lobster bugs..." Amanda yelped. "Can I please start off by turning into a nice duck? They're pretty cool, and they're cute, and they can swim, and they can fly... "

Lyssah ignored her and commenced the lecture, "Some of your transformations are instinctual; however, if you do not deeply understand how something is built with the components of biology, you risk creating abominations. Devices and creatures that are sterile, broken, and add nothing to history. Study this creature's anatomy. Understand how its poison is made. Slip into a deformed transformation and wager losing your life."

The woman continued to the next angel. She gently took Ezekiel by the arm and brought him to his own corner of the room. This area was filled with plants, small stone gargoyles, strange machines, and colorful, mystical charms. Timidly, Ezekiel tiptoed behind the woman and leered at the hanging animal skeletons.

"Command of God. Uriel, Light of God. The Prince of Tartarus and Sacred Angel of Death," Lyssah Rhamiel solemnly spoke, "you are the connection between this world and the hereafter. As you grow, your abilities continuously hover over you like a desolate cloud."

"T-that doesn't sound too good," Ezekiel mumbled and pulled his sleeves over his twitching fingers.

"If you don't want to do it, go back to your old life," Lyssah snuffed. "No one cares about us, not even our mothers! We have done nothing to deserve this life, yet we remain pieces in a celestial board game. Wellness is not found in a fruitless life."

Ezekiel's chest filled with air and confused he asked, "So how do you suggest I handle this?"

"It is manageable," Lyssah answered and laid Ezekiel flat on his back, "because you are a conduit. You emit a steady progression of symptomatic electromagnetic fields."

Ezekiel apprehensively watched Lyssah Rhamiel flip the necessary switches on a machine that reminded him of an old-fashioned radio. The three meters on the machine wiggled while the device statically cried. She informed him, "When you release these electromagnetic fields, they attract and excite spirits. Soon you should be able to summon them and their ectoplasm for your defensive and offensive advantage. This is an Electromagnetic Field Detector, and it will document your progress. My recommendations:

Commune with the spirit realm. Psychotherapy must be forthright and honest if you ever hope to survive the Apocalypse."

"B-but I-I don't know if I can," Ezekiel murmured as Lyssah Rhamiel darted away, "do this…"

He closed his eyes in unsure concentration. Before, he summoned spirits in his sleep, but to consciously call apparitions proved more difficult. Ezekiel pulled from an inner reserve of strength and anxiously gritted his teeth until he felt a chilly cloud enter the room. The Electromagnetic Field Detector screeched loudly as its meters flipped about.

Ezekiel opened his eyes to see the familiar white tadpole creatures flutter and flash in and out of visibility. The room filled with more swirling apparitions than he could count. His heart thumped in his tight throat. Somehow, he could feel every one of the spirits bounce about in his mind. Upon closer inspection, he sensed the souls within them and thought he saw human faces flash in the floating ectoplasm. "Blessed, be Uriel!" the moving shadows whispered in voices only Ezekiel could hear.

Repeatedly and unsystematically, they all shouted phrases and sounds he could barely make out. "Save the world, Uriel! Help us! You must stop the Apocalypse! For the sake of this world and all others. Uriel Sacred Angel of Death, you must deliver us!"

Ezekiel wavered, then sat upright and gaped while the phantoms gilded about like bubbles. "Okay. No pressure."

Finally, Lyssah Rhamiel regrettably approached Aurora. She took Aurora by the hand, but the model swiped it away. The nun led her to the West corner of the room. In this corner hung several large clocks of all shapes and sizes. Digital clocks broke down time by the millisecond and more massive clocks recorded by years. There was a clock for every time zone on Earth and possibly one or two for the otherworldly.

"Sit," Lyssah commanded.

"I think I'd rather stand," Aurora smirked sarcastically.

"God is my strength. My Archangel Gabriel, powers of prophecy shouldn't make you so paranoid." She studied Aurora and sulked, "What are you wearing on your feet? I told you to dress comfortably."

Aurora placed a hand on her hip and retorted, "Listen, anything I can do in sneakers I can do in heels. Now, why are we here?"

"To expand your abilities…" Lyssah shuddered.

"Yeah, nothing too much, I just got out of the shower," Aurora scoffed below her breath. "Can we get to this training thing or whatever?"

"Why are you so angry?" Lyssah began to tremble as she spoke. "I can hardly control myself."

"I'm not angry! I'm just..." Unable to come up with an answer, she sat on the floor.

The older woman pulled out a sizable orange scale with fifteen pendulum crystals. She placed them before Aurora and muttered, "To gain control over your power of the future, you must first gain insight into your past. The more familiar you get with recognizing temporal patterns, the better you can control your celestial triggers." Lyssah Rhamiel shook the crystal pendulums till they danced in an uneven frenzy. "With the right aim and preciseness, you should be able to manipulate time so that the pendulum waves are uniform and fluid."

Aurora fixed her hair. She concentrated on the wild pendulum, and her eyes began to heat up. Slowly, time warped around the crystals. Smoky lights covered the scale as some gems sped wildly, others sluggishly rocked, and a few stopped movements altogether. She struggled through nausea and released her power, but the tool returned to normal.

Lyssah Rhamiel glowered down at her, disappointedly, "Understand your power's limitations. You can temporarily manipulate the timeline of a small area only if it is in your vicinity. Work on summoning visions of the past; they will help you with predictions of the future. Think back to your personal history; perhaps you can trigger a vision of the past. Match your memory with the truth and see it plainly and without judgment... if you can help it."

"I'll do my best," Aurora snidely retorted as Lyssah Rhamiel marched away.

Aurora closed her eyes and unclenched. She cleared her mind and breathed deeply. "Yoga I can do," the model mused. The dark-haired model readily flashed through her memories without consideration for several minutes.

Then she felt it. A creeping. A tingling in her spine. The sense that told her something was coming.

Aurora's wedding was a week before her eighteenth birthday. Her eyes drooped heavily while her mother brushed her overly glossy hair back into place. The middle-aged woman wiggled fabulously in her designer lavender dress as she excessively sprayed Aurora with hair spray.

"Cheer up, it's embarrassing!" Rebecca Haith demanded while she primped Aurora's fluffy and luxurious wedding gown. "You look beautiful! Biff will make you a

good husband, so cut the bull. He loves you, and his family is respectable and very well off. Don't you dare even think about..."

There was a knock at the hotel door, and Biff entered. He was an extremely tall, attractive, cleanly shaven dark-skinned man with a suit that fit him exquisitely.

He smiled charmingly, "Hello, soon-to-be Mother-in-law. I know it's against the tradition, but may I have a moment with my future wife?"

"Of course! Who believes in that, anyway? Nowadays, there's no such thing as bad luck. Only bad choices." Rebecca threateningly glared at Aurora before she plastered on a smile and winked at Biff when she exited the room.

Immediately he started towards her, "The guys have been drinking a ton to relieve the nerves and ME. And guess what? Nerves not relieved." He stumbled toward her and grabbed her shoulders. "That's where you come in, baby! Relieve my stress. Remind me why I'm marrying you! I want what you stole from me. Give me back my power."

"Biff, get off me." Aurora stood from her chair. "You'll mess up my makeup. I have to look nice."

"Don't you ever tell me what to do," Biff threatened. *"You will be mine, I will get back what I want. You can't keep it from me."*

Her violent vision abruptly ended. To her dismay, she remembered the moment clearly. In a frantic bolt, Aurora left the room before the streaming tears could smear her face.

The White House was just as busy as he imagined. It buzzed with electric energy that excited the Horseman of Pestilence—so many important decisions were made here. Covered in his extended white cape, he adjusted his pale crown and scoffed at the White House attendants as they rushed through the halls on their cellphones like bees in a hive.

None of them was innocent; not a single one.

Invisible to the crowd, he stepped into the auditorium.

The White House kept hidden auditoriums solely for these secret meetings. Monthly, representatives of every world power occupied the rowed seats and discussed necessary future arrangements. Like a shadow, Pestilence slithered onto the main stage. Great wars began with the White Horseman. He planted kernels of annoyance that grew into massive trees of abhorrence in the hearts of men. Careful to remain quiet, Lyssah Rhamiel's owl watched diligently through the thin holes of a vent and took note of every detail.

Pestilence's boney fingers gripped his bow tightly. This moment was something he had dreamed of years ago. He had never been so happy. Soaking in each second, he raised his enchanted bow and opened fire. Unbeknownst to the officials, the arrows hit their hearts and melted away to nothing. The demon felt the loathing rise within the private politicians. He grinned as his unholy arrows damned their souls.

Ezekiel refused to go to work the next day. He was unsure he could ever go to work again. Lyssah Rhamiel counseled them all night and showed them how to use their new abilities more naturally. Neil telekinetically rolled around boxes; Aurora temporarily froze time around small areas, Amanda had a great time mimicking the people she knew, and Ezekiel hesitantly astral projected.

Though slightly more comfortable with his fresh skills, he was in a paralyzing dysthymia. Ezekiel spent the entire day in the library—researched and contemplated the world he was thrown into. He spent his time reading every frightening religious and demonic reference that seemed legitimate. Angels, Gods—they all had their daunting mysteries. Most books were old and held horrific depictions of naked demons raping women and eating children. He shivered and closed a book, unable to find information on the Cherubim of the Throne. When Lyssah Rhamiel said that their origins were shrouded, she was right, and Ezekiel anxiously slid his fingers under his sleeves.

Amanda sat in her living room as the images of cartoons played on the television screen. She panted and sobbed between handfuls of her sloppy sandwich. Her eyes moved across her roommate's open door. Olive had been missing for two days—ever since she had seen Amanda transform.

Amanda wiped her lonely tears, and the front door suddenly opened. Olive entered the room with a skirt made of burlap and a purple tie-dye tank top but stopped short when the two locked gazes under her rose-colored glasses. Amanda stood abruptly, knocked over the pile of dishes on the coffee table, and crawled over the couch. "Olive..."

Olive swiftly started toward her bedroom door, and Amanda jumped before her and reassured, "Don't be scared! Please, I can explain everything... Just sit down and talk to me for a little while. It's not what you think!" Amanda cautiously entreated, "Look, I made lunch! Eat, I'm sure you're hungry... Did you know that you can make Philly cheesesteak locally? I'm making some, vegan of course—I didn't have to travel out of state for the ingredients or anything... I'm thinking about adding it to the truck... I could make some...just please don't leave! I have so much to tell you, and I need the opinion of my best friend."

Olive's mouth dropped open as she forced the words to come out, "I saw you transform right before my eyes. How can you logically explain that? Explain why you chose to not disclose this information."

Amanda was apologetic, but couldn't hide her excitement as she spoke, "Because Olive I just found out! I don't think I'm supposed to tell anyone but since you're *totally* my best friend and I *totally* tell you everything and you kind of already saw. Olive, I'm an angel."

"An angel? Interesting. I've never believed in anything I could not see right before my eyes, but how could I deny solid evidence? You literally defy everything I know and learned in my life. If I'm going to succumb to this, I need a drink." Olive pulled out two animal-shaped mugs from the cabinet and filled them with red wine. Hesitantly she asked, "Shall I add a little Nectar in yours as well?"

"Nectar...?" Amanda raised an eyebrow.

"It's a calming formula... all-natural," Olive readily answered before she fished out a small brown bottle from her pocket and poured a golden powder that smelt like honey into her glass. "It's been around for centuries; I'm surprised you never heard of it. Sort of like CBD oil, only stronger. Yet I digress, just continue..."

"Just a little wine is fine," Amanda nodded vigorously. "It's actually kind of cool! I've been itching to tell somebody. I can do all this cool stuff. I have these powers. I mean, people have tried to kill me in the past couple of days, but I have powers!" Amanda was delighted. "I can show you."

Olive's brow wrinkled while Amanda walked closer to her. Amanda's smile grew more full, and she took Olive's hand and welcomed, "Buckle your seat belt because what I'm about to show you will blow your mind!"

Later that night, Aurora's eyes refused to shut completely. Her fingers tightly gripped the edges of her thick, expensive comforter. Aurora's lower lip dropped as little noises from her living room stirred into her chambers. The wooden floor under the white carpet creaked as though someone was walking on it. Not so long ago, Aurora would have ignored the minimal sounds, but things were different now. Each creak seemed louder and more suspicious than before.

She held her breath in fear. The demons probably had some magical way of figuring out where they lived. Why not? What stopped them from coming into her home and seizing her any instant? Aurora lowered the sheets slowly then leaned over towards the small dresser beside her.

Her heartbeat loudly while she opened the bedside drawer, and unsteadily pulled out a nine-millimeter revolver. Since her first encounter with the Horsemen, she had the sudden need to protect herself and enrolled in a handgun training course. Freezing time was great, but her range wasn't far, and she never knew how long she could hold someone.

Aurora placed her cold feet on the floor and walked into the living room. Glimmers of sleepless Manhattan lights flowed through the silk curtains. She held the gun close to her chest, and her large auburn eyes investigated the corners of her home. In a moment of relief, she took comfort to the fact that there was no bursting cow.

She dashed towards the light switch and quickly illuminated the entire room. Nothing. Aurora brushed some hair from her face, livid. This was too stressful. She needed to get some sleep—her job required it.

Neil's laptop was scarcely used for anything but writing articles. Lately, however, he just couldn't put it down. The Horsemen of the Apocalypse were out there and were capable of attacking at any moment. He studied late into the night until an urgent knock sounded at his front door. Neil jumped a bit as the sound blasted into his still condominium. He pulled himself to the entryway and greeted her, "Aurora,"

Armed with a thick yellow blanket and pillow, Aurora marched in without an invitation. The model was dressed in a white cotton form-fitting pair of pajama bottoms and a button-up shirt, both printed with small red hearts, underneath her designer jacket, of course. She turned to Neil and snarled a bit as if it were difficult to speak, "I know you can't tell by the way I look, but I'm a mess. Neil, I don't know when I'll have a vision or what creepy crawly will attack me in my sleep! I tried Neil, I really did, but I can't! I just keep thinking about that damn bloody cow in my living room. I know it was just a vision, but all of my furniture is white, Neil, it's stressful. You have the best power and can defend yourself. So don't take this the wrong way, but can I spend the night? Or maybe a few nights until I get used to this thing."

Neil watched her for a few moments; his lip quivered, then he nodded, "Nice monologue. Y-yes, of course. Mi casa es su casa."

"Okay, I don't speak Japanese." Aurora examined his apartment and looked back to Neil. "But thank you." Glancing him over a bit, she noticed how extremely nervous he looked in his checkered boxers and his white t-shirt. She arched an eyebrow and smiled, "And don't let the name brand pajamas fool you: try something, and I will claw your eyes out."

"I wouldn't think of it, and I'm not Japanese, my mother was Italian American, and my father was Chinese American, so let's not talk about race if you have no idea," he corrected her with a grin. "You come here, in the middle of the night, and barge in before I invite you. I'm surprised you didn't try to take my bed! Why have evil demons when we have you, Aurora?"

"I know it must be difficult being around a woman like me this late at night," Aurora said and exhaled. "I do understand that men have their urges, especially if they haven't been touched in a while… So I think it's best if I take the bed, just to avoid any confusion…"

"It's my house," Neil's nose wrinkled and responded with disgust, "You can take the couch."

"Ugh," Aurora narrowed her eyes, defeated, and she threw her sheets on the couch before concluding, "well, you're no gentleman, are you?"

Neil shrugged his shoulders and admitted, "Nope. I mean, you'll end up protecting me. One look at you, and the demons will run away screaming."

She folded her arms, unamused, then retorted, "I would say you're funny, but your looks aren't everything."

"You're one to talk," he quickly combated, "With your kindergarten insults…"

"You're really pushing it. Stop making fun of my outer beauty," Aurora snapped as she placed her hands in her pockets and noticed Neil's computer screen. "Ugh, Horsemen? Take a break; you don't want to have bad dreams." He lowered his head as Aurora continued, "It's a little too late for that stuff."

The two locked gazes for a moment. She still smelt of warm cocoa.

"It's been like this for the last two days. I don't really know anything about the Horsemen. I don't know when they're going to attack, or how they're going to attack when they try to end the world." Neil scratched his slightly ruffled black-brown hair and announced, "So, my plan is…"

"To throw that freak show off the rooftop, then book it the Hell out of there again because even Lyssah said we're not ready to face them?" Aurora folded her arms and confessed, "She's right, but I still don't trust her."

"Why?"

"You know those chandelier earrings I wore to that training session?" Aurora's temperament turned accusatory, but she tried to hold her composure while she spoke, "I put them down for just a moment… I haven't seen them since."

"Sometimes she tells me she really isn't into fashion," Neil objected.

"Those are very expensive earrings," Aurora urged. "And it's not like the woman is working."

"She's tough," Neil commented, "but you have to admire her work ethic."

"She's weird," Aurora snarled, "and I don't have to admire her for anything. She won't tell us anything, really! Like those evil symbols on the walls! And what's up with that bird? She wants us to keep coming for sessions, but I don't think we should see her again unless we know what's going on. Maybe you should read her mind!"

"Maybe." Neil shrugged. "But it doesn't always work. At least it doesn't work on you guys."

"What do you mean?" Aurora's neck coiled like a snake as she accused, "You tried to read my mind without my permission? That is just…distasteful. Don't you know that a girl's thoughts are supposed to be her own? Look, I know I come across as an angry black woman, but these are weird circumstances, I'm really not this high strung. Why would you need to read my mind?"

Neil turned from her and admitted, "I didn't know who you were. I couldn't trust you."

Her eyes rolled as she scowled, "But you trust me now?"

Before he could answer, however, she felt a familiar sensation run down her vertebrae. Her body heaved as though something inside of her was desperately trying to escape. Aurora's mouth dropped, and her eyes enlarged. It was the coming signs of a vision; she could feel it. Aurora coughed a bit as she forced her mind to open the projection. All her strength and energy was required to push through these predictions, but she had no control over what played in her mind.

The Donald Woods Library on 48th street. It is the most extensive library in Manhattan and holds a restricted section of the rarest and most unique texts. Aurora had never been, but she noticed the enormous lion statues that guarded the entrance. She struggled to remain standing—her prophetic visions were like seeing through a video recording on a drone—in fast motion.

Hidden, deep inside of the library, was the unmistakable Horsemen of the Apocalypse. In their signature armor, fur, and capes, the four surrounded a pile of books laid open on the ground. The ancient texts were turned to specific pages and strategically placed so that the random words drew the letters of an unknown language.

The Horsemen lowered their heads around the puzzle. Volumes suddenly burst into flames while a large metal box covered in prehistoric warnings appeared. When the fire died down Hunger, the Black Horsemen discovered an engraved metal box in the ash's center. With a flip of the latch, the box was open.

Rapidly, thousands of small naked creatures leaped from the chest. Four inches tall, bald and covered in gray skin, the tiny men hit the floor and rushed off throughout the building. They gnawed and snapped at the air with small mouths of teeth like broken glass in rows. A cloud of flying insects swarmed the room. Fleas, mosquitoes, and wasps flew from the box in a single stream, biting at the air with mutilated human faces and sharp teeth.

Aurora blinked her eyes several times as her vision ended, and she realized she was in Neil's arms, unharmed. Saliva ran bitterly through her mouth. Without thinking, she knew that the insects were somehow related to disease, sickness, and—the event was going to take place the very next night.

"I don't need you to touch me." Aurora pushed her way out of his arms and fought the urge to vomit. Finally she found the strength to alert, "Those horse-guys… I think they're about to do something…"

Chapter 7: The Box of Morbus

> "Will it be three years of Famine; or three months of fleeing your enemies, with the sword of your foes ever at your back; or three days of the Lord's own sword, a pestilence in the land, with the Lord's destroying angel in every part of Israel? Therefore choose: What answer am I to give him who sent me?"
>
> **Chronicles 21:12**

"And they were." Amanda paused and leaned in closer to Aurora and Neil. "Naked men? Gross..." her voice trailed off in a whisper. The next afternoon the four had a chance to meet with Lyssah Rhamiel d'Youville. Neil rapped on the wooden entrance loudly. Aurora nudged him and pointed up to a small camera lens that hung hidden in a corner above the door. She rolled her eyes and placed a hand on her hip before turning to let Amanda finish. "And bees with human faces? That's strange."

"Yes!" Aurora shouted, "Why would I make that up?"

The door swung open. Lyssah Rhamiel's delicate hands fished in and out of a can of sausages while she scrambled around the room. Lyssah refused to acknowledge anyone or even waste time with pleasantries. Aurora gazed at her suspiciously, then nodded to Neil.

He closed his eyes and reached out into Lyssah Rhamiel's mind.

Pictures of a large scaly creature flashed in Neil's head. Memories mixed with thoughts and ideas melted together in chaos. "I will get my revenge!" bellowed the grave and terrifying voice of the creature. "Stolas! Stolas!" It was Lyssah Rhamiel's voice now. "Where's Stolas? Where is Stolas? Stolas, what the Hell is taking so long?"

Neil blinked, confused. His mental link with Lyssah Rhamiel severed. It was strange: although he wasn't completely blocked from her thoughts, they were jagged, unclear, and harder to get.

Lyssah Rhamiel plucked and devoured the last sausage from the can. A tapping at the window began, and immediately, she opened it, and the small gray owl hopped in. She lifted it on her finger and removed a little blinking light from its leg. Lyssah Rhamiel tossed the broken tracker into the trash and silently held her pet for a few moments before placing him in the cage.

"The Horseman of Hunger and Disease is attempting to open the Box of Morbus," Lyssah glanced saltily at Aurora and revealed. "You had a vision, and that's why you're here. You don't have the power to take on the Horsemen yet. You know that. You will retrieve the box and bring it back to me so it can be mystically destroyed."

"You sure know how to bark to orders." Aurora frowned. "What are you going to do?"

"What exactly is in this box?" Ezekiel bit his lower lip and asked.

"The Box of Morbus contains creatures called the Withers—small yellow demons, invisible to the human eye. They find human bodies and hang off of them like parasites, infecting them and slowly killing them with rare, untreatable viruses. Once the Wither is full, it gestates and bursts—multiplying itself. You mustn't allow it to pass."

"But the things I saw were gray," Aurora interrupted.

"Withers 2.0," Neil suggested. "A new disease?"

"So, that's just it?" Ezekiel waved his arms in an outcry, "W-we walk in the door, you give us some f-footnotes, and we're supposed to feel comfortable fighting for our lives?"

"Oh my God," Amanda gasped before placing a hand over her chest, "oops... shouldn't be breaking commandments now..." There was nothing she hated more than seeing people (especially children) deathly ill because of the time and care she put into her volunteer work at the hospital. "We can't let that happen... are we gonna have to fight?"

Neil faced them grimly, almost as if he was expecting this, and declared, "We have to stop them from opening that box."

Ezekiel fumbled about nervously, "So, you want us just to go down there and fight them? Neil, we can't do that; we could get killed."

Neil answered with his head between his palms. "We're going to have to fight," Neil's voice trailed off. "We need to come up with a game plan. Aurora's vision is happening later tonight."

"Fight?" Ezekiel disputed, "Easy for you to say Mr. I-can-throw-people-off-rooftops…"

"We all have our abilities…" Neil reaffirmed.

"Wait," Aurora interjected when she felt a chill in the back of her mind. "I-I think we made a mistake. This is happening sooner than I thought."

An hour later, they were on-site. Two massive stone lions greeted outsiders from the steps at the extensive Donald Woods Library. Neil jiggled the handles on the front doors, but they were locked, as expected. He turned toward the members of the Alpha Omega.

"Well," Aurora shrugged her shoulders and urged, "You didn't expect the door to be open at night, did you?" Aurora nodded towards the door, "Use your—"

"Get ready, everyone," he warned. Stay together and watch each other's backs. We get the box, then we leave."

"Great plan!" Ezekiel sarcastically quipped.

"Well," Neil shrugged and recoiled, "it's not like we had a lot of time to plan."

"So somehow, this is my fault," Aurora assumed.

"Shh!" Neil warned. He braced himself, then telekinetically snapped the lock and opened the doors to the large dark room.

"I hope there's no alarm," Amanda wished as she quietly tiptoed through the sizable empty library.

"Be quiet," Neil ordered while he led them through the shadows, "Don't say anything unless it's very important.."

Amanda nervously bit her lower lip and uttered, "Well, I don't know if I should be mentioning this right now, but my roommate works in life insurance—so if anyone has any loved ones they're thinking about..."

Aurora shot her a silencing glare. A constant yammering eventually crawled through the halls. The crackle of fire whispered beneath foreign verses as its shadows bounced around the walls. Neil slipped into the room with the others behind him.

Suddenly, his heart sped up. He could feel the presence of the Four Horsemen. Amanda emphatically pointed as the copper smell of a dead body entered their nostrils. A security guard was sprawled across a bookshelf with a large open wound that cut across his abdomen and soaked his navy blue tie and badge in blood. The murder looked unreal and artful—right out of a film. Amanda hyperventilated and turned away in shock.

Ezekiel's stomach ran up in a bubbly war then—his lunch resurfaced. He leaned over and vomited on the carpet, digested remains spreading over his shoes. Neil patted Ezekiel on the back, while he finished heaving then turned to Aurora. She had been watching the dead body with swollen eyes and parted full lips.

"Come on," he summoned his confidence and pushed forward, "let's pull it together. We don't want to give up a surprise attack." Neil turned from them and walked toward the whispering demons.

Moonlight shone from the windows, but the light from the fire lit the ransacked space. The Horsemen stood tall and ominous around the pile of books and chanted in a different tongue. It was just as Aurora had seen it. Hunger was there, he smiled a peculiar grin as every fold on his body rippled, and drool fell from his lips. When the ring of fire died down, Hunger wobbled through the ashen remains like a polar bear through the snow.

Neil targeted his hand and prepared for the next steps. He would never allow Hunger to unleash the thousands of small naked demons and insects that would spread sickness throughout Manhattan. He stepped out from behind the bookshelf and raised an open palm. Slowly, the metal box slid across the floor away from Hunger's meaty grip.

The Four Horsemen turned all at once. One after the other, the demons readied their weapons. "E.Z., get the box," Neil ordered.

Pestilence aimed his ivory bow, but Neil telekinetically held the weapon in place against the White Horseman's strength.

Ezekiel astral-projected across the room. His ghostly hands swiped through the metal box several times. He was incorporeal and struggled in the heat of the moment—but he eventually worked up enough concentration to become tangible long enough to snatch the metal object.

War drew his sword and charged at Neil. Aurora tackled the angel to the ground and saved him from the blow before the demon continued towards Amanda, who could do nothing but shiver. War pointed the sword at her throat. Frozen in her baby blue bubble jacket, Amanda dropped her jaw helplessly. Betrayed by her body, her mind fell blank. Her ears deafened. Then slowly the rest of her senses escaped her while War approached.

"Hey!" Ezekiel grunted with the box tight at this chest. He caught the attention of the Horseman, which gave Amanda enough time to take cover.

Hunger's tiny balanced scales shifted. As an enchanted weapon, this magical item had unique and often mysterious ways of attacking. A warm sensation wrapped around Ezekiel's astral body, then it burned. In his spirit form, he had no physical senses but somehow could still feel pain. He dropped the box and tried to return to his host body but was quickly shoved through the nearest bookshelf.

Pestilence fired an arrow, and Neil fought his way to his feet with just enough time to send the flying blade into War's shoulder.

Death snickered and charged at Aurora. Abruptly, she turned to escape, but her burgundy high heel snapped, and she fell to her knees. Her irises reddened, and she summoned her power, but Death was too quick. He swung his scythe, and a rush of invisible energy sent Aurora flying into the wall behind her.

The blow was suffocating, and for a second, she thought she was dead—had the assault been any more substantial, she would have been. She hit the ground and was out cold.

An explosion of dusty air gushed into the room.

Hunger held open the engraved metal box. Just as Aurora had foreseen, several thousands of naked, miniature, bug-eyed creatures ran freely into the shadows. The tiny men had three rows of snapping sharp teeth—they cursed and cheered as they jumped over each other and rushed to the darkness.

Hunger pulled back the lid of the box further, and a cloud of black human-faced insects escaped. They wept sorrowfully while they buzzed. Cries of distress filled the room as the small demons' woeful faces looked for a way to avoid them. Countless wasps, mosquitoes, and fleas swarmed like a dense gas until they found an open window to exit. Pestilence's raspy voice was mocking as the Horsemen faded, ghostly, crepuscular: "Nicely played, Seraph,"

"We have to leave," Neil exclaimed loudly and ran his frustrated fingers through his thick spiky hair. He picked up Aurora's unconscious body and headed towards the exit.

"Does she need to be taken to the hospital?" Ezekiel mumbled his suggestion.

"I think she's just unconscious," Neil disagreed and shook his head. "She's a strong girl; She can take it. We need to get out of here; I'm sure plenty of people heard the noise we made up here."

Amanda frantically ran behind Neil. "What are we going to do about everyone getting sick? We have to do something!" she shouted. "We can't just let thousands of people get infected by the Whitneys!"

"It's *Withers*. You do have powers of your own, you know," Neil retorted while Aurora shifted uncomfortably in his arms.

"What did you want me to do?" Amanda asked roughly. "Hit him?"

"That's the general idea!" Neil countered. "You could have helped!"

"I tried to tell everyone about health insurance, Neil!" Amanda cried. "I am a pacifist. I never threw a single punch in my life, and you can't expect me to go sumo overnight! I froze Neil, alright, sue me!"

"You better learn quickly. Pacifists don't win wars. One of us could have died tonight," Neil scolded her before he kicked open the doors to the entrance of the library.

"Freeze!" a hollering voice commanded.

Chapter 8: Frozen

> "Make them like chaff before the wind, with the angel of the Lord driving them on. Make their way slippery and dark, with the angel of the Lord pursuing them."
>
> **Psalms 35:5-6**

"I said, 'Freeze!'" the voice got louder. A tall man with a chocolate five-o'clock shadow and bright green eyes aimed his gun. From his black suit, he fished out a small leather wallet and flashed his badge. Several police officers backed the young detective and pointed their pistols at Neil, Amanda, and Ezekiel. He smiled confidently and sarcastically, then arrogantly exclaimed, "I'm Detective Rhion Galloway, and you've just been arrested!"

"Cuff 'em," he instructed the other officers as they tackled Ezekiel and Amanda. "Ever hear of a silent alarm? Most places have them nowadays. Welcome to the present."

"We didn't do anything!" Amanda shouted as the police officer locked her hands in metal cuffs. "And we're not telling you anything either! Breaking in here was the only time we ever broke the law!"

"You are at my crime scene," the green-eyed cop declared. He placed his gun in its tan jacket, and the policemen snatched Aurora's unconscious body from Neil. "That's good enough. What happened to her?"

Neil thought quickly, "She fainted. And there's a body of a security guard inside."

"A dead body?" Rhion repeated. "Really? That's interesting. Here we thought this was just a robbery. And you're seen running from the crime scene with a fainted girl because why?" He let Neil stumble for a moment before he commanded, "Get in the car."

Police shoved Neil into the cop car beside Amanda and Ezekiel. He watched the ambulance arrive through the dusty police car window but bound at his wrists, Neil was powerless. He didn't want to leave Aurora alone, but Rhion insisted she go to the hospital.

Ezekiel managed to slip his cuffed hands underneath his sleeves. His eyes welled up, but he held back his tears. He gazed at Neil quizzically.

"We need to come up with a solid story right now," Neil whispered.

"Just say we were out for a walk, and through a crazy and random turn of events ended up in the library!" Amanda offered, then wiggled urgently in her seat as the policeman started the car.

Neil murmured angrily, "That doesn't make any sense!"

"I've never been arrested before," Ezekiel gasped for air. "They just caught us with a dead body! It's done—no more Cherubim. I-I told you we should have told them. They could have been helping us o-out right now. They would have understood..."

"Or they would have handed us over to the FBI and have us sliced and diced," Neil whispered as the car pulled into the police station moments later. "Tell them we were going to the park when we heard a scream and checked it out..."

An hour later, Ezekiel quivered on the monochrome plastic chair in the small bland interrogation room. The angel nervously pulled his sleeves over his anxious fingers. He was the first to be questioned. His eyes welled, and his heart beat so loudly he could hardly hear. Sweat wet his palms, and he wiped them on his sleeves as two intimidating officers sat across a large white table.

Detective Martin was a middle-aged chubby man with no hair on his face or scalp. He had gentle eyes and a peaceful demeanor. His partner, however, sat feverishly in his chair. Rhion Galloway's brow tensed as he silently reviewed the paperwork on his desk.

Rhion arrogantly folded his arms while the other officer took notes before the sizable two-way mirror. Ezekiel swallowed a rock in his throat as a bead of sweat raced down his forehead.

"So, Ezekiel Wallace, I went Santa Claus on your ass and personally checked your record twice. And may I say, you have a squeaky clean ass! Did you know that?" Rhion's solemn voice echoed. "Unlike some of your friends… what'd that blonde girl really get arrested for? An aggressive topless protest at… a Build-a-Bear?"

"Maybe she was confused by the name…" Ezekiel swallowed hard.

"What were you doing in that building?"

"I-I was walking by... saw that the doors were open... because I was, w- we were going to the park, and the d-doors were open, and we heard a scream, so we went inside..." Ezekiel stumbled tearfully through his story.

Rhion raised his bushy eyebrows inquisitively, "You just see an open building, and you decide to walk in?"

"No," Ezekiel shook his head stuttered, "th-there was, s-somebody screamed..."

Rhion's stern expression was unchanging. It was clear he was an expert at his job. His poker face was like stone and made Ezekiel tear up whenever their eyes met. Rhion tapped his fingers on the table then began, "Are you scared of me, Ezekiel? You should be. If you were a smart guy, you would be pissing your pants right now. I control the rest of your young life, so if I were you, I would be terrified... I've been in this game for a long time, and I can tell when I'm being lied to. You look like you've just seen a dead body." The young cop said flatly, "The dead body of Bill Peirce, forty-six-year-old security guard, a happily married, hardworking father of two, to be more specific."

Rhion placed a bent hand on his chest and continued, "The way he was murdered. It was a lot, even for someone who's seen as much as I have. It takes a real sick bastard to do something like that... I know it wasn't you. But I'm going to need you to be completely honest with me if I'm going to catch whoever did this."

"I-I am being honest with you..." Ezekiel's voice cracked, and he nervously jerked his knee.

"You're not!" Rhion interjected quickly and stood from his chair. "I said if you were smart, you would be scared of me. But I guess I overestimated you." His emerald eyes pierced Ezekiel as he ordered his partner, "Call in a confession..."

"But, I didn't confess anything!" Ezekiel exclaimed.

Smugly, Rhion looked at his very expensive designer watch and apologized, "I'm sorry, my very expensive designer watch is about five minutes fast. Confession time."

The second officer left the room and shut the door behind him. Rhion leaned in and urged, "Look, it's late. Both my partner and I heard a confession... Now you have five minutes. I want to go home, sleep in my nice warm bed tonight, have sex with my beautiful wife, and live out the rest of my life with my family; whether you ever get to do that or not is up to you. Like I said, I don't think that you did it; a little man of your size couldn't possibly... But I'm not an idiot. You obviously know something that you're not telling me, and that stupid half-ass lie will only get you locked up. Who are you covering for? Are you guys a part of the Blood Wolf?"

Ezekiel shook his head, and adrenaline desperately pumped through his veins. He bleated, "No, we're not a part of any gang. I'm not covering for anyone!"

"Then you killed Bill Peirce!" Rhion accused.

"No!" Firecrackers went off in Ezekiel's mind.

"Liar!" Rhion shouted and slammed his hands down on the table.

With a heavy thud, Ezekiel's heart stopped. His head fell, and his eyes rolled back into his head. Reopening his unfocused vision, he floated like a gray haze. He watched Rhion frantically shake his lifeless body from his astral form. Ezekiel struggled for balance but managed to land his ghostly spirit. He was scared, but physical repercussions were no longer—no sweaty palms or beating heart. Petrified and confused, Rhion turned from Ezekiel's dead body and stumbled into his ghostly one.

"What the Hell!" Rhion screamed as he fell into Ezekiel's astral self.

Ezekiel's shadow filled Rhion like water soaked into a sponge. He reopened his eyes anew and stumbled. His body was not his own. As the disorientation subsided, Ezekiel stood, possessing the flesh of Rhion Galloway. Erupting with uncertainty, he threw open the door and rushed out into the station lobby where Neil and Amanda sat on a bench and waited to be questioned.

Neil frowned defensively as Rhion walked towards him, "I'm not speaking without a lawyer."

Ezekiel walked up to the other cops and spoke apprehensively, "Th- they're free to g-go."

"Wait, how are they just...?" an officer questioned.

"There are n-no fingerprints on the door, and an s-sword o-obviously did the murder... I think," Ezekiel stuttered. "There is not enough evidence or whatever! You guys get out of here!"

The other officers looked puzzled, and Ezekiel urged Neil and Amanda. "I said you're free to go, so get out of here!"

Neil and Amanda exchanged confused glances.

"Now!" Ezekiel screeched through Rhion Galloway's body, "J-just promise me you'll w- wait for Ezekiel outside..."

Neil and Amanda nodded suspiciously but quickly left while Ezekiel returned to the room and his soulless body. Like wading through jello, Ezekiel stepped from Rhion's flesh and entered his own. Rhion fell to the ground, unconscious, and Ezekiel rushed out of the room and shut the door behind him.

"You don't look so good," Dr. Deveen advised Aurora to stay in bed.

"Long day," Aurora groaned, unleashed her power, freezing the doctor in place. She answered her cellphone as Neil called, "If you only knew..."

"You can answer your cellphone... I assume you're good?" Neil stood outside of the police station with his cell to his ear.

Aurora narrowed her red eyes, her gold and silver cellphone pressed tightly against her. She snuck around the corner of the hospital and across the street while two cops were paralyzed in a smoky white light. She held her sore and bandaged abdomen. "Yes," Aurora winced, "I'm leaving now."

Amanda smiled while Ezekiel sped onto the streets. Neil and Amanda followed Ezekiel as Stolas, the Maniae Owl, flew above, then quickly out of sight. "That was sooo effing freaking awesome! How in the heck did you do that?" she exclaimed.

"I don't know," Ezekiel anxiously rushed down the stairs, "but I think we should leave right now."

Chapter 9: Tragedy and Sickness

> "At the resurrection, they neither marry nor are given in marriage but are like the angels in heaven."
> **Matthew 22:30**

Salty sea air licked the shore like a million frozen tongues, then twisted grains of sand into small whirlpools. The moon was large, white, and ethereal over the ocean as flakes of snow fell gently into the water below. Nathaniel Robinson wiped away the powdery, eerie specks that landed on his eyelashes and dropped his substantial black bag onto the sandy, cold ground. Photography never paid the bills, but it was his lifelong passion.

He peered through his camera and turned the focus knobs. The mysterious ocean was a chilly navy blue and a hair-raising wonder. As he focused his lens, he noticed a suspicious darkening in the sea. It expanded quickly and blackened the water. He dipped his fingers into the shadowed liquid as it ran onto the coast—it smelt like copper.

In the distance, an object rose from the tar. A man, he thought, but as the figure walked closer, Nathaniel saw that it was anything but. The creature was skinless and bled so thick and profusely it was hard to recognize. It opened huge empty eyes and inched toward him.

He stood, unmoving, frozen in a state of fear. The blood suddenly parted where this creature's mouth was and revealed two rows of smiling teeth. Nathaniel jolted backward, but the creature grabbed him. It was more durable than it looked, and the demon's tight grasp overcame Nathaniel. Immediately the unknown creature pressed his bloody lips onto Nathaniel. It was like pressing his face into boiling water. Acid-like venom rushed through his veins. His life was sucked from him, and within a few moments of struggling, he was dead.

Nathaniel was dropped into the water as it started to boil. The monster threw his head back and slowly dissolved. All the blood in the water twisted and moved unnaturally—it swirled and seeped into the dead human body.

Hours later, the dark red in the sea filled Nathaniel's carcass, and when the last drop was absorbed, his body rose.

Nathaniel looked at his hand anew to ensure himself that it was there. He smiled, then noticed that two fallen angels had appeared on the shore. Pale Typhon wiggled his thin fingers; his skinny frame arched with anger and dementia. He had greasy black hair that draped over his crooked shoulders and a twisted face. His eyes and mouth bled black liquid that steadily dropped and added new stains to his ripped white shirt.

His wife, on the other hand, was a vision of perfection. Giselle was close but was careful not to touch him. Her model blonde hair curled just before her shoulders, and her eyes sparkled like blue jewels. She wore a white dress with pink polka dots and a red heart pendant around her neck to match her lipstick. Breathlessly, the beauty took a step towards the man when he approached.

"Forgive me; I thank you for coming," the demon dressed as Nathaniel uttered. His thick winter clothes dripped excess blood and saltwater while he crept onto the shore. "It's a beautiful night, isn't it? Wouldn't you like to see it, Typhon?"

Typhon batted his head about wildly, "This curse... I long to see the agony I cause—but I found a new muse in screaming."

Nathaniel purred, "When's the last time you saw your wife? Gave her a bloodstained kiss? Groped her? Can you feel her love?" Typhon shamefully turned away. Nathaniel smiled wickedly, "I can feel this blood pumping through me; it's warm." Giselle and Typhon stood silently as he continued. "This world has been eclipsed; the Horsemen have taken the first steps toward Armageddon, and I can feel this Earth dying. The deeper power that separates all worlds is unraveling; the walls that separate dimensions are melting. I can feel it, can you? Lilith, have you done as I instructed?"

Giselle parted her rosy red lips, "Oh hush now, you know if there's one thing I understand, it's how to take an order! I christened the Horsemen just like you asked, each and every one! Though, honey, I have outgrown my old name. Giselle is a much better fit than Lilith or Echidna, don't you think?"

"It's taking everything in me not to fry you where you stand," Typhon snapped, pressing his bare feet into the icy sand. "Tell me why you called us here."

"I need acolytes," Nathaniel answered. "But not just any ordinary acolytes. We three share a bond. As angels, you were bathed in the rapturous light and were granted Everlasting Glory. But that wasn't enough, was it? You were denied forgiveness. Ironic how the Lord's devoted angels are beneath his spitting and shitting… impure creations."

"I hear a crackle in the sky," Typhon muttered a threat.

"You were also denied true love," Nathaniel spoke. "As heavenly attendants, you were forced to love all of his creations, but that's not the love you desired, was it? You wanted to love on a deeper level, and you were punished for your love and cursed, with poisonous lips and eyesight.

Thrown from Heaven, because you wanted a life—with her! See, we are connected because we understand that when you rub a white horse against its hairs, you see deep down it is black."

"As the fallen angel who blessed the Horsemen," Giselle began inquisitively, "why did you ask me to bear the White Horseman's child?"

Nathaniel laughed, "You'll see."

Aurora didn't bother to show up to her shoot that day with a back full of stitches. Though the wall's fragments were removed and almost completely healed, she could not take photos in a bikini until the stitches were also gone. Nevertheless, she listened to her empowerment speech this morning, and she could not let this day go to waste. Shimmering red lip gloss colored her lips as she stood flawlessly at the shooting range. She threw a lock of her dark hair behind her large headphones. Aurora cocked her hip and pointed her pistol at the target.

Round after round, her aim greatly improved. Aurora confidently destroyed the paper head of her target. Her cellphone began to vibrate. She flipped off her headgear and shuddered as her employment agency called.

Hesitantly she answered the phone, "Hello?"

"Aurora!" Sentrin, of the Maize Modeling Agency, bellowed. "Why didn't you show up for the Diana Cerqueira Suntanning lotion shoot today?"

"Family emergency," Aurora answered flatly.

"Family emergency?" Sentrin screamed at the top of his lungs. "This is the second shoot you didn't even call for! Do you realize that every shoot you miss cost everyone money?"

"I-I know, but," Aurora barely got her words out, "I've been going through a lot of personal issues lately..."

Sentrin interjected, "We're dropping you from the agency Aurora. We just can't afford this irresponsibility!"

Aurora felt her heart drop in her chest as the pistol dropped from her fingers. Her dream career as a model was dying in its infancy. She had left home and given up everything to do this job. "Are you serious, Sentrin?" Aurora sassed angrily. "I have worked my ass off for this agency, and you're letting me go now?"

"You cost us too much money!" Sentrin shouted back. "I'm sorry, Aurora, but your contract has been terminated."

"It's whatever!" Aurora slammed her cellphone shut, and she fell to her knees. What was she going to do now? Aurora fought the tears with her hair between her fist but failed when they rolled down her cheeks. What was she going to do now?

Chapter 10: Yin and Yang

> "Exult with him, you heavens, glorify him, all you angels of God; for he avenges the blood of his servants and purges his people's land."
> **Deuteronomy 32-43**

The Black Horsemen smiled through rotted teeth as he appeared at his last stop for today. Alberta, Canada, where the wheat ran for two-hundred and forty-two kilometers. Hunger revealed his marble scales from his dark slacks in the center of the several large open pastures. Breaking off a piece of wheat, he placed it on the scale's golden dishes. The pearl scale's more massive saucer dropped, raising the other plate higher into the air as he murmured a forbidden language. Slowly, the tall wheat withered and died around him in an outgrowing circle.

Within moments, the once large and flourishing field of tall and healthy wheat plants became ash. Most of North America, if not the world, depended on these fields—areas that were now rendered useless. These fires were only a beginning.

Blaring traffic and belligerent echoes leaked from the sleepless streets into an immaculate living room. The noise crossed over the perfectly mopped stone ground and crept over hundreds of loving family photographs, large and small. Each picture held a different member of the family, yet they shared no resemblance. Their physical traits, styles, and even races dramatically varied as the pictures cluttered the walls and every surface.

Giselle's finely styled blonde hair swayed while she rocked the screaming infant in her arms. She sang sweetly to him and gracefully danced around the apartment.

With a grimace, Typhon pressed his bare toes solidly on the stone ground and snarled, "Doesn't that thing ever shut up? What is wrong with that thing? One second it's crying, and the next, it just sits there like it's dead. Why the fuck is that skid mark so loud?"

Giselle stopped pacing and smiled sweetly, "Because silly, that's what babies do when they're happy! Especially our little Legnanu! He's going to grow so strong! I can already tell! "

"Legnanu? Echidna, don't tell me you've named the little shit already?" Typhon frowned.

Giselle turned towards her husband, "My name is Giselle now. And what's wrong, honey? Do you not like your son's name?"

"He is not my son!" Typhon roared as the earth began to shake under them. The room trembled, and the walls vibrated as the blind demon sent cracks through the marble ground. "It's not my spawn. It's not a baby. We've eaten babies. That thing... it creeps me out. That is the Horseman's child. Why did it take you so long to give birth to him? You're usually pregnant and spitting out kids in a day!"

"Typhon," Giselle begged amidst the quakes and falling picture frames. "Please calm down; honey. In my heart, all my children belong to you. I love you, Typhon. Now, I realize this muffin took a little longer to bake in the oven than they usually do, but that's just because I think our little Legnanu is an extra special little boy! I just wish you could see his face! Biologically he may be a Nephilim, but he definitely takes after you! I know it within me that he's gonna do great things, just like his real Daddy, you! I know you can't look at him, but he loves you—and so do I."

The quaking stopped. Typhon turned away and retorted, "Do you really think I care who fucked and left their sour waste in you, only to be born into a bigger, more annoying piece of shit? All I care about is regaining my strength, and for that, I need to concentrate. So, happy baby or not, shut it up before I smear these walls with him!"

"Oh, Mr. Grumpy-puss, you can't. He told us this child was going to be helpful in his rising. He gave me the borrowed power I needed to release you from your prison. Honey, you're sweet, and I know a strong and compassionate man, such as yourself, also has the patience to deal with the cries of a small child, at least until dinner gets..." The doorbell rang. Giselle smiled and tossed her model blonde hair backward, "Here."

She drifted across the living room and opened the door to a young pizza boy in a red outfit. Before he could speak, she grabbed him by the back of the neck and lifted him off the marble ground. The demon winked at the child in her arms. She swung the delivery boy over her head and ripped his neck into dangling red pieces of stretched skin. Giselle wiped her red fingers across her white apron and gently closed the door.

Amanda laughed loudly, "Honestly, crazy lady, just go away." The clown lowered her head and walked away. The themed restaurant was shaped like a haunted house. Cobwebs decorated the ceiling, fake bones lined the floor, and the saltshakers looked like monsters.

"You were saying?" Amanda asked as she turned to Henry and forced a big debutant smile.

"I was just saying I think you look great tonight," Henry smirked.

"I feel great," Amanda's heart dropped into her stomach. "Well, you know, everyone keeps telling me I'd make a beautiful bride." She batted her eyes and blew a kiss. She didn't think it was possible, but recent, more dangerous experiences made her love him more each day.

Amanda spent extra time and energy getting ready for this date, and she felt she would explode. She forced a smile through her frown and ogled the sensational man she knew would make an even better husband.

"Today, I read that..." Amanda started then paused, "you know, I read today in the paper that if you're going to get married, that now is the perfect time to do it... With the economy and everything..."

Henry flatly nodded and shoved salad down his throat. Amanda continued, "You know, it just makes sense for... boyfriends of a few years, to ask their completely ready and willing girlfriends of a few years, to get married... You know, my friend Wilma? Her fiancé totally just asked her to marry him in the cutest way! There was this adorable puppy with a ribbon there, waiting where they had first met..."

"That's sweet," Henry dully spoke. "Are we going to order entrees or just sit here staring at each other? I could do either."

"Oh," Amanda rested for a beat. She got the hint and needed to change the subject, "Did you know that vegan Philly cheesesteak can be made locally? Philadelphia is so far, but I didn't even have to leave the city; I found all the ingredients right here in Soho! I was thinking about adding it to the food truck… or maybe some vegan pork ribs…?"

Amanda dropped her head in defeat as her eyes welled. Henry wasn't going to ask her to marry him, not tonight and not ever. The CTN News report on the television above the bar caught her attention. It was a story at the hospital she volunteered. She viewed from a distance but could faintly hear Jackie Adams as she spoke, "This is just one of the many hospitals tonight filling to their max capacity with patients suffering from an unknown illness." The newscaster continued, "It is unclear how this mystery illness is spread, but time has shown the sickness is eventually fatal, already claiming seven adult victims and over two dozen children. The infected grow bruises on their skin and behave hysterically. If you know anyone experiencing these symptoms, it is important to get them to a hospital while maintaining your distance."

"Not now," she cooed. Amanda's guilty fingers clawed anxiously at the table cloth. The Withers were free because the Cherubim of the Throne failed to stop the Horsemen. She knew it had to be them. Innocent children died because she was too weak to act. She had to go volunteer. It was the least she could do. "I feel really bad."

"I thought you said you feel really good," dumbfounded Henry squinted.

"Not anymore," she said with a shake of her head. With plans to start a family soon, Amanda had a soft spot for children, and her heart felt like it was put through a juicer. She had to go. They needed her help, and the Withers waited. But she worried that she would die without ever having found true love if she got infected or killed.

Before she left, she had to know.

"Henry!" her unsteady shrill voice exploded with excitement, "isn't there anything that you have to ask me tonight?"

Confused, he raised an eyebrow, "What do you mean?"

"Don't you love me?" Amanda's eyes were large white saucers of blue water as she cried.

"You know I do, sweetheart…"

"Then what is taking so long?!" Amanda shrieked and tugged at her blue dress. "Why haven't you asked me yet? What will happen if I die tonight..."

"Amanda!" Henry exclaimed. "What are you talking about? You're not gonna die."

"Why won't you marry me?!" Amanda slammed her fists on the table, and her heart swelled as she exclaimed.

Henry stuttered, "Y-you want me to marry you?"

"Yes!" Amanda wailed. "I want you to marry me!"

"I-I didn't know," Henry gasped. "Yes! I'll marry you!"

"No," she muttered. Amanda's gushing heart rolled down her chest and oozed onto the floor. "This isn't how it was supposed to be. In my fairytale, you asked me... I'm sorry," she retreated. She planted a small kiss on his lips and ran out of the restaurant before saying another word.

Amanda raced into the humid and crowded hospital, traded her fluffy jacket for a white coat, and instantly began lending a hand where she could. She held and lifted the wounded, recorded temperatures, and fetched tools for the doctors. It wasn't much, but she needed to do her part. She was college-educated, but her doctoral skills were limited to what she had learned here.

Amanda was very dedicated to her volunteer work, but this particular night, the hospital's eerie feeling kept her constantly distracted. She ducked into the empty hospital cafeteria for a quick break when a small boy appeared by the cafeteria benches. He had a head full of black hair, pale skin, and a white hospital gown. The boy deliriously curled himself around the bar.

She approached the child and knelt to his level. "Hi," she beamed. "You know, benches are fun and everything, but I think a nice warm bed and some ice cream are a lot more fun! Wouldn't you say?"

He failed to respond.

"Strawberry!" Amanda cheered and winked, but the boy remained silent. In the distance, she could hear a strange song whisper into the air.

The medieval flute and string tune steadily grew louder, and the boy finally unraveled himself from the bench and took off in the direction of the song. "Wait!" Amanda called and chased him into the hallway behind the cafeteria.

Several children in white gowns marched in a haze before a ghoulish fire. The unnatural inferno silently enthralled them, and the children willingly walked into it. Amanda screamed as the small boy ran from her side and into the flame.

Two figures faded in like specters. They swirled and danced in the air. Tall and lanky with light blue hair and forest green skin, the male played gentle music on a small violin. The female gracefully bounced his opposite fair blue skin, dark green hair, and a piccolo to her lips. Dusty and torn rags covered their humanoid bodies, and they glared with sharp pink eyes.

Holding back the urge to scream, Amanda reached for her coral cellphone and saw that it had no signal. Her mind scrambled to make a decision when a little girl passed her. The song taunted the girl, and she headed towards the fire. Withers, she finally noticed, were attached to the children by their teeth. The miniature gray men hung onto them like parasites.

Amanda tried to grab the girl, but her hand slipped through. She was a spirit, as were the other children in the fire. Amanda watched helplessly as the girl continued to walk.

"Stop!" she implored, and the girl stepped into the fire.

"Okay, fine," Amanda stammered, her chest expanding with fear. "Then you stop!" she commanded as the demons ignored her and continued to frolic. "Excuse me; I'm talking to you!"

The dark green male lowered his instrument and spun toward her. "Do you think she sees us, Lilin?"

"I'm not sure, Drekavac," she responded.

Their cooing feminine voices chilled Amanda's skin. She felt helpless, unskilled, and weak. Her power was passive; she couldn't kill in a blink like Neil. Her jaw dropped in horror, and she struggled to find her voice, "Um... Guys, this doesn't look safe... Maybe we can go somewhere else? I-I have money... and a gift certificate to Mermaid Cafe... it's for fifty dollars..." Amanda nervously went through her wallet spilling gift cards and coupons. "Okay, so I lied! I'm sorry! It's twenty-five dollars! But that's still good, right? It's twenty-five more than you got!" She paused as they refused to respond, "Does anyone else want their parents right about now?" Amanda muttered the question while her eyes dampened, and panic sunk in. Finally, she ordered, "Leave those little kids alone!"

"Do you think she's a witch, Lilin?"

"I'm not sure, Drekavac," Lilin's blue lips cracked.

"She is not a ghost," Drekavac murmured. "What else would she be, Lilin?"

"A demon? An empath?" Lilin frowned. "I'm not sure, Drekavac."

"Lilin and Drekavac..." Amanda mumbled. "No, really. It's okay; you don't have to repeat yourself... I think I get your names."

"Whatever she is," Lilin spoke, "she ridicules us, Drekavac. We are the Monogram. We come from Hell."

"I am Mandy Randall…I come from Staten Island, but I was born in New Jersey." Amanda momentarily summoned her confidence, "The Angel of Amends! Oh." Amanda scrambled to apologize, "Sorry, I mean... I am the Angel of Amends, Drekavac, and I am the Angel of Amends, Lilin? How was that? Is that how you guys talk to each other? I really don't wanna be rude at a time like this..."

"The Alpha Omega. How do you think they'll pay for her soul, Lilin," Drekavac muttered, turning to his sister.

"Sacred Angels. Only one way to find out is Drekavac."

A sudden burst of wind forced itself through Amanda's hair. It cast the flower from her locks then knocked her to the ground. Before she could stand, they were at her sides. Lilin and Drekavac grabbed an arm each and systematically kicked her body and face, bruising her. Then they slashed at her torso.

Amanda yelped in pain, and her skin tingled with electricity. She was morphing. Her lips hardened, and she shrunk until she fell into a pile of her clothes. Discombobulated and terrified, she reopened her eyes and screamed, "Ack!"

She wiggled through her clothes and flapped her disoriented brown feathery wings. Powered by adrenaline, she ricocheted down the hall. Unsure how to fly, the new duck nearly knocked herself out while she escaped. Amanda crashed into an empty dark room and landed on a bed to catch her breath. Without a thought, she felt her skin shiver as the feathers retreated inside her. Gradually, she transformed into her naked human self. Before she knew it, she was cornered.

Drekavac wrapped a clawed hand around her throat and shoved her into the wall behind. She could feel her body change again. Adrenaline excited her, and her pigment shifted. The morphing felt as natural as breathing. It was satisfying and instinctual yet took a tremendous amount of concentration.

Quickly Amanda reviewed the lessons she learned in her training sessions and finally picked a transformation she could handle.

As a black scorpion, she crawled across Drekavac's hand. She summoned her strength and injected her potent poison into him. Drekavac angrily tossed Amanda aside. She smashed into a large water cooler in her human form and spilled it across the bare tiles. Drekavac and Lilin absorbed the moment as they slowly inched closer by foot. The angel found a device she had seen Dr. Devanne use around the hospital several times. Grateful, she lifted the treasure and slowly flipped the necessary switches. She inched onto the bed.

"She is scared, Lilin," Drekavac spoke.

"She would be the first angel we bring to Hell with the children, Drekavac," Lilin answered.

Amanda lifted the device in her hand. "Y-you should have taken the Mermaid Cafe card..." she muttered as she dropped the defibrillator into the spilled water. "Clear!"

Electric surges burst as Drekavac and Lilin's bodies smoked till their eyes exploded in flames. Amanda watched nervously as their flesh flaked into ash and then the ash into dust.

Her hands covered her body as she strolled into the hallway. The fire was gone. The children's spirits floated and shimmered away in white lights. The Withers that attached themselves to the apparitions fell from their hosts and shriveled into nothing.

"D-did I really do that..." she finally managed to speak over her pounding headache. "Yes." She giggled and fell into uncontrolled laughter. "YES! I did it! I did it!"

Her shoulders sunk with disdain, "But all the poor babies are dead... But at least they went to Heaven! I think..."

Icy rain shattered across the raw concrete. Amanda didn't have an umbrella that night, but she couldn't go home just yet. Cold, soaked, and tired, she steadily knocked on Henry's front door. She shivered and jumped when he opened it. Her large blue eyes were wetter than her wet hair. "Is it just me, or do all of our dates totally seem to be ending up like this?"

Henry forced away from his smile, "Do you want to...?"

"I wanna say something," Amanda cut in. "Growing up, my parents totally had the best marriage ever. My dad asked my mom to marry him on the beach on the night of her birthday. Lightning bugs were blinking, and the weather was warm. She remembers it as the most magical moment in her life! It was like something I only heard about in fairy tales. I grew up admiring them, fantasized every day, waiting for it to be my turn! I watched love movies and read romance novels all the time... I loved how the prince always came from a big, expensive castle, riding a magnificent noble white horse. He had a huge beautiful ring, and he wanted to take care of his princess forever and give her the world. That's the dream I always had... But now I realize none of that matters anymore. Sometimes you're just a girl; next, you're a duck or a scorpion... It's a new crazy year, and you're never gonna know what will happen, so I just... I don't give a darn anymore!" She blushed awkwardly but couldn't stop yet—Amanda fell to a single knee and asked, "So, do you mind if I forget the stupid horse?"

Chapter 11: Beneath

> "Do you not know that we will judge angels? Then why not everyday matters?"
> **Corinthians 6:3**

Aurora clutched her smartphone between her ear and shoulder as she fiercely brushed her teeth. Her eyes rolled through the conversation, and she silently rehearsed her Empowerment recording that played in the background before she spat into the sink. "I know, I know." Smiling, Aurora drifted to her ivory couch and flipped through a newspaper-covered in red circles then asked, "Where are you getting your dress?"

"Duh!" Amanda cheerfully snapped through the telephone. "I'm gonna wear my momma's! She got it from her momma and so on. It's huge and full of frills! It has dozens of silk flowers on it, so cute! It'll have to be taken in a bit, but..."

"Are you serious?" Aurora shook her head and disagreed, "On your wedding day, you want to wear some taken-in *used* dress that's older than you? Heads will turn..."

"Aw, Aurora," Amanda beamed. "You're so sweet."

Aurora slammed the newspaper on her lap and mocked, "I meant away from you!"

"Well, in that case, ew Aurora, you're mean!" Amanda mimicked herself. "It's called 'Family Tradition.' Join the club."

"The only club I want to join with is one large enough to beat a sense of style into you. Listen, honey, just because I say it, the 'Aurora Way' doesn't make it any less accurate! We'll talk about Vera later." Aurora ended the conversation and continued through the classified section in her newspaper when a familiar feeling grasped the base of her back.

She knew this touch and prepared herself when all her energy rushed to her eyes.

The empty street looked different at night, but she instantly recognized the church across it. A tall, attractive police officer prowled around the block. Lyssah Rhamiel's eyes burned through the blinds of her window. She raised a handgun steadily and shot Rhion cleanly in the forehead. With the small pistol in his claws, Stolas the Maniae Owl landed near the body and dropped a gun in the cop's hands. The little bird pecked and pulled until he manipulated the weapon into the cop's grasp.

Aurora shook off the slight delirium and reopened her eyes. Her visions were less painful now. She flipped her cellphone open; she knew she had to call Neil.

Rhion firmly pressed the paper coffee cup to his lips. He narrowed his bright green eyes and rewound the recording, and played it again. He watched the footage eighty-seven times but was still unsure of what he had seen. He wasn't an idiot. Although the other officers told him that he freed Ezekiel, Neil, and Amanda, he knew it wasn't right.

He would remember that. He watched the recording of his interrogation of Ezekiel over and over, but the taping only proved what his partners had said. It clearly showed him get up, leave the room, and return with Ezekiel planted in the seat before him. How could he explain that? Though Rhion was unsure if it was the recording's bad quality, he could swear a gray shadow jumped from his body.

"I can't believe I'm missing work for this," Neil uttered as they approached Lyssah Rhamiel's front door.

"I already told you," Aurora reminded him, "I saw her kill someone. We might have to shoot this bitch." She tapped her purse and nodded, which indicated she was armed, and confessed, "I never liked her from the beginning... Her or her pigeon."

Neil snickered in disbelief, "Let's stick to the plan before you start busting caps… so just wait."

"For what?" she rolled her eyes and spat, "So you can give a long-winded seminar about the importance of proper vaginal health care? We need to go in."

"You know, ever since the Apocalypse started, you definitely gained weight." Neil defended his bruised ego, "But something's not right. There must be a reason I'm having trouble reading her mind."

"I know... I was half-joking... You ready?" Aurora continued as they arrived at the door. "Let's go through her shit..."

Lyssah Rhamiel answered her door and rushed the two inside. She wrapped her knotted hair around her shoulder and perched onto her couch. When she shoved her fingers into an open can of corn, she finally asked, "You never scheduled an appointment. Why are you here?"

Aurora walked closer to the woman. She forced all her energy into her eyes and could feel her pupils fill with crimson. When her pupils filled, Lyssah froze, covered in a smoky white light. Aurora shook her head and cleared the euphoria, and recovered some of her lost energy.

Impressed, Neil walked over to her and looked into her red eyes. "Scary."

"Come on..." Aurora sighed. "I never know how long I can keep this up."

They were never given a full tour of Lyssah's home. She kept things very private, and they had never gone beyond the living room and the basement. However, now with Lyssah suspended, Aurora had free range through her house. She ran to the first locked door she found and gestured for Neil to open it telekinetically.

He snapped the lock with his mind and entered the room with Aurora close behind. The room was small but entirely covered in computers and file cabinets. Neil's eyes dashed around the computer screens. He learned Lyssah had cameras set up all over the city, and even further, there was one on his block, one by his job and one by his son's mother's house. "What the hell?"

"What is this?" Aurora's voice was shrill as she tore open a folder with her name scribbled on the front. "She has folders on all of us!" Aurora read out loud. "'Surprisingly air-headed, with a bad attitude and the unwillingness to accept her future. The patient is a fashion model. This job is too public for a sacred duty and must be relinquished. I will deal with this shortly.' She got me fired from my job? How did she...? What the...? Neil!"

Stunned and confused, Neil struggled to speak, but before he could come up with an answer, a loud squawk came from the living room. The owl screeched and tugged at the suspended Lyssah. Aurora's influence was broken with enough interference, the white mist faded away, and she was freed.

Puzzled for a moment, Lyssah Rhamiel saw her locked door was left wide open. The bird cawed for a few moments, and Lyssah furiously listened. "You used your power on me! How dare you? How dare you! HOW DARE YOU?"

"Oh no!" Aurora clenched the folder between her hands. "You got me fired from my job! How dare you!"

Stolas the Maniae chirped frantically before Lyssah charged, "You've breached patient confidentiality!"

"No!" Aurora spat and ran towards the door with Neil close behind her. Dodging Lyssah, Aurora slipped through the door with several folders in hand.

"Wait!" Lyssah desperately cried. "Please wait!" She stopped suddenly at the foot of her door. Hopelessly she bawled, "I need those papers! Give me those papers! You've breached confidentiality!"

Aurora stopped short. She lifted the files to taunt the older woman. Lyssah Rhamiel fell to the ground and gripped her doorframe. She refused to leave her home.

"Do you want them? Here..." Aurora taunted and watched her for a moment as the woman refused to leave her doorway and walk into the halls. "Okay, confused again."

"Lyssah Rhamiel," Neil demanded, "why were you planning on shooting a man?"

Lyssah's face wrinkled in defeat, "Rhion Galloway has access to some valuable information. He has the means to expose you. Come inside, and I will explain..."

"Rhion Galloway," Neil growled.

Aurora questioned, "Who?"

"Let's talk," he entered and closed the door behind her. Lyssah retreated to her favorite chair and gazed blankly as the angels stood around her.

Neil nodded to Aurora. Assuringly, she took out her nine-millimeter and aimed it at Lyssah's head before alluding, "Way ahead of you."

"A pistol. Bad angels want to hurt me. Is that necessary?" Lyssah asked coldly.

"When your life and the lives of others are in danger, it is very necessary," Neil cautioned. "What information does Rhion have on us?"

"The detective Rhion Galloway has video evidence of Ezekiel's..." Lyssah Rhamiel paused before she retorted, "incident...The envious scribe tapes all of his interrogations.

Though I am unsure he understands what he has, he is very suspicious for obvious reasons. The detective investigates you still and, with his recording, has the beginnings of the means to expose you. I was simply trying to eliminate the problem before it started."

"By killing an innocent man?" Neil scowled.

"Do you realize what can happen if you are exposed?" Lyssah cut in sharply. "Not only will it be impossible for you to do your duty, but there will be a tremendous uproar! Even I wouldn't be able to keep you safe. There is a reason why things such as these are kept from the general public! Demons and angels disintegrate upon death for this reason! I had to arrange for Aurora to lose her very public job for this reason. Killing the detective is the only way to ensure that he discontinues his investigations. We have no time to worry about him becoming a potential enemy."

Neil watched Lyssah Rhamiel blankly as he replayed her words in his mind but affirmed, "We can't let you kill a man for something he didn't even do yet. It's not right."

"I have thought about it, and it is the only way," Lyssah reassured them.

"Well, let me think about it," Neil proposed.

"Wait," said Aurora as she pointed her gun coiled with frustration, "don't relax yet; I haven't asked my set of questions. How did you make me lose my job? Are you human? What's up with that bird? And why won't you walk outside your house? I don't care which one you answer first, but make it quick before I lose my temper."

"Hmm." Lyssah Rhamiel straightened her back for the first time in front of the angels as a crooked, confident smile turned her lips. She declared, "I will not tell you anything that you don't need to know. I am not on trial here. I have done nothing wrong, and you will not shoot me."

"Sure about that?" Aurora asked. "You were going to kill that man."

"You can't kill me for something I haven't done yet." Lyssah Rhamiel grinned at Neil. "By your logic, it would be the wrong thing to do."

"You hurt anyone," Neil threatened, "we'll have to stop you, whatever that means... But Rhion isn't going to be a problem. I have an idea." He grabbed his cellphone and dialed.

Rhion's eyes worsened with fatigue as he watched his computer. He gathered papers from the printer and shoved them into his briefcase along with the video file of his encounter with Ezekiel. He arched an eyebrow and gasped, "Internal affairs? Really? Sir, Jormun Gandr, how may I help you this evening?"

The tall bald man wore a suit on his thick body and a bold mustache above his lip. "This evening," Jormun Gandr started, "you can hand over that tape you have on Ezekiel Wallace along with any other information you have on him or any of the three that came in that night."

"What?!" Rhion interjected. "Why? Gandr, I could be on to something. I don't think they're a part of Blood Wolf at all."

"Calm down!" Jormun yelled. "The investigation is totally being handled by another department, and they want the information. We're told by internal affairs that we don't have the authorization even to investigate this any further—so just totally hand it over."

"That's ridiculous," Rhion objected, then opened his briefcase and handed Jormun the video file and the stack of papers. "Why would they do that?"

"I don't know!" Jormun smirked. "Oh well, these things happen or whatever!"

He slipped the items into his bag, and giddily turned on his heel, and exited the building. He put his pink cellphone to his ear and babbled. "Done and done!"

"Are you sure you got everything, Amanda?" Neil asked from the other end of the phone.

"Yes, Neil!" Amanda spoke, hidden in her guise. "I told him to give me everything! Mission complete!"

Rhion watched as his chief left the building. He flared his nostrils and fell deep into his chair. Determined, he reopened the windows on his screen containing the background and records of the four angels. When the pages reprinted from his computer, Rhion shoved them into his briefcase and left the building.

Chapter 12: Past Winds

> "Whereas angels, despite their superior strength and power, do not bring a revealing judgment against them from the Lord."
> **Peter 2:11**

A stuffed toy bird rose under Neil's telekinetic control. Zachary wiggled his arms up and down and giggled as spit bubbled onto his bib. A slow month idly slipped by since Amanda destroyed Drekavac and Lilin. Lyssah Rhamiel insisted on daily training sessions, and though they were exhausting, they were both beneficial and necessary. The lives of the angels regressed toward the somewhat routine.

The media, however, cautioned everyone about a food shortage. New Yorkers were instructed not to worry but to consume less before it became a full-blown problem. Neil was suspicious. Like the new illness that was slowly spreading, he knew that somehow the Horsemen were involved.

He moved the stuffed yellow bird, slid across the armrest of the couch, and Zachary coughed up a small laugh. Neil eased back into his chair and ran his fingers so that the bird plummeted to the ground. Jokingly he begged, "Please don't tell your mom that your daddy is a super-powered angel sent here to save the world."

These weekend visits often tired him, but Neil loved them. Unfortunately, this vacation was coming to an end. Victoria was near. She was beginning to collect her son... He could feel it. He could hear her footsteps in his mind. Odd. He stood from the couch and walked over to his front door. His power slowly removed the chain that latched it.

"How did you know I was out here? I didn't even knock!" Victoria demanded as he swung the door open.

"I didn't. I was just about to throw out the trash," Neil lied softly.

"And you were going to leave Zach by himself?" Victoria snarled.

"No," he whispered slowly.

"So, in addition to rarely seeing your son, you leave him alone when you do have him." Victoria hissed. "You're a deadbeat father. I don't know why I even bother to send him over here in the first place. You don't pay attention, and you don't give a damn!"

"Victoria, I take care of my son!"

"Financially," she placed a hand on her hip and continued, "but a boy needs more than that!"

Neil lowered his head, "I've just had a lot of responsibilities lately. I... have a lot of dangerous... personal... issues that are consuming my life, and I don't want my child anywhere around that."

"Oh!" Victoria snapped. "Poor little tortured you. Your son should be your world, and nothing else should matter!"

"I don't know what matters anymore..."

Suddenly, the thought to erase her memory entered his head. Why not? His power was still developing. Neil focused on Victoria and blocked out everything else. He willed for her to forget. Victoria shouted in pain and fell to the ground. She clenched her head and rocked as the terrible migraine attacked her mind.

It was Saturday, Amanda's lazy day. She emerged from her room with a yawn, and the television blared afternoon cartoons. The massive, sugary smell of honey surged through her nostrils as Olive crushed small golden crystals recklessly with her cellphone on the coffee table. She cut the rosin into pale yellow sloppy piles with a parking ticket. Broad-eyed and alerted, she tugged at her strawberry-blonde hair.

"Girl, if you weren't an angel, I'd say you looked like a bat out of Hell! Please, you're not going to tell me how you" (Olive raised her fingers in quotation), "'Kentucky fried' those two demon people again are you? Or ask if I would like to try some of your" (raising her fingers again) "'Original recipe.' I laughed so hard, I almost queefed! There's nothing worse than being a regular person! Oh, my God... I hate it... I wish I could fly or start fires or something... how great would that be in bed? So sexy, I can't take it... Oh my God..."

However, Amanda had already fallen asleep, and Olive was talking to herself. This was beginning to happen all too often. With a heavy exhale, Olive turned back into her room and allowed Amanda to get her rest.

"Yeeeeoooooow...." the green-eyed Maine coon dragged his empty food bowl to the couch where Amanda had slept for hours. Repeatedly, he slammed the bare dish on the ground and failed to call any attention. Purrson's thick brown hairs stood as straight as needles when he resonated in annoyance. He was a big cat—knew what time he should be fed and refused to suffer tardiness.

For a second, Purrson circled the reupholstered patched-up couch and cried before he quickly lost his nerve. The enormous feline rubbed his dry pink nose against

Amanda's cheek. However, the blonde angel was a heavy sleeper; Purrson had to step up his game. With more force, the fuzzy brown cat pressed the short black hairs around his mouth across Amanda's lips. When that failed, he swept her face with his eighteen-inch fox-like tail.

"Spider!" Amanda awoke with a jolt—slapping Purrson into the air and behind the kitchen counter. Her disorientation lasted only a second as she jumped to her feet. "Oh, no!"

"What's going on?" Olive asked as she rushed out of her bedroom in just enough time to see the large cat fly across the living room and into the kitchen.

Purrson landed with a thud and screeched in violent dismay.

Amanda rushed to his fallen body, but what she saw stopped her immediately. Her palms began to sweat as her eyes widened but could not turn away. Purrson howled in pain as he tossed it on the kitchen floor. His face twisted with convulsions Amanda had never witnessed. She covered her mouth and took Olive's hand. The angel could feel it within her—Purrson was transforming.

The smell of bile filled the air. Her stomach ran up in knots as she could feel her cat's organs liquefy underneath his flesh. His skin hardened into a shell. Amanda trembled, and her eyes welled. She could sense his bones crack, hollow out, and change shape. Thermal energy ran off Purrson, and his body steamed like hot spaghetti in a strainer.

His hind legs grew bulkier and longer.

Simultaneously, four fully formed limbs extended from his torso. It was like watching him give birth to himself. The Maine coon shrieked as his eight wet legs took shape around him. In a final cry, Purrson shook his head to reveal a second pair of green eyes right above his original in the last cry.

"Oh my gosh," Amanda gasped in astonishment, "Purrson... are you okay?"

The mutated cat shook off the bodily fluids that clung to its bushy brown coat. Purrson stood a little taller with much longer legs and let his long feathery tail curl over his back like a fluffy scorpion.

"P-P-Purrson?"

"HUrrRarah!" Purrson unleashed a guttural hiss. Amanda reached out a hand, but before she could touch him, the cat's new legs made it even easier for him to scurry beneath the torn couch.

Olive and Amanda clung to each other's clothes as they examined the smelly wet spot left on the floor from Purrson's mutation. Amanda was silent, but Olive had never seen anything like that. Stunned, her lips parted, "Mandy… did you just morph our cat into a huge tarantula-feline hybrid?"

"I-I think so…" She fought the urge to vomit.

"Oh," Olive accepted and slowly nodded. "Why?"

Ezekiel enjoyed his bedroom view with an apple and a basket of unfolded laundry. His window opened to a picturesque old wall with crumbled brick and magnificent vines. At ease, he took a bite of his apple and focused his attention on his unfolded clothes; however, it wasn't long before he was interrupted.

"Didn't I tell you to throw away the garbage?" his drunken father yelled and kicked open Ezekiel's bedroom door. The intoxicated underachiever swung the black bag of trash in his hand and taunted his son.

"No... I-I don't think you did..." Ezekiel answered in dismay.

"I did so!" Fred bellowed. "You don't ever do shit in this house! Nothing—and yet you live here rent-free!"

Ezekiel stuttered, "B-but I'm doing laundry now, and I don't live here rent-free... I give you and M-mom money every month... You k-know that..."

"What I know is that I told you to throw out this trash!" Fred confirmed. The drunkard ripped the plastic bag of waste open and flung it into the room. Moldy garbage and smelly unknown liquids covered the clean laundry, carpet, and bedsheets. He emptied the entire bag throughout the room. He concluded, "You like living like a pig, then sleep in your filth!"

Ezekiel's mind fell blank. At this point, he was used to being frightened, but his father's wickedness stunned him so acutely he could not think. He viciously rose off the ground. The angel dealt with this abuse for years, and he was sick of it. All his father needed to do was ask, but because his father got drunk again, Ezekiel's life was made that much more difficult.

The curly-haired angel shook with so much anger he could hardly speak. Why did his father have to do this? As if he wasn't exhausted enough! Ezekiel's lower lip quivered with vexation, and his brow wrinkled in disbelief. Every hair on his arm stood straight, and the blood in his veins ran hot.

"Oh!" Completely unthreatened, Fred laughed a little bit, "Look at you, you're a m-m-man now. Standing up to your D-D-Daddy..." Fred couldn't hold in his laughter anymore. Hugging his stomach, he burst into a mocking laugh that bounced loudly off the walls. He began poking Ezekiel on the forehead. "What are you gonna do? Draw another faggoty picture about it?"

Ezekiel's fist tightened around the apple in his hand. He panted heavily. A fever rose under his skin, and everything inside him wanted to explode.

"Get out," Ezekiel finally spoke.

"This is my house! To Hell with leaving!" Fred roared and refused to back down from the angel.

Ezekiel's nostrils widened. In seconds, the once fresh apple in Ezekiel's hand rotted and blackened. A vinegary coil of adrenaline bathed Ezekiel's tongue. The wild vines on the brick wall behind him withered until they were black and broke off the brick.

Fred dropped to his knees

His father's skin constricted and shriveled. Green veins grew irritated and thick on his red neck. Ezekiel felt the energy drain from Fred's tensing muscles when a bead of dark blood oozed from the man's nose. He knew Fred was suffocating, but the energy flowed effortlessly from him, almost needed to be released.

He fought through his trance and broke his derangement.

The dead fruit fell from Ezekiel's cold fingers; Fred's pulsing eyes rolled to the back of his head.

Ezekiel hyperventilated uncontrollably. His sight shook and blackened around the edges. He pressed his fingers against Fred's wrist.

No pulse.

Reality rushed in like water bursting through a dam. The adrenaline in his mouth suddenly turned into another liquid. He grabbed his turning stomach and vomited all over the trash in his living room. His eyes shut tightly, but tears forced through. His hands slipped into his sleeves, covered his face, and he wept in shame.

Ezekiel had just killed his father.

His heartbeat was in his throat. His power drained the life of his father, and it was too strong for him to control. He still radiated. He knelt on his cold hardwood floor and covered himself completely. Now dirty socks, gloves, jogging pants, a sweater, scarf, and hat—anything that would fog the range of his new power. He took a deep breath, dressed in most of his laundry, and closed his eyes. Firecrackers went off in his mind, and he could still feel the cold touch of his power on his skin.

Ezekiel knew what he needed to do. Whenever he concentrated, he excited spirits and summoned them into this world. Maybe if he focused hard enough, he could bring back Fred's soul. Then perhaps, they could communicate somehow? He knew he was grasping at straws, but he had to try. A chilling shiver rose from a place of power. He called for his father.

As tadpole-like creatures faded into existence and filled the chilly room, a different feeling gripped at his insides. It was cold and bitter. The atmosphere darkened. He almost threw up again. Could I be pulling him out of Hell? he thought. Throbbing pains punched his throat as he choked. His eyes burst open while his head cocked backward. Summoning ectoplasm never hurt him before, but when his vision cleared, there he was.

The transparent soul of Fred hovered right before him.

"Dad!" Ezekiel desperately screamed, "I am so sorry!"

"You," bewildered, Fred spoke, his voice rang with a softer tone. "You killed me..." Fred lowered his head in disappointment.

Her face was like a lattice crust cherry pie. Amanda dabbed her wounds with a white disinfectant cloth as Purrson hissed in his carrying cage at her feet. It took Olive and Amanda nearly an hour and a half to get Purrson into his carrier, he never liked it before, and now—with eight legs, space was even more cramped.

Lyssah's fixed stare met Amanda's unwavering orbs. The basement was cold and seemed bigger when she was in there alone with the older woman. Amanda wrapped herself in her arms as Lyssah leaned forward and finished the sardines from the can.

"So, what brings you in today?" Lyssah sighed as she swallowed the fish whole.

"This is Purrson," Amanda started to tear up when she spoke. "Like 'person' in cat language… And if it looks like he's a mutant creature, it's because he is one. I did this to him. Now, look at him! It's not that he's evil exactly… he just that he likes to destroy stuff, hurt people, and doesn't care who is in his way. I know he loves me even though he did this to my face. Oh," the angel wiped her tears, "Olive says that we developed an unhealthy codependent relationship, but he NEEDS me! And I-I..."

"Please," Lyssah interrupted, her eyes rolled deep into the back of her head. "Before the next ice age..."

"I made a Spat!" the angel confessed.

"Tell me you're referring to what's in the box and not in your pants because if you—"

"A spider-cat," Amanda interrupted. "Somehow, I... I think I changed my cat into a monster."

Lyssah folded her arms, "If you have changed him, then you can revert it."

"I don't know how." She gulped. "I already tried. I did it while I was asleep."

"You're an alchemist," the older woman frowned, "not a child playing with clay. Yes, some of your transformations are instinctual, but to build something, to alter something, you have to understand how it is constructed. You don't know how to build a car, so why would you think you could just pull one out of the air? To create something without deformity, you must understand each and every working piece. From the ground up! Metal? Stone? Blood? Gas? Sing in every element."

"What if I don't understand anything?" Amanda gulped again. "Could I just skip that part?"

"No, or you risk creating flawed concoctions." She nodded, "Like that beast in that cage."

"He's not a 'beast in a cage!'" Amanda objected and fisted her hands. "He's a kitty muffin that's alive, and you don't eat him because he's your best friend who has to do everything you say because you feed him and are pretty much his boss… but if he had a choice, he'd still love me all the same."

"It no longer belongs to you," Lyssah narrowed her eyes and declared, "'Bring me a sword. Divide the living child in two and give half to one with enough interference and a half to the other.' Separate the animal and risk destroying it."

"No!" Amanda swallowed a rock in her throat. "I'll take him home. I'll take care of him. Just don't kill him."

"'And all Israel heard of the judgment with much longer legs which the king had rendered; and they feared the king, for they saw that the wisdom of God was in him to administer justice,'" Lyssah whispered melodically.

"Huh?" Amanda shuttered and raised an eyebrow.

"Get out of my house," the woman frowned before she hurried stairs. "And take it with you now!"

Ezekiel's eyes swelled with water. "I-I didn't even k-know I-I could do t-that..." Ezekiel paused before he could continue, "Daddy, I don't know what to do! Are you okay? I'm scared! I-I'm so..."

"You're sorry," Fred finished Ezekiel's sentence. "I know." He paused and turned away from him, then glanced over the garbage that he had thrown over Ezekiel's folded clothes. "It's just," his non-corporeal lips reluctantly continued, "things are much clearer where I am, and I'm the one who needs to be sorry."

"Clear?" Ezekiel asked as he scrunched up his nose, and the water from his eyes poured down his face.

"I could see my path from up there, and trust me," Fred admitted, shaking his head, "I'm better off dead. All my life, I was a loser. Kind of like you..."

Ezekiel buried his head in his hands.

Fred went on, "Always drunk, always angry. But I'm better now. If I would have kept on the road I was going, I would have brought you and your mother down with me. I've always loved you both."

Ezekiel nodded.

"That's why I'm okay with being dead. It's," Fred sighed, "for the greater good, and I'm willing to make that sacrifice. The only question is: Are you?"

"Huh?" the words stabbed Ezekiel.

"When you die, they let you see your path. Your would-be future if you hadn't died," Fred explained. "Why not? I mean, you're dead; there's nothing you could do about it. I saw your future and Ezekiel; it's not good. I love you... but I was given a message."

Ezekiel shook his head in disbelief and asked, "What?"

"The power that you have," Fred warned, "it's greater than you. You don't have the strength to control it. The angels thought you did, but you don't. With your new power, you're going to kill. I was your first, but there will be others… so many others."

"No," he refused to believe it. Ezekiel shook his head. "I-I can control myself! If I just relax, I'll be able to c-control it, and no one will die! I can start going to more sessions with Lyssah Rhamiel and Neil and..."

"You won't," Fred shook his head. "Ezekiel, you don't know what I saw. I never tasted such dark power in anyone I have ever met. You can't control it. You didn't do it on purpose. It just started happening! And you don't have much time. Soon as your mother walks through that door, she will shrivel up and die just like I did! I love you—but it will all be your fault."

Ezekiel bit his lower lip and bleated, "I never even wanted this fucking power!"

"I know," Fred assured him, "I'm sorry, so sorry. You can feel the evil inside you. You're the Angel of Death, and it will always surround you. The Lord made a mistake, Ezekiel, and he knows that now but he is powerless to change it. Your powers are rooted in darkness. It's what you've been afraid of all along... You're the only one who can stop it."

"How?"

"Before any of it happens," Fred answered, "before your mother walks through that door and falls to her death... before you murder both your parents in one day and become a stone-cold killer... you could do the noble thing and become a tragic hero…"

"Death is not that bad, Ezekiel," Fred muttered.

Woefully he continued, "You of all people should know that. It's peace. All your life, you've serviced others; now it's about time you do something for yourself. You deserve that peace. Peace that I was never able to give you before I died. You're an unfortunate boy, Ezekiel. Look at how death changed me. I'm much happier than I ever was."

Ezekiel's eyes narrowed, and his voice wavered, "Y-you w-want me to kill m- myself?"

"It'll only hurt for a few seconds,"

"But if I-I," Ezekiel released a deep breath, "...if I d-die, the Alpha Omega would be broken and the world..."

"There are other forces of good out there, Ezekiel," Fred cried. "They will find a way to gain back their powers without you, and they will handle the Horsemen. Do you honestly think that you would be any help in fighting them? Come on, Ezekiel, you're the weak one. You know that I know that the whole damn world knows that. If you do this, it would be the only strong thing you have ever done in your life. It takes great power and courage to end your own life, Ezekiel. Show the world you have that strength."

Ezekiel bit down on his lower lip and, with hysteric eyes, shook his head. But disagreed, "I-I c- can't..." Chalky saliva curled in Ezekiel's mouth. His father's essence felt different from others. Fred was dry and empty—unlike anything he had experienced before.

"Why not?" Fred wrinkled his brow.

"Because," Ezekiel took a step backward and spoke between sniffles. "I'm vulnerable right now, not stupid..." He gritted his teeth, "W-who the hell are you?"

A burst of hot air entered the space and knocked Ezekiel into a large mirror in his bedroom. He raised his head fast enough to see the phantom dressed as Fred jump into the flesh of his dead father.

When the winds subsided, and the carcass stood.

"I guess I poured it on a little thick, huh?" his lips broke into a smile. Wiggling his eyebrows, Fred sneered, "Boy, are we going to have fun." With those words, he sped through the apartment with inhuman swiftness and out the front door, slamming it so hard the metal frame bent.

Ezekiel bled from pieces of the broken glass and placed a hand on the doorframe as his only leverage. What did I just do? He asked himself repeatedly as loose papers and clothes that were caught in Fred's gust fluttered to the ground.

Chapter 13: Undercover

> "But now the anger of God flared up at him for going, and the angel of the Lord stationed himself on the road to hinder him as he was riding along on his ass, accompanied by two of his servants. When the ass saw the angel of the Lord standing on the road with a sword drawn, she turned off the road and went into the field, and Balaam had to beat her to bring her back on the road."
> **Numbers 22:22-23**

Pedestrians crowded the streets, walking and chatting in uniformity. Adolescent boys on skateboards weaved rudely between them and shouted obscenities. As the New Yorkers made room for the speeding skaters to pass, the traffic did not. The first teen realized the danger, and he leaped off his skateboard then rolled to the ground.

The second skateboarder, however, was too slow. Traffic continued to rocket as he moved through it. Neil lifted his hand from his pocket, and telekinetically threw the boy to the sidewalk. He fell to the floor scraped but otherwise unharmed. The car shattered his skateboard into pieces. Neil lowered his hand apprehensively and grinned at the small fact that he saved the loud teen from death or severe injury, but there was an unsettling feeling that worried him. Though no one saw, he felt like he was being watched.

Later that night, the feeling of paranoia grew louder as he lay in bed. Demanding sleep, his eyes closed. It was his regular job to be prepared even when the other angels were negligent. It was his regular job to be smart, to protect the innocent, be the hero. But on weary nights such as these, he often wondered who would protect *him*?

It took hours, but Neil finally fell asleep. Then the hidden demon showed itself. It took the form of a rotten and eyeless decaying pig. The demon's mouth dripped live worms, maggots, and centipedes. Rotten skin hung off the cow-sized beast as he abnormally snickered over Neil's body. The creature stood on the bed above him. With the squirming insects in its jaws, it was a foul sight, but it was odorless and weightless. A few worms dropped from the demon's mouth and burrowed themselves into Neil's cheeks.

Neil awoke.

He jolted from his bed and onto the sturdy hardwood floor. This demon was unlike any he had ever seen: huge, gaping, black eye sockets, hefty appearance, and a harrowing crooked smile. Neil shot an open palm, and the dresser flew. The boar toppled over in pain. A splintered dresser leg snapped through the air and plummeted into the skull of the fallen beast. It opened its mouth wide, the demon squealed loudly and burst into flames. The fiery tongue burned brightly, scorching the ground beneath it. Neil exhaled leisurely as he watched the fire fizzle out, and the carcass quickly turned to ash.

"Kicked his fat ass," Neil mused to himself.

Chapter 14: The Blinded

> "Then, the angel of the Lord took his stand in a narrow lane between vineyards with a stone wall. When the ass saw the angel of the Lord there, she shrank against the wall; and since she squeezed Balaam's leg against it, he beat her again."
> **Numbers 22:24-25**

Apprehensively, Ezekiel second-guessed his knock at Sister Lyssah's door. When the entryway peeled open, he slid hesitant fingers beneath his sleeves. Dappled sunlight trickled in from the windows and lit up floating dust particles like the stars in a milky way. The older woman unnerved him. Her faded blue eyes were always judgmental, and her movements were erratic and bird-like. Nervously, she wrapped her knotted hair away from her face and welcomed, "Lurk in doorways and risk offending your host."

His eyes widened as he crossed the threshold apologetically and the nun guided her to the basement as he apologized, "Sorry, I was jus—"

"Petrified…" She stopped at the doorway and announced.. Lyssah's expression fell earnest as her body started to shake, "A liquid bubble filled with bees! Anxious creatures—they buzz and buzz and sting! And I don't know… I don't know where they will go—how they will spill!"

Ezekiel rushed to Lyssah's aid as she tumbled to the ground. He attempted to lift her to her feet, but it quickly became apparent that she intended to stay. Thoughtful he asked, "Can I get you a glass of water or something?"

Lyssah grabbed Ezekiel by the sweater and pulled him closer to her, "'And the Lord said to Satan, 'Have you considered my servant, that there is none like him on the earth a blameless and upright man, who fears God and turns away from evil.'"

"What does that mean?" he asked. Invisible needles pricked at his skin, and his heart dropped into his gut, "D-do, you know what I did?"

Her breath reeked of rotten bananas as she answered, "I know what you feel…"

Confused, Ezekiel's heart rate rose, and he bit his lower lip to distract some of the tension. As his chest convulsed, a sharp bleating sound cut into the room. Lyssah dragged Ezekiel over to his respected corner of the basement. This time, however, it was completely redecorated.

Ezekiel instantly locked eyes with the tiny lamb. Bound by the hoofs, the fifteen-pound creature struggled in its rope. The angel could taste the fear in the young sheep's mouth. Overwhelmed, Ezekiel turned to see the ghost tracking systems and computers replaced by colored stones and rocks painted with the Chi-Rho. White grains and sprinkles of the meal were assorted with burning sage and wine-soaked crystals.

His hands trembled.

"'Take your son, your only son, whom you love and go to the region of Lyssah. Sacrifice him there as a burnt offering of a mouth I will show you,'" Lyssah whispered whimsically.

"Wha?" Ezekiel was stunned.

"What seems to be the problem?" Lyssah frowned impatiently, "I believe I made myself clear. You do not control death; you are an instrument of it. Do as you're told. Take this creature's life."

"You want me to k-kill that thing?" The small-framed man could barely get out his words, "I-I-I'm Noooo… I can't do that."

Lyssah paused for a moment as though she were caught off guard by his refusal and inquired, "Why not?"

"Because," Ezekiel shook his head in disbelief and muttered, "It doesn't deserve to die. This lamb didn't do anything."

"And it makes you feel useless?" she threw up her hands in frustration when she responded. She quickly stammered around the room to release pent up energy before she crawled closer to Ezekiel's face. "Trapped, powerless, and oh yes, irrelevant? So self-righteous! None of us can control life. We simply have our roles to play. You, myself, and the lamb."

Lyssah slid a rusted blade into Ezekiel's hand so abruptly he nearly dropped it. He breathed heavily through his words, "Wait, you want me to use this? Hold on Lyssah—no…."

"Alarms, you do not get to decide!" Lyssah ranted. "Trumpets, horns, you never get to decide—only act!"

Tears clung to Ezekiel's eyes like a sap on a tree. "I'm not killing this lamb, Lyssah!"

"Why not?" Lyssah's voice bellowed through the basement.

"I'm a good person!"

"You're already a murderer!" Lyssah broke down into tears only a moment after Ezekiel started to cry. Channeling his emotions, she continued, "But deep down, I know he deserved it! He tortured me, my mother! He betrayed me! I always wanted him dead!"

"That's not true!" Ezekiel bawled. "What does this have to do with this lamb? This lamb is innocent!"

"My mother was innocent! We were innocent when we had to fall asleep to the sounds of him beating her! Innocence means nothing!" Lyssah screamed at the top of her lungs, "You are an angel of death! Now be strong for once in your life and do as you're told, you poor, insignificant piece of shit."

The first slice was the hardest.

He didn't know where to cut or how to prevent the ear-splitting bleats. But once he started—he had to finish the job. After a while, he couldn't tell if he or the lamb were screaming. Repeatedly he tore at the baby sheep with the rusted blade. Seconds felt like lifetimes as the creature's struggle weakened, and its last moments of breath evaporated into the ether.

The angel had never seen this much blood. It was still hot with energy. Unable to breathe, he dropped the knife and fell to his knees simultaneously. Everything in sight was covered in red—his mouth widened, and he gasped—finally able to inhale the warm copper fumes.

Lyssah rushed to Ezekiel's side and took him into her arms as he bawled. Slowly, she brushed her fingers through his curly hair and comforted him as he cried, "'Do not do anything to him. Now I know that you fear God because you have not withheld from me your son, your only son…'"

Amanda, Aurora, and Neil enjoyed their lunch breaks the following day in one of Manhattan's busiest restaurants. They munched on entrées at small iron tables set on the cluttered street before the eatery. Neil took a quick sip from a mug of coffee. "So anyway," he said dryly, gulping his drink, "my dresser started shaking. So I broke off my dresser's leg and shoved the sharp part into the pig's head. And he screamed." Neil paused. "Then turned into fire."

"Yes, yes," Aurora nodded and reluctantly agreed, "All hail the mighty Neil. Without whom, we would all be dead. Blah, blah."

Amanda mocked Aurora with a mouthful of chocolate cake, "I'm Aurora, all hail me for I am the princess. Everyone is stupid except for me!"

"That's the smartest thing I have ever heard you say." Aurora toasted Amanda's comment with a glass of diet ginger ale. "Anyone hear from Ezekiel?"

"No," Amanda shook her head and continued to eat her dessert, "You know what's not fair? I kill the most annoying twins on Earth, Linen, and Denzel or whatever, and I get nothing. Neil kills one fat pig, and he gets this whole little fiesta! Where's my fiesta? I should be having like a million because I had to kill twins, and I was in the nude."

Aurora raised her nose in disgust and rebutted, "Like we need the image of your butt while we're eating."

"Oh please, as models eat," Amanda chuckled.

"We do eat; we just don't stuff our faces with chocolate mousse..."

"There's no actual moose in this thing," Amanda corrected, eyes widened, "Vegan, remember?"

Neil grinned, "Cut it out, Aurora… "

"How could I?" Aurora shrugged and continued, "I've never seen a butt so square. It's like someone built your ass out of Legos."

"Hey," Amanda shouted. "Legos are cool! You don't have to hate everything, you know!"

"But you make it so easy," Aurora confirmed.

"On that note," Amanda beamed, "I got us all a little surprise."

Aurora rolled her eyes as Amanda reached down to a plastic bag at the side of her chair. With a smile as sweet as honeydew, Amanda handed out her gifts. "Do you remember a few years ago when someone burned down that fur factory in New Jersey? Well, the way we got away with it is because we were all wearing masks. I figured, since we are sneaking around and stuff and that we're sort of like a team, then we should be too! It would be cute and fun and just in case for the police and stuff..."

"That actually makes sense..." Neil agreed as Amanda handed the thin plastic lion's mask.

"I searched every costume shop in Manhattan to get just the right ones!" the blonde explained as she passed Aurora a cow's mask.

Aurora held the cheap disguise, betwixt her fingers with a grimace, and retorted, "A cow?"

"Sorry," Amanda apologized, "It's the closest thing I could find to an ox..."

Proudly, Amanda held up her mask, which was simply a featureless white face. Finally, she whipped out the final costume she had reserved for Ezekiel, the mask of an eagle. "It's what we all saw in our visions, remember? Lyssah said it represents the four faces of the Cherubim? I just wish I could give Ezekiel his; he hasn't been answering his phone..."

Aurora set down her glass and sighed, "Alright, not that this reunion wasn't fun, but unlike you, I have that little thing called...oh yeah, a life to get back to... I hardly have a job, and I would hate for my new boss to kill me."

"Come on, no one is going to kill you." Neil shook his head and disagreed. "It takes some holy water and a silver bullet to do that."

"Funny!" Aurora snapped sarcastically, "you think it's that easy? Many have tried, dear boy, many have tried. Now, if you don't mind, my lunch break is almost over." She hoisted her burgundy designer purse over her shoulder the then slipped her cow mask inside. "And I have to get back to work before I lose another job."

After trading departing pleasantries, Neil found himself rushing down the street once again. He continued through the crowds when a chilling feeling trembled at the base of his spine and stopped him in his tracks. An arrow whizzed past him and plunged itself into the side of a building. Neil turned to see Pestilence standing behind him in a white cape that looked like it was flowing through the water. The White Horsemen tucked his greasy black hair behind his pasty ears and greeted him, "You look surprised to see me, angel."

Neil was amazed as to how the man on the horse went unnoticed by the public.

He briskly swatted his hand at the demonic rider. He missed. The glass covering the showcase window behind Pestilence shattered.

"Gun!" someone shouted. The people of Manhattan scurried in chaos. The Horseman turned down the street. Neil ducked behind a corner, slipped on his lion's mask, and sprinted after him.

Aurora paused before she re-entered the lobby of her new job. Her body trembled. There it was again. She lost energy and grabbed the door to support her. Another vision. Being that she had no choice welcomed the power because to resist, she learned, was ineffectual.

Neil frantically threw his arms around in the middle of an empty construction site. In the main skeletal frame of a building, he convulsed. A spasm knocked him off his feet onto a concrete pot and then the floor. His mouth bled profusely.

Aurora awoke from the unsettling vision. He was under attack and lost the battle. She raced urgently towards the site.

Neil stopped short when the demonic Horseman leaped over large planks surrounding the metal frame of the building. He frantically surveyed the empty area; it was a large construction site. In the center stood the cold metal skeleton of the building and several construction tools left about haphazardly. Neil was now in an enclosed space with nowhere to run. "Holy hell, what the hell did I get myself into?"

The demon folded his arms, and his white cape covered him like a robe. He raised an eyebrow and smirked snuggly, "My sacred seraphim prince, why have you lost all your color? A bright future is ahead: Michael, 'the lion,' the most powerful of the Alpha Omega, will save us all as the fated hero in this epic journey. Fool, I know that you and your little band of infant angels have been plotting against me. I just want you to know that what you've always feared has always been right. You cannot stop what must come to pass."

"Is there going to be an intermission?" Neil spat coyly.

"You have access to such power, but you quiver at its costs. I see no leader here, no matriarch of the people. Just a pawn who is ignorant enough to believe that good triumphs over evil still."

The White Horseman armed himself with his small bow promptly loaded it, and fired. Neil's palm redirected the arrow, but the White Horsemen averted the blow.

Instead, Pestilence's attack was like a strike from a rhinoceros. Neil fell to the ground and cracked his head over the flower pot. He tried to stand, but the demon kicked Neil in the abdomen so hard he skidded several feet across the gravel. Neil bled from the mouth when the beast lifted him. The Horseman held him high by the throat and squeezed. With another hard blow, Neil was sent into a metal beam of the unfinished structure. It was a searing blinding pain; his entire body hurt, and his temples pounded.

"Neil!" her voice cracked his unconsciousness. Aurora reached down and removed the mask from his bleeding face.

"Where's the Horseman?"

Aurora shook her head and asked, "Who?"

"White robe," Neil squinted his eyes in pain as he attempted to answer.

"Neil, there's no one here." Aurora threw his arm over her shoulder and whined, "Damn, you're heavy."

"Y-you must have scared him off," Neil struggled. "We're more powerful when we're together, right? Two against one?"

Aurora limped slightly under his weight as she carried him out of the construction site. She warned, "Don't talk."

After he visited with Lyssah, Ezekiel needed some time alone. He was prone on his floor for over a day. Too weak to stand and too empty to form a thought. He listened silently as someone entered the apartment. He shivered, and the tiny hairs on his arms stood straight. They placed the jingling keys on the kitchen countertop. His skin crawled. Two voices were chattering in the living room. He recognized his mother's laugh. It was a while since he heard it, but he would know her chuckle anywhere. What would she think when she learned the truth?

Ezekiel forced his wobbly legs to attention. He curiously followed the voices but stopped at the foot of the doorway.

Fred and his mother cuddled on the dirty couch. Ezekiel's heart raced.

"Ezekiel!" Fred's strange smile was sharp and icy. "We're going to watch a movie; come sit with us." Ezekiel's mind was blank. He could feel his eyes well up, and he froze in place. What was going on?

The past few hours were surreal. This was a dream. A nightmare. Whatever it was, it couldn't be real. Stunned, Ezekiel pulled his sleeves over his trembling fingertips. Fred's tone suddenly flattened, "Ezekiel, is there something wrong? Sit down."

He repeated, "Sit, please. Now..."

Ezekiel treaded slowly to the small yarn armchair and sat ungracefully.

"It's a romance," Lauren giggled joyfully. "Isn't your father good to me?"

Ezekiel was shamefully silent and self-conscious.

Fred pulled Lauren closer to him and questioned, "Ezekiel, are you sure there isn't anything wrong?"

Ezekiel bit his lower lip to keep from crying and uttered, "N-no..."

Chapter 15: Please

> "The angel of the Lord then went ahead and stopped next in a passage so narrow that there was no room to move either to the right or to the left."
> **Numbers 22:27**

"And somehow he deflected my power and was able to take me out," Neil said flatly, his body and face covered more cuts and bruises than he could count. He was supposed to be the most powerful, the leader. How could he lose? The three angels sat around him with caring gazes and he confessed, "I-I don't know how he did it. He just waved his hand and was able to; I don't know, bounce my attack. I wasn't powerful enough to take him."

Concerned, Amanda pouted. Neil's scars and bruises were already starting to heal, but she was still worried. Quizzically, she asked, "Any idea what he was doing right in the middle of Times Square? Shopping for a new fancy robe?"

Neil shook his head in response, "No, it was more than that. He was planning something. I don't know what. And it was weird. It was like no one else on the street could see him. He must have put up some type of glamour or was invisible or something."

"No," Aurora sighed, "what was weird was in my vision. I didn't see a Hood. What I saw was Neil falling on the floor."

"He was there," Neil knowingly argued. "Obviously, look at what he did to me. Maybe he was invisible."

Aurora reached a hand out and ran her fingers over his bloodied lip. She paused for a second and retracted her touch and answered, "Yeah, well, I didn't sense any sort of glamour or invisibility when I had the vision. And my predictions are getting stronger, I can sense more in them, and they don't really hurt as much as they used to. Trust me; there was no glamour. I'd know; who's more glamorous than me?"

Dragged out of his apartment, Ezekiel's eyes were red with stress. His hair was messy, and his clothes unwashed. Agitated, he twitched with discomfort. Amanda narrowed her brow and placed a hand on his shoulder, and he jittered as though he suddenly realized he was in the moment. "Hey babe, you okay?" she asked.

Ezekiel nodded. He wasn't ready to tell them what he had done. Still, he was unable to admit it to himself. Ezekiel had killed his father, but somehow, it was easier to believe in fantasy and keep distracted.

Neil shot Aurora a resentful look, "I don't know why you didn't see him in the vision. Your power must not be working because he was there. Look at what he did to me!"

Aurora surrendered with an eye roll, "Alright, he was there."

"What we need to do is find some way to hunt him down and take him out!" Neil slammed a fist into his hand and spoke commandingly, "I mean, four against one, right? He did run when Aurora came."

Ezekiel bashfully shook his head and struggled to speak, "D-Do, we all realize how little we know about the White Hood and his Lord of The Rings friends? I r-researched so much about them, but I still feel like we're going into this thing b-blind. If w-we knew about how he deflected your power, then we'd be able to get through it or be better p- prepared for it. Maybe there's something in those files Aurora stole from Lyssah Rhamiel."

Scowling, Aurora retorted, "Stole?" Neil retrieved the folders from his desk, and she continued, "What about the future she stole from me? From all of us? I was going to be somebody!"

"I was reading some of this before." Neil retrieved a stack of papers from his desk and examined them. "But it's good for us all to know." He read aloud, "'For centuries, the four laid dormant in spiritual slumber, repeatedly reincarnated until the Four Horsemen of the Apocalypse revealed themselves and their destinies were awakened. The angels once stood at the throne of God but descended only to protect the Earth. Blessed with human souls, the depths of their powers are unlike any angel's but bound to the earth; they remain tangled in mortal mentalities.

'When the planet was created, and great powers existed, a war sparked between the benevolent and the wicked. It took thousands of years for the light to overcome the darkness, but the light was powerless to eradicate it. So, the benevolent forced them to sign a pact. It was a treaty that said the Earth belonged to the many allied Heavens for two thousand years after God's son was born. However, evil will always exist and has waged celestial war.

'Glory be to Michael, Neil, head of God's army of angels born as men and bestowed with extraordinary powers, the guide to salvation.

'Alone, their powers are to be feared, but it is only together that they form the Alpha Omega, the most powerful force there ever was and ever will be. If one-fourth of the circle is broken, the ring is broken, and thus all powers are gone.'"

Amanda yawned and ran a hand through her long fair hair, "If I could interrupt this meeting of the Neil fan club: I don't see what this has to do with that guy blocking your powers... especially if you're sooo cool Neil..."

He stood abruptly, "If no one else is going to take this seriously, you can leave, and I'll handle this myself."

"Are you kicking us out?" Aurora cocked up her eyebrow.

"I know what I saw," he muttered as he opened the front door. "I don't need you telling me something different."

Aurora threw her pocketbook over her shoulder and stomped towards the exit. With a snarl, she twisted, "I swear this is the last time you'll ever see me in this apartment!"

Amanda glumly retreated close behind her, "No need for a temper; I was just joking, Neil... I really do think you're cool..."

As she exited, Ezekiel followed suit. "Yeah, me too..."

Unsympathetically, Neil slammed the door.

Chapter 16: Images

> "When the ass saw the angel of the Lord there, she cowered under Balaam. So, in anger, he again beat the ass with his stick."
>
> **Numbers 22:27**

Neil suffered a sleepless night pressed between the sheets of his bed. His room was unusually warm, and he experienced a stubborn headache. The migraines came more frequently now. Constant drumming in his brain kept him from sleeping or getting comfortable. Paranoid, every corner looked dangerous. The Horsemen of the Apocalypse were trying to kill him, and they could attack at any time. Neil shut his eyes in frustration and gritted his teeth but the attempt to sleep only prolonged his restlessness.

A strange, chilling gust blew through his window. Neil opened his eyes to a dark figure before him. A tall man cloaked in a white-hooded robe, with a bow at his side, came into focus. The Horseman of Hatred aimed his arrow at the center of Neil's forehead. The angel crawled back on his bed, hitting the post with his back.

"Lovely apartment," the white devil taunted in a hoarse voice. "I hate that journalists make more money than good, honest working people."

"How do you…" Neil gasped.

"We are connected," Pestilence suggested. "Not that it would matter in a few seconds anyway."

Neil flashed a palm and telekinetically directed the sheets off his bed onto the demon. Then he mentally tossed the mattress from under him and at his intruder. The Horseman flung the cushion aside and aimed his bow once again. Neil dashed off to the window to escape, but an arrow landed on his shoulder.

It was a sharp, hot pain that fell in and out of numbness. Neil grabbed the arrow and felt lightning strike throughout his body. He inched around his windowpane as the blood on his hands made his grasp slippery.

"Let us end this once and for all," Pestilence spat over Neil's barrage of moans.

Bombs exploded in Neil's mind as he mentally reached out for help.

Aurora's eyes burst open. It was like a gunshot to her stomach. For a moment, the pain was blinding and her belly coiled with a shredding pang. Every inch of her quivered with the worry but it wasn't a vision.

As the pain subsided, she reached for her cellphone. All she could think about was Neil. There was something wrong. Neil would answer his phone if nothing were wrong. Soon after her calls reached voicemail, a cold shudder ran down her spine. If Neil was in trouble, how could she save him?

Slowly, Aurora opened her drawer and collected her small handgun. Would this even work on a Horseman of the Apocalypse? Covering her pajamas with her designer robe, Aurora ordered herself a car and rushed into the streets. Frantically, she sent out text messages as the vehicle pulled off.

Amanda's cellphone blared Broadway tunes. With a groggy yawn, she silenced the device and quickly retreated to slumber. But when the ring repeated, she jolted to attention with a tremendous amount of energy. She scanned Aurora's texts with intensity as Henry stirred beside her.

He looked at her with tired confusion and concluded, "It's late...Who is it?"

Amanda was never a great liar. Aurora's text panicked her, and she needed to leave immediately, but

Henry's longing gaze was loving and questioning. What was she going to tell him?

"I..." Amanda bit her lower lip and searched her brain for a lie. "I have to go to the bathroom!" she yelled before she stormed out of the apartment.

Thrown against the kitchen cupboards, Neil crashed onto the hard chilly marble floor, knocking dishes from the cabinets. The angel struggled to stand, though large pieces of glass cut through his bare feet, and the kitchen tiles were painted red. He psychically conducted the fallen shards of broken dishes towards Pestilence, who dodged them gracefully, allowing them to crash into the hallway.

Neil winced in pain while his shoulder continued to bleed through his white t-shirt.

"Stop!" he screamed as he moved backward and cut himself on pieces of broken ceramic.

The Horseman fired another arrow from his bow, aimed at Neil's forehead. Neil anxiously threw his arm across his torso, sending the arrow astray. Quickly, Pestilence fired another. His palm aimed at the shaft, the angel supernaturally held the weapon a few inches in the air from him.

However, the demon was relentless, and he discharged the third arrow. Neil re-positioned his other hand but could only psychically hold the needles a few inches from his face. Pushed by an invisible force, the blades drew closer to him every second.

Neil howled and used every bit of strength he had in him to banish both the arrows from his face. Then Pestilence attacked. The naked, chest white, robe-wearing demon planted a solid kick in Neil's gut. Blood gushed from Neil's mouth as he coughed through the pain.

Neil grappled with consciousness. The angel sent wave after wave of telekinetic energy directly at the crowned Horseman, but the man was able to wince his way through each assault.

Pestilence took a fist full of Neil's brown, black hair and placed a stable knee in his back. Confident he had the angel bound, Pestilence cooed, "I hate that you've given up so easily. I thought there would be a real challenge here. After all, the Alpha Omega, Sacred Angels, Descended Radiance or whatever the fuck you overgrown pigeons want to call yourselves are suppose to be the strongest."

Pestilence laughed, "If only my Mom could see me now, killing an angel. She'd be so disappointed!"

Restrained and in pain, Neil was powerless to move until a distant banging borrowed into his eardrums. Aurora pounded heavily on Neil's front door. "Neil! Neil! Open the door!" she cried out in anguish and momentarily distracted Pestilence.

Neil telekinetically unlocked the front door, and Aurora spilled into the room like an unruly storm. She scanned the room. Broken glass, bloodstains, ransacked furniture—everything was wrecked, but there was no sign of the angel. "Neil!" Aurora shouted, "Neil!"

She ran to the kitchen, where Neil was face down on the floor. Carefully, she placed his back against the wall and surveyed the area. Seeing Neil like this shook her to the core. She pressed a hand against his chest and examined his wound, "Neil. Oh my god. I-I called the others. They should be here real soon. Who did this to you?"

Neil coughed, "Horsemen."

"White Hood?" Aurora muttered. "Where is he?"

Neil flinched, "He's here, he ran off somewhere."

"Neil," Aurora murmured suspiciously. "There's no one else here but me and you. Are you sure it was him? I did some thinking."

"Of course, I know it was him!" Neil firmly objected through coughs of spit and blood, "He shot me in the shoulder with a fucking arrow!"

His tone resurrected a memory within Aurora. She shuddered at the sound of a man's screaming voice. Aurora looked at Neil's bleeding shoulder, where no arrow was lodged. He was indeed wounded, but there was no weapon to be seen. Almost hesitantly, Aurora asked, "So where's the arrow, Neil? It's not in your shoulder."

Neil felt his wound and explored the hole created by the weapon but quickly realized she was right. There was a wound but no gun. What had happened to it? "What do you think, Aurora? I did this to myself? I wouldn't hurt myself!" Neil shrugged away from her in denial, "Get off me! Someone has to kill White Hood, and if you're not going to, then I am!" He forced himself to stand using the kitchen counter as support.

An eerie chill rattled through Neil's bones, and pins shot up through his veins.

Pestilence stood in the doorframe between the kitchen and the living room. Ignoring Aurora, who stood in front of him, Pestilence aimed his arrow directly at Neil. The angel could hardly move, but he managed to speak.

"There!" he warned, "Behind you! Do you believe me now?"

Aurora's eyes danced around the ravaged kitchen but saw no immediate danger. Sheepishly she admitted, "Neil, there's no one here."

"He's going to kill me," Neil distrustfully pressed as he struggled to hold up his body. The angel held out his hand as if trying to focus on an invisible target.

"Neil! There's no one there!" Aurora exclaimed as she grabbed hold of his shoulders. "You have to believe me!"

"This is for your protection," he revealed before he summoned a bout of strength.

Violently, Neil managed to break her embrace and throw her to the ground. He glared at the Horseman, his hand raised and aimed at his foe. As his nostrils flared, he could feel his body vibrating from the base of his feet as he focused.

Hurt and now bruised, Aurora looked in the direction Neil had been watching but still did not see a Horseman; in the corner of the room, however, something did catch her eye.

"What the..." she murmured as a tremor ran down Aurora's spine.

A cattle-sized, blind, infested hog lurked in the shadows and studied Neil with hollow sockets. The mere sight of it was like nothing Aurora had ever seen. Ghostly and almost zombie-like, the mound of animated, rotting flesh dripped maggots from every pink and gray opening it had.

For a moment, she stared in awe. Unable to pull up the courage and concentration she needed to create a temporal fold, her restless fingers inched toward her coat pocket. Without much thought behind it, Aurora opened fire. The magical beast wailed in pain, and Aurora fired again, this time hitting it in its head.

In an attempt to escape, the demonic animal limped and squealed, but as Aurora fired the final shot between the eyes, it finally fell to the floor. Unnaturally, the demon's body fell apart. It began to decay within seconds until there were no bones or skin, only loose, bubbling organs lying openly across the ground. The steaming mess burned as it fizzed and stained the wood floor in shades of red, purple, and blue.

She could hardly take her eyes off the demon's death but only broke out of her trance as stirring behind her got louder. Aurora grabbed Neil just before he lost his grip on the countertop. Worms dug up from inside Neil's face and to the surface of his skin. They, too, dropped to the floor, motionless and dead as Pestilence faded from Neil's eye. The smell of the pig organs scattered across the floor curled Neil's stomach. He recognized the demon instantly as his assault from just the night before.

"It was a trick. The White Hood," Neil admitted as he realized the truth. "He was never really there, was he?"

Aurora shook her head and agreed.

"Y-you tried to tell me," Neil trembled. "I was hallucinating, and I hurt you..."

Aurora bit her lower lip but shook her head in agreement a second time. She had saved him. If he had continued fighting nothing, he would have ridden himself into the ground; if he had kept going, he would have killed himself. Aurora had never met a man as powerful and determined as Neil and never witnessed masculine weakness this raw or vulnerable.

"I'm sorry," Neil admitted. His head fell into Aurora's chest, and she hugged him. She allowed his blood to seep onto her clothes. He took a deep breath of her cocoa butter skin and apologized. "I'm so sorry."

Aurora parted her lips to answer, but before she could, Neil moved in closer. She could feel his hot breath on his face before their noses touched, and her face became wet with blood. He hesitated for just a moment before he gently brushed the rim of her mouth with his lips.

It only lasted a millisecond before he was thirsty for more. Leaning in, he took hold of her cheeks, and as his tongue entered Aurora's mouth he felt her body stiffen and the tension in her touch rise.

Now completely covered in blood that was not her own, Aurora shuddered. Her eyes welled up as her brain struggled to make sense of the scenario that just played out before her. Slowly, her hand loosened around her firearm. Gently, Aurora pulled back and softly conceded, "I-I can't."

In disbelief, Neil inched backward.

"I'm sorry," Aurora whispered, paused, then asserted, "Don't ever touch me like that again."

Chapter 17: Sealed with a Kiss

"Then the Lord removed the veil from Balaam's eyes so that he too saw the angel of the Lord standing on the road with sword drawn, and he fell on his knees and bowed to the ground. [32] But the angel of the Lord said to him, 'Why have you beaten your ass these three times? I have come armed to hinder you because this rash journey of yours is directly opposed to me.'"
Numbers 22:31-32

"Okay." Embarrassed, Neil scoffed and pulled back, "I won't." It was almost as if time had slowed down. He could hear her heartbeat in his temple, and even through the scent of his sweat and blood, he could swear he still smelled the cocoa butter on her skin.

"You're bleeding everywhere," Aurora told him. "You need to go to the hospital."

"No," he countered and turned from her, disappointedly, "They're going to ask too many questions. And we have to be careful with Rhion, right?"

"Yeah, but," Aurora disagreed before Neil cut her off.

"We're stronger, remember?" he reminded her as he tried to stand, "Maybe just help me to bed?"

She hesitated but agreed before throwing his arm over her shoulder and leading him into his room. After replacing his mattresses on the box spring, Aurora laid towels on his bed and rested the angel in it. Sharp pangs shot through his torso as he struggled to get comfortable.

"Alright," Aurora concluded, "take off your shirt."

"Wha?" Neil snorted.

"And where is your first aid kit?"

Suspicious, he curved a thick and bushy eyebrow before he asked, "You know first aid?"

"Only what I learned in rugby," Aurora announced, " asic, but it's better than nothing. I can also help you cover it up in case you have a hot date that evening."

"No hot date," Neil confirmed, "under the bathroom sink."

Just as Aurora stood, the doorbell rang. *This must be Amanda and Ezekiel,* she thought, as she left Neil's side to answer the door. As she walked through the dismantled apartment, she was surprised to see how much damage Neil had done by himself. Aurora answered the chime at the front door but was disappointed by who she discovered. A portly, older woman with her hair in rollers displeasing examined Aurora through small green glasses.

Her tiny lips bent with disgust. "I need to speak with Neil." The woman adjusted her polka-dotted pajama suit as she divulged, "I'm Sylvia Goldenblatt." She announced this proudly as she buried her fists in her muffin top, "I live next door."

"He's a little busy right now," Aurora misled her as she placed a hand on her hip and stepped in front of the door. "Can I help you with something?"

"It is three in the morning!" the woman hissed. "I don't know who you are but what's with all the noise? This is ridiculous! What are you having a party over here? I have a son, you know, and a growing boy needs his rest! It sounds like gunshots or a car wreck over here! I will call the police!"

"The party's over. Okay, Karen?" Aurora retorted. "We'll keep it down."

"I'm actually not a *Karen*," Sylvia corrected, "I'm a retired judge, okay? And I'm tired! So I'd watch the tone if I were you. I have a young boy at home who needs his rest, so I would appreciate it if—."

The apartment door next to Neil's swung open.

A twenty-seven-year-old strawberry blonde man with large red glasses and pajamas printed with cartoon spaceships stuck his head out. Annoyed, he shouted, "Mom, what are you doing? Come and stop harassing people! What did I tell you about being a Karen?"

"Cody," Sylvia instructed, "I'm just talking to Neil's mistress. Go to bed, honey! You need your full twelve hours, or you'll get cranky again! Now hurry away so I can get you ready for tomorrow."

"I already told you, Mom!" the man shouted. "I just don't need you to comb my hair anymore!"

Sylvia giggled to herself condescendingly, "You'll never be able to get that part right. Why not just let mommy help you?"

"Because of Mom!" Cody stomped his feet. "I'm perfectly capable of..."

Aurora tapped her foot and interrupted, "Listen! I said we'll keep it down. Don't you have anything better to do at three in the morning than crowd other people's doorsteps? Get out of here!" Aurora slammed the door and took a deep breath before releasing it. "I don't need to see into the future to tell there's a lot of problems there…"

She sat at the side of Neil's bed while he slept. His wounds were deep but stopped bleeding once she patched them. Aurora observed Neil— watched him as he recovered, studied his every breath, and counted them. She was unsure why she gazed so intently; was it just to make sure he was still alive or was it something else? Her eyes crossed his chestnut hair and ran down to his blistered face. The doorbell rang again, and Aurora scowled, then nervously pulled her hair back. Ezekiel and Amanda were at the door almost an hour later than Aurora's phone call. Greeting them with a pout, she allowed them to enter Neil's home. "Wow, you're late. Come in and welcome," she hissed sarcastically.

"Is everything a-alright?" Ezekiel asked.

"Now it is," Aurora shrugged.

Amanda shook her head in disbelief and asked, "We rushed over here 'cause you said you thought a demon was after Neil. Where's the hideous beast?"

"Have you tried checking the mirror?" Aurora scoffed then folded her arms across her chest. "Seriously, Neil needs his rest. Remember that pig Neil said that he killed?"

"The Notorious P.I.G.?" Amanda questioned.

Aurora inhaled and summarized, "Cliff notes: Turns out he wasn't so dead. This whole time that pig had been pulling this imagery or something, making Neil see White Hood and kick the crap out of him. So I shot the thing; it turned into a bunch of rotted organs. I...flushed them down the toilet."

"Wow," Amanda nodded surprisingly, "Aurora, cleaning. I never thought I'd see the day."

Aurora scowled, "It was disgusting. But seriously, you guys should get going; he needs his rest."

"Shouldn't we get him to a hospital?" asked Ezekiel.

Aurora shook her head, "Neil's strong. He'll pull out of it. We don't want to draw more attention to ourselves with Rhion Galloway in our business. Plus, we heal faster than normal people, right?"

"I guess," Ezekiel thought for a moment. "Are you going to stay with him?"

Aurora nodded.

An hour later, Ezekiel cautiously snuck back into his now immaculate apartment. It was years before he had seen his apartment so spotless. Eerily dirt-free... Ezekiel cleaned regularly, but he could never get the stench from the walls. He instantly noticed the difference in scent. Fresh pine never turned his stomach before. His mother was too weak to tidy up, and he knew he didn't do it. That only left one person.

It was 4:30 in the morning, and so he tried to remain as quiet as possible as he slipped into the apartment. He tiptoed to his door as the unsettling scents of fresh pine and vanilla tickled his nose hairs. Fred waited for him in the living room. He pursed his lips and blew Ezekiel a haunting kiss.

Ezekiel jumped back a few steps. He lost control of his breath again. Fear crippled his stomach. His temples hammered in his head, and sweat ran down his forehead.

"Hey there, E-z," Fred spoke, his voice gentle yet daunting. "And how are you doing this early in the morning?"

Ezekiel stumbled back a few steps.

"What?" he sneered.

Whatever this thing was, it was not his father.

Fred spread his arms open to taunt Ezekiel with the body of his dead father. This Fred stood straighter, looked cleaner, and thinner, but his eyes always squinted to not let too much light in.

"You're not going to answer your father?" Fredrick continued as he moved closer. "That is just rude. You know, I might have to lay you over my lap."

Ezekiel gulped.

"But you might like that a little too much," Fred winked a dark eye and snickered. "You didn't tell anyone about me." The silence between the two stretched, and the demon assumed, "So, what were you doing out so late tonight? You weren't going out killing my friends, were you? Or out partying? Wait, no. That's not you. You're too busy not getting girls or having friends and sitting here in this rat hole, drawing pretty little pictures that nobody cares about. As if that's actually going to get you somewhere in life. Where were you tonight? I won't ask again."

"I was," Ezekiel bit his lower lip and grappled with his wits to force out an answer, "N-Neil n-needed help."

Fred laughed mockingly, "'N-n-Neil n-n-needed help...' The most powerful of angels. What could he need your help doing?"

"There was a demon," Ezekiel answered.

"Right, of course. Another demon," he acknowledged. Fred turned his back and walked toward the small window in the living room. Ezekiel turned toward his room, but the thing that looked like his father commanded, "Stop, don't go in there. Come here."

Ezekiel slowly marched into the shaded living room. Fred stood at the windows with his hands folded behind him. He looked out onto the streets as the lights flickered, the cars moved by, and the people crowded.

"We can feel it, you know, us demons," Fred explained. "We can feel the darkness within the Earth. We know what's going to happen. The Four Horsemen and their guardian, the Hallowed One, they're starting the war. Hell does not have to hide now that the treaty is broken. We're here to unleash Hell upon Earth, and one of us will succeed, sooner or later. Trust me; you will die. Demonic appearances are on the rise since the Horsemen came out. No one can stop what must come to pass." Fred paused then asked, "What kind of demon attacked Neil?"

Ezekiel hesitated to speak, "H-he was this large pig. He p-put illusions inside Neil's h-head. I never got actually to see him."

"Smart," Fred mumbled, "they set a bounty hunter after you. The Horsemen are too important."

"A bounty hunter? B-but what would a demon bounty hunter work for?" Ezekiel asked.

Fred shrugged his shoulders before he related, "They work for friends. They ally themselves with power so that they can pull in favors. Have buddies in high places... or low places."

"Is that what you're going to do?" Ezekiel's voice was hoarse.

"No," Fred turned to Ezekiel. "What I'm going to do is much worse. You know what I'll do to your mother if you open your mouth, and you know I will know if you do. Go to bed."

The sun shone through the white curtains and glared across the hard wooden floors and throughout the room's white walls. Bright rays moved across furniture and finally onto Neil's bed, caressing his face and stirring him from his slumber. He blinked awake and threw the sheets off his bed. Beside him, Aurora was just waking from Neil's fussing.

Aurora fixed her hair and stretched her arms above her head. She yawned loudly and neglected to cover her mouth or face before expressing, "It's like sleeping on... I don't know... something not very comfortable. I can't believe I slept here and left my inspirational speech at home... You okay?"

Neil nodded slowly, "I'm fine."

"Yeah, it looks like it." Aurora studied his smaller cuts that had already closed. "You don't look as bloody and gross."

"Look Aurora," Neil cut off her words and placed a hand on hers, "about last night,"

"The kiss?" Aurora blurted out and moved his hand off hers. "Oh, psst. Forget it. It's okay."

Neil nodded, "I was going to apologize again but not for that. For getting you in danger and for not believing you. For putting my hands on you the way I did... I also wanted to thank you. For all you've done. For cleaning up my home, saving my life, killing that demon."

"It was the first thing I ever killed," Aurora boasted, then gazed away and fought away the urge to shiver. "Not gonna lie, it was kind of fun. Maybe killing isn't an actual sin, huh?"

"Not according to the Catholic church," Neil muttered a bitter joke. "Speaking of… we should let Lyssah know what happened."

"Can't we just send her a text?"

Chapter 18: Able

> "For if God did not spare the angels when they sinned, but condemned them to the chains of Tartarus and handed them over to be kept for judgment…"
> **Peter 2:4**

Ezekiel was breathless. He had never seen his home so incredibly immaculate. The walls were newly painted, and pine's fresh smell had replaced the scent of cat urine. In the frighteningly spotless living room, a new forty-two-inch flat-screen television was surrounded by new expensive-looking furniture. Frederick had gotten a job, stopped drinking, and found a way to pay for his wife's medical bills, all in a matter of a week. Ezekiel ran his fingers across the new soft daunting leather couch and felt uneasy.

Something was very wrong here, he knew, but he had never seen his mother so happy. He dropped his pencil and gave up the hope of drawing anything. After all, no one cared.

The faint sounds of a fire burning rumbled into his ears. The room began to shake, and suddenly he felt the slight flux of flames touch his skin. His eyes dashed around the area. There was nothing out of the ordinary, yet the rolling feeling in his stomach refused to settle.

A few feet before him stood a woman with long brown hair reaching down her back. She was completely naked underneath the hundreds of live snakes that clothed her. Serpents of different sizes, colors, and species hissed and clung to her body as she held an apple in her right hand. Without a word, the woman pulled off an orange snake from the many that slithered on her thigh. She dropped the animal onto the now polished tile floor. Before Ezekiel could scream, the serpent launched off the ground and sunk its teeth into his cheek.

"Hello!" Amanda announced herself, then cheerfully pulled out a chair across from Neil's desk and sat. Disappointed, she took in Neil's tiny office's blandness but was then shocked he even had an office at such a young age. She placed her giant kitten-shaped pocketbook on her lap. On her lunch break, she was short for time but desperately needed to speak with Neil. Amanda anxiously grinned and held on tightly to her pocketbook.

"It's crazy to see you back at work so soon," she deduced.

"It's been a little over a week," Neil confirmed. "I may not be a hundred percent healed, but I'm feeling much better. What's up?"

"Promise me you're not going to be mad," Amanda warned.

"No," he answered firmly, almost annoyed that he had to make time to meet with her.

She cleared her throat. "Okay, I don't know how you're going to react to this." Amanda paused.

"But..." She paused a second time, "I want to tell Henry about us being angels!"

Shocked, Neil erupted, "Okay, have you completely lost your mind? Amanda, you know you can't tell anyone about us."

"Okay, just about me then," Amanda answered readily. "Look, I understand how you, a journalist, could stand here and lie, but someone like me? Neil, I can't keep lying to him. I am an honest person. I love him, and he loves me too, and it's just really awkward. He can tell something is different with me. We talk every night, and I just, I really need to tell him. Did you know I had to leave his bed to go over to your house when Aurora called us the other night? He's super confused. I don't want him to think I'm cheating! If we're going to get married, I have to be truthful with him… not to mention he misses Purrson… and you know… it's not that Purrson is exactly evil now… but if he looks like a mutant, it's probably because he is one...but that's beside the point...it'll just be hard to explain."

"If you understand so well, you should know how I, a journalist, know how this thing could blow up," Neil warned. "If word gets out about what we are, we'd never get a moment's peace! People would bang down our doors. We wouldn't be able to do what we're supposed to do. Not to mention the government chopping us up into tiny pieces to see what we're made of. I know you want to tell him but you can't. Thanks for leaving his bed to come to save me, but how many times have I saved you?"

"Neil," Amanda disagreed, "this isn't your decision."

"The hell it isn't!" Neil's voice rose.

"That's right!" Amanda blurted loudly. She was shocked as to how loud her voice had actually become, but she clenched her pocketbook and continued. "I love Henry; someday soon, I will marry him! We're going to have kids and a family! He won't tell anyone; I can promise you that! I mean, my roommate knows, and she hasn't told anyone!"

Neil paused, "Your roommate knows?"

"Neil, she saw me turn into Henry the first night we had our powers; there wasn't much I could do!" Amanda frowned. "And hello, she lives with me! Do you think I could hide an eight-legged Maine coon?! I'm just asking you to understand that I cannot keep lying to Henry!" She walked toward the front door and opened it. Before she could exit, the door suddenly slammed shut. Amanda turned toward Neil; she knew it was under his control.

"And I'm just asking you to understand that I will do everything in my power to keep you from telling him even if I have to follow you and hold you down." Neil stood from his chair. "It's not just your life you're putting on the line here; it's mine, it's Aurora's, it's Ezekiel's, it's the world. Don't you think this changed my life as well? That I am scared to be with my own son for fear of what might happen? Don't be selfish, Amanda."

"Neil, you are the biggest jerk butt I have ever met!" the blonde screeched. Her lips pursed together as she threw the door open and exited. Amanda's eyes were like arrows in Neil's face as she declared, "We are not cool!"

Beads of sweat ran down Aurora's cheeks, and she breathed forcibly. Massive headphones covered her ears, but they did little to obstruct the vibrations she felt when she fired her pistol.

Her gun fired several times, and she shredded the center of her paper human target. She took a sip of her water from her canteen and felt that familiar shimmer down her spine. It wasn't long before the vision had taken over her body and forced her to let go of her handgun mid-fire.

Ezekiel was in the dark, steaming tar trench. Embers sparked and exploded in the raging wind as intense heat rose from the boiling muck and tremoring sand. An aroma of brimstone coiled down from the sky as reptilian creatures soared through the thundering atmosphere and snapped with an insatiable hunger.

Under them, Ezekiel shivered in an endless pit filled with thousands of oily mutilated bodies. The black soup of twitching human organs came to his waist, and though dismembered, the limbs squirmed about aggressively. Full of life, they reached miserably toward him. Beside Ezekiel stood a woman, naked and covered in snakes. She placed an arm onto Ezekiel's shoulder and forced him forward.

Aurora rose from her vision with several people from the range crowded around her. Her eyes widened, and something uncontrollable rose. She leaned over and began to vomit.

Chapter 19: Welcome to Hell

> "The angels too, who did not keep to their own domain but deserted their proper dwelling, he has kept in eternal chains, in gloom, for the judgment of the great day."
>
> **Jude 1:6**

The Cherubim of the Throne held a vigil in Ezekiel's living room. Sprawled on the couch, he was still breathing but motionless and unresponsive to all techniques the angels used to wake him. They had no idea how long Ezekiel had been this way, nor did they know how they would explain this to his mother and father, should they return. Aurora slapped Ezekiel again, but still, he lay unresponsive.

"Damn it," she cursed. "Nothing is working. He's comatose!"

Amanda narrowed her eyes and tightened her folded arms before hypothesizing, "How do we know he's just not ghosting out or something?"

"Because," Neil answered, "he usually returns to his body if it's in some sort of danger, and Aurora has been smacking him in the face for the past fifteen minutes."

"Okay," Aurora nearly shouted, "well, we need to get out of here before we have to explain this to his parents."

"Aurora, are you sure you have no idea where he was in your vision?" Neil asked.

"No," she told him, shaking her head, "but maybe I should ask one of those people crawling on the floor around him. Oh yeah, they're too busy having a slight case of being ripped the hell open." Aurora exhaled and explained. "I can't control when I have my visions, how long they are, or what I can see. I just get information. Flashes. Feelings. Sometimes I hear things, even taste them. Wherever that place was, it's somewhere disgusting and evil. I could smell… rotting bodies."

Amanda examined Ezekiel's face. She turned his head over to see the snake bites and exclaimed, "Hey, what are those two things on his cheek?"

"Do you think someone attacked him?" Neil asked.

Amanda turned toward him and scowled, "Okay, first off, I still hate you, and you will be punished in the near future, and second I was talking to Aurora, not you."

Stolas the Maniae frantically pecked at the window. Neil opened it, and the bird hopped in. Quickly, Stolas feverishly freed the note attached to his leg and hooted deafeningly before leaving the same way he entered.

"Why doesn't she ever use the phone?" Amanda asked.

Neil unfolded the paper and read aloud, "'Beware of the Sealers, angel executioners! Banish them, my patients, first destroy what links them.'"

"This is what I mean!" Aurora ranted, "Why be cryptic for no reason?"

"Oh my Go—," the words barely left Ezekiel's lips before the shock caused involuntary convulsions. A burning numbness attacked his senses, and a thousand electric tweezers yanked out his veins. His vision faded in and out, and he was unsure if the unbearable screaming he heard was his own. Each wail was more intense than the last, and he could feel them vibrate on his skin.

It was like breathing acid, the smell of offal and waste melted inside of him, but his body heaved so heavily that he could not help but take in large puffs of poison. Sour coils of rotten meat and blood twisted around his tongue and immediately turned his stomach.

Ezekiel fell to his knees and took in handfuls of the hot sand. As the substrate slipped through his fingers, he felt starvation in the grains and a leeching pang that intensified the longer he held them. Overwhelmed and close to unconsciousness, his mouth dropped open, and his eyes adjusted to the peppery air.

Forests of twisted trees with tormented human faces in their trunks cried out in sorrow for miles. Hot ashes crashed through the air like hail, and Ezekiel struggled to cover his face to see through the soot.

The sky was black and full of harpies—hairless winged creatures. They screamed like parrots and fought over bones with taloned feet and wide mouths full of sharp teeth. Ezekiel was familiar with violence, but this new world was more than he could handle all at once. His brain was overloaded and blank as he struggled to process this moment. In horrific astonishment, he attempted to stand but fell to his knees. The burning sand below him throbbed freakishly and surged like it was alive and bloodthirsty.

Swarms of wasps with human faces flew over his head, and he ducked in fright. He watched them pass above and quivered before the naked woman wrapped in snakes. At first, he thought to run, but there was no energy in his legs. When he realized he wasn't being chased, he managed to sputter, "W-where am I?"

The woman looked down at him but said nothing. The largest snake on her body coiled around her in brown scales. He whipped out his fiery tongue and seemed to smile at Ezekiel. "Look around. You know where you are; you can feel it. We are standing on the cusp of Hell: welcome."

Though its mouth was still, Ezekiel knew that the voice came from the large snake and was horrified. Hesitantly he addressed the animal, "W-who are you?"

The snake twisted abnormally, black eyes were like needles as it spoke, "You can call me Eve."

"Eve?" Ezekiel gasped, stood from the ground, and walked over to the creature while the snake followed him with its head. He examined the woman; her expression was frozen in terror. She held an apple in her pale right hand. Suddenly, it made sense to him, and he assumed, "You're Eve? Like Adam and Eve? Eve, the woman who committed the original s-sin?"

"I said you could call me that," the snake hissed and slithered. "I didn't say that was my name." The reptile looked forward, "Come, the sinful one."

Just as she turned, three creatures materialized like spirits before her. Savagely they trampled across the hot sand to block Eve and Ezekiel's path in the fiery black desert. First, a large leopard, then a lion, then finally the wolf. Immense. The ground shook as they ran, and when they sat, they were sixteen feet tall. Each roared ferociously with godly knowledge in their eyes. The terrifying howls drowned out all the tormented screams around them.

Ezekiel's heart fell into his chest, and he was momentarily deaf. Thunderstruck and panicked, he was out of touch with his body. His vision blurred with alarm. All his senses numbed. He needed to vomit but couldn't...

"Linger not before me," Eve the serpent spoke. "Away with you!" She reached to one of the various serpents around her body then pulled a white and black snake from her waist. She dropped it onto the surging dirt, and the reptile rapidly grew several times its size. It hissed and snapped at the demonic animals before it.

Suddenly, Ezekiel remembered to breathe, and sound rushed back into his ears. The reptile whipped and struck at the leopard. With supreme roars, the lion and wolf tackled the serpent and buried their teeth into its flesh.

The talking snake that called itself Eve turned to look at Ezekiel and ordered, "Come now, walk with me. As your punisher, you must obey me or face something much worse than I."

"Why?!" Ezekiel begged, his eyes filled with tears. Terrified, Ezekiel paused in hesitation, then followed Eve. She strolled past the snake, wolf, lion, and leopard as they shredded each other to bits.

The snake-beast turned to him, "I am the Angel of Retribution, the renegade spirit! Balancer of the Celestial

Order that governs all and Capturer of the Fallen, that betray the Gods! You have taken a human life, broken the most sacred of commandments, and brought you to Hell... So to speak... 'Abandon all hope, ye who enter here.'"

"B-but, it was an accident!" Ezekiel cried, "I-I didn't know that I could do that! I loved my father!"

"Whether you knew what you were doing or not, you were granted free will as all living creatures are," the snake informed him.

Hot tears spilled down his face as he grieved, "So you're just going to bring me to Hell? I didn't even die yet! What about the Alpha Omega?! Please, you can't do this to me! I'm a nice person! I didn't mean to! I swear, please!"

Emotionless, the snake commanded, "Because you are what you are, does not make you impervious to the deeper religion that governs all! Ancient rules still apply. Angels may not lie with humans, *alive or dead*. They may not lie with their kin. They may not disobey orders, and when an angel kills a human without divine permission, it is fallen and brought to Hell! What's done is done; you no longer have a choice. Let me show you your punishment."

Several hours passed in Hell, and he spent most of them walking on the scorching dunes beside Eve or the thing that dressed as her. She finally led him to a mile-long black pool of thick tar-like water. Ezekiel could smell the gore of the disfigured human forms while they rolled in the black muck.

Hacked pieces of people wiggled with life and bubbled like boiling water. The swamp's inhabitants cried out like living lobsters in this disheartening soup.

Ezekiel had never seen something so alien, so disturbing, and devoid of love. Humanity was almost unrecognizable; some human frames lacked limbs, and others dripped flesh. He felt his mind struggle to take in the incredible amount of pain he witnessed. His knees buckled under the weight of his empathy, and he fell to the radioactive dirt.

"Get up," Eve ordered. "Walk into the black pool. Here you see murderers. Men, women, and children who have killed their kindred, whether by accident or intention, all suffer the same fate."

Ezekiel shook his head slightly and stuttered, "I-I..."

"Make haste!" Eve commanded and stepped into the pool. Slowly and hesitantly, Ezekiel followed. The ooze was thick and heavy, like blood mixed with oil. His eyes watered as he waded more in-depth into the lake with the woman. The gel enveloped his body like a thick meaty glove and sunk into every curve. Those with eyes watched him, then those with movable parts crawled after him like spiders.

Ezekiel waded through the greasy reservoir then abruptly halted in disgust. He tried to turn back, but Eve placed a firm grip on his shoulder to stop him. As the detached limbs approached, they all progressively became more human to him. He looked directly into their forlorn faces, which told of torment, suffering, sadness, and pain. They cried out to Ezekiel and reached to him with whatever body parts they had left.

"W-what are t-they d-d-doing?" Ezekiel asked.

"They can sense your power," Eve spoke. "They know you are the Angel of Death, and they think you have the power to free them."

Ezekiel's heart ached in his chest as he asked, "Do I?"

The deity dressed as Eve the serpent uttered, "Yes, you do."

"Then I will," Ezekiel shouted and waded through the water toward them. "It's not fair! No one deserves this! Things aren't so black and white; some people kill in self-defense!"

"You mustn't free them!" Eve cautioned. "Yes, it is true that some are here because they have killed in self-defense. I know that is what you sense, but they have still killed. Perhaps your father is better off dead. Perhaps the years he had left were full of nothing but sin and wastefulness. Still, that wasn't your choice to make. Without divine consent, it is wrong to kill even in self-defense. But with free-will comes forgiveness. No matter how unlikely you believe it, Fred could have turned his life around, and he would have been forgiven. Within every human soul is the potential for greatness and must never be taken for granted or wasted. In the few seconds you had, you still had a choice to be strong enough and control your power without letting it control you! But you failed. A sin, no matter how justified, is still a sin. Those you see here have committed the foulest of sins, and now they must be punished, as do you."

Ezekiel's large brown eyes turned from Eve, then back to those who squirmed through the slime and pleaded for his help. His heart tore itself apart. A man particularly close to him groaned for his attention. He had a single arm and no lower body; his face was cut and filled with dirt and grime. The man outstretched his only arm towards Ezekiel, and his mouth hung open in agony. Pieces of his jaw dropped off into the liquid, and his fingers broke apart as he stretched them.

"Follow me," Eve spoke. "We must wade through these sinners."

Chapter 20: Eve

"But the angel of the Lord went down into the furnace with Azariah and his companions, drove the fiery flames out of the furnace."
Daniel 3:49

Ezekiel followed the creature dressed as a woman into a cave. At first, the cave was dark, but Eve waved her arm, and a small campfire sparked in the center of the cavern. She sat on the rocks around the fire. He looked outside to the endless black dunes against an angry, now red sky.

Shriveled black trees with branches twisted like claws and trunks that resembled human faces cried in distress. He shivered, sat on a rock opposite Eve, and pulled his sleeves over his hands.

Ezekiel bit his lower lip and looked down the cave; Eve had rushed him in here, but she had not given him a reason for their swiftness. His heart beat heavily and he was finally brave enough to ask, "I-is there something in here?"

"No," the reptile spoke abruptly. "There is nothing here but blood-drinking rocks."

Ezekiel suspiciously eyed the boulder he sat on. After a moment, his shoulders sunk, and he questioned, "So why did you…"

A clap of thunder cracked through the sandy dunes. The red sky swirled until the clouds formed a violent multi-horned face. Commanding, ferocious eyes glared over a thin and pointed nose made of fire and smoke. The cyclone was the size of a skyscraper. It stretched its jaws open for a bone-chilling screech.

Ezekiel flinched as the sky thundered, sand stirred into multiple whirlwinds several yards away from the cave. Tornados twisted off the ground as lightning and fire churned from the sky.

Ezekiel choked, "What's happening?"

The serpent snorted and turned its head toward the outside of the cave, "Who do you think? This is the way he reminds us of his power. Just in case anyone tries to get stupid and cross him, they'd know what they're up against. Do you see what you're up against?"

"The Alpha Omega," the snake laughed. "You're a joke to everyone down here. No one takes you seriously. As the benevolent sat high and mighty for all these years, what do you think we were doing? Relaxing? No, they were waiting for the moment when they could finally rise. A skinny, pathetic little boy. How old are you? Twenty-five? Twenty-six? What exists down here was set into motion long before your species crawled up from the scum pits. Do you really think you stand a chance? You murder your father, try to bring back his spirit by dragging him from Hell, and in the process open a connection just large enough for a demon to jump through...Then, even better... you provided it with a beautiful fresh warm body for it to use. You were pitiful on Earth. This is where you belong."

"T-this m-must be an n-nightmare! I'm dead?" Ezekiel toppled over with tears. He tried to be strong but painted uncontrollably. His brain was unresponsive as the circumstances piled tons on his shoulders. His bottom lip quivered hopelessly. This was unreal.

The brown snake wiggled with a sinister grin. Sorrow burst out of Ezekiel while he wept wildly, "It was an accident! I didn't know I had the power! I didn't ask for it! I didn't ask for any of these powers; I hate them! I just want a normal life! If I could take it back, I would! I loved my father and would never hurt him! When he passed..."

"Stop lying to yourself," Eve challenged him. "He didn't pass; you killed him! Life isn't a pretty picture, Ezekiel. You can't erase your mistakes and draw over them! You killed your father, it happens..."

"B-but, it didn't happen like that!" Ezekiel protested.

"That's exactly how it happened!" Eve countered.

He tried to speak up. Ezekiel's nose ran while tears saturated his face. There was nothing left to say. He pulled his sleeves over his fingertips and conceded, "So this is just my p-punishment then? He was a drunk... he tormented me my entire life..."

"You think you're the only person on Earth with a drunken and irresponsible father?" Eve asked him with defiance. "There are millions of people who would do anything to have what you have and would have never thrown it all away as you did! You're in Hell because..."

"I killed my father!" Ezekiel acknowledged. He screamed through sobs, "I killed him! At first, I didn't know what I was doing. I-I didn't know I had that power, but when I saw him start to die... I knew... but I-I couldn't stop. I was so angry I wasn't thinking. I pretended like I didn't know what I was doing but deep down... I was so mad at him... and now... That's why I'm in Hell..."

He pulled the sleeves from off his fingertips.

"Maybe we *should* just take him to the hospital?" Aurora mumbled as she watched Ezekiel on the couch. They managed to sneak Ezekiel's body into Neil's apartment but spent hours trying to wake him.

Tears hung at the edges of Ezekiel's eyes as he wept in his coma.

Amanda put her cat-shaped pocketbook on a side table and sighed, "Except hospitals aren't fun anymore. Go there now, and you might end up butt-booty naked and fighting ridiculous twins!"

"We have to bring him to Lyssah Rhamiel," Neil finally disclosed after he paced back and forth. The angel ignored Aurora's glare and continued, "She's a loon, but she might be the only one that could help us right now. We tried it our way, and now I'm just worried about him."

The air filled with static, and the angels suddenly became queasy. When the room began to shake, Neil huffed in aggravation. "What now?"

Mid-air, a tan trio of skinny beings in loincloths materialized, backs pressed against each other. Their skin was tight like a rhinoceros but was damaged and had bits of muscle and bone exposed in open bloodless wounds. Tiny leather belts covered the eyes, ears, and mouths of the hairless creatures.

Bound together by a large strap across their ankles, they were identical in every way except the objects in their hands. The demon in the middle held a golden chain with a tassel at its end. To his right, his brother owned a hand mirror outlined in gold to his chest. The final demon held a golden cup with red and blue jewels encrusted around its rim to his left. The silent trio stiffly glided toward the angels.

"Okay," Neil whispered and looked back. His teammates slunk further away from the disturbing sight. Neil tried to throw the Sealers with a jerk of his arm and the might of his mind. The mirror flashed gold light and enveloped the three floating demons in a transparent sphere that shielded them from the attack.

"Okay..." Neil repeated before urging Aurora, "my power isn't working; you try."

Aurora's eyes heated up, and her irises slowly became scarlet. As her eyes blazed like rubies, her powers rifted through time, but the invisible cloak that surrounded the trio flashed gold. They continued to inch toward them, unaffected by Aurora's assault. Neil gravely looked over toward Amanda.

Amanda focused. Changing the shape of objects was way harder than altering her form and required a great deal of concentration, but she needed to hurry.

Puppies!

She saw the image in her mind. She reminded herself of their smell and touch. Quickly she struggled to recall their biological makeup. Amanda directed both her arms and separated her fingers. Her new transmogrification skills needed practice, and like the others, she was quickly overpowered by the invisible shield.

"What now?" she gulped.

Ezekiel trekked with the snake for hours. Finally, he was led up a tall hill with a thick white vapor cloaking the crispy grass. Ezekiel stopped walking when Eve signaled with an authoritative arm. They stood on the edge of a cliff above a lake of fire. The bold flames spun, and Ezekiel trembled in awe. Excited, the blaze rose miles above his head and contained tormented and mangled flashing faces.

"Here lies the Lake of Chastisement," the snake spoke. "In it burn the sinners, those who've committed crimes against God. Here is our final trip and the end of our journey."

He was in a constant state of dread. Everything was new and threatening. His energy was spent, and his nerves were so tightly wound that they threatened to pop at any moment. Yet, there was beginning to be a level of comfort in his familiar fear. He took a breath, then calmed himself and expected the worst. However, he remained unprepared when a suffering spirit struggled into clarity. His father screamed as he pushed through and stormed past the burning souls trapped within the flames.

"No..." Ezekiel pleaded.

"Ezekiel!" Fred's voice was hoarse and broken as if he'd been screaming for years. "Let me out! Please! Ezekiel, son!"

Aurora and Amanda laid Ezekiel on Neil's bed, and his bureau slid in front of the door. Neil bombarded the exit and bounced readily.

"Are these the Sealers?" he wearily exhaled. "They're immune to our powers."

Aurora scowled, "Damn it, Neil, how does everybody know where you live?!"

"They kill angels, but we're like, super angels, right?" Amanda asked. "There's three of them and three of us, right?"

"But there isn't supposed to be," Aurora countered. "There's supposed to be four of us, and we're one down; that's why they decided to attack now! Do you think they got Ezekiel?"

Neil shook his head and thought out loud, "We're supposed to break them up, but I don't know how since we can't get through that shield." He surmised, "We can't just stay trapped in this room... You two take Ezekiel towards the door, and I'll hold them off... I'll meet you at the church."

"Neil, no," Aurora protested. "So it's three against one?"

"You think they can't get through that door within a matter of seconds? The best defense is a good offense. We don't have time to talk about this. Get ready!" Neil warned. He swung his arm in the air and bewitched the dresser across the room.

Warm tears streamed freely down Ezekiel's face and crept into the cracks of his lips. His mouth gaped and let the salty tears drip against his tongue, "Free him. I could. Couldn't I?"

Eve nodded.

Ezekiel paused in a moment of realization. He bit his lower lip and wiped his noses with his sleeve. He acknowledged, "I could release myself too?"

Eve nodded again.

"I could..." Ezekiel admitted and struggled to see through glassy eyes. This cruel place was limitless. It made him feel so small and powerless. Bad people were sent here. That was reality; the rules. He did not make them. It was, however, his job to enforce them and his responsibility to obey them. "B-but I can't... Redemption, huh..."

Ezekiel stepped toward the fire, he could feel the flames' warm licks across his chest and face. His eyes burned with tears, and he let himself go. The angel convulsed with emotion. He forgot to breathe again. He was again, but queasy but knew what he needed to do.

Eve blankly stared.

Arms spread back, Ezekiel jumped into the warmth. The fires stroked his skin with high intensity and engulfed his body. The naked woman smiled then finally opened her mouth. "It has been a pleasure being your guide, Ezekiel Wallace."

The golden chain flew towards Neil, and he blasted his living room chair to defend himself. It wrapped around the piece of furniture, and the angel held the whip in his power. The Sealer yanked the other end of the chain, and Neil refused to release his telekinetic grip. Aurora and Amanda followed instructions and carried Ezekiel's body out of the room.

Tadpole-like white ectoplasm squiggled through the walls and into Neil's apartment. Ezekiel stirred then broke from Aurora's grasp. He stood, tattered and beaten, as the spirits floated around him. His eyes were red from the tears, he was pale and looked half-dead, but he stood without Amanda's support. Through his grief, his eyes struggled to refocus.

"What the hell is going on?" he asked as he realized they had brought him to Neil's apartment, then jumped as he discovered the monsters. "Did anybody know there were demons in the apartment?!"

As the translucent spirits phased through the walls and objects, in and out of the room, Neil had an idea. "Ezekiel," he shouted, "ghost through their shield and rip that leather strap off their feet!"

Ezekiel fought through his delirium and immediately followed Neil's instructions. His astral spirit appeared inside the Scalers' shield just long enough to become corporeal and untie the black leather rope that bounded their ankles.

A millisecond after the strap loosened, heat and invisible energy burst into the room like water from a balloon. A wave of radiation exploded, the force tramped through space and crashed through the furniture. The demons split and spun off in different directions. Separated, they were now free from their binds, and their heads moved in constant, sharp motions. They shook, rolled, and jerked their skulls as the shield dissipated, and they were no longer protected.

Neil rushed to his feet while the creatures twisted with confusion. In delirium, they knocked over his trophies and awards until they found their feet. Neil aimed at one of the Sealers and threw his arm, launching a telekinetic blast. It deflected Neil's efforts and redirected the energy with its mirror. The sheer power bounced off the glass and blew out the living room windows, blowing pieces of the window frame, and designer curtains fell into ash.

Within seconds the trio floated through the broken window and took to the streets.

He gasped as he surveyed the area. Neil couldn't care less about the expensive damage that was just done, nor did he care if the battle woke his neighbors. He dusted off his pants and asked, "Is everyone alright?"

"I almost peed myself, but I'm okay," Amanda answered and watched the others recover.

Neil looked over to Ezekiel and inquired, "You okay? Where were you?"

Nervous, Ezekiel misled, "I... was just... astral-projecting...meditation… training and whatever. I-I didn't know I could do it for that long..."

"Aurora said she saw you in a pool of mutilated bodies," Neil retorted.

Ezekiel paused for a moment before he shrugged sheepishly, "Go figure...Glad you guys saved me and prevented that vision from happening..."

"Well," Neil sighed and stretched his arms behind his back, "let's go get them."

"W-wait, we're going after those things?" Ezekiel petitioned and raised a brow. He was emotionally exhausted and struggled to speak, "I think I need to b-breathe!"

Neil walked to the closet and threw on his brown leather jacket. Unwilling to listen, he announced, "Yeah, we have to crush them while they're weak. We can't just let them run the streets."

"Neil, I know, those looked like costly curtains. I'm as pissed as you." Aurora collected herself, "But those guys, maybe we should just let this one go."

"So, what do you want to do?" Neil turned to her and urged, "Let them escape, come back with their shield, and kill us when we're separated? I won't let that happen. Whoever is too scared to go can stay, but I am going... Don't forget your masks." He slipped the plastic lion disguise over his face, rushed out, and left the door swinging.

Chapter 21: Reunion

> "Another angel came out of the temple, crying out in a loud voice to the one sitting on the cloud, 'Use your sickle and reap the harvest, for the time to reap has come because the earth's harvest is fully ripe.'"
> **Revelation 14:15**

"What did I tell you?" Amanda whispered as she rushed alongside Aurora and Ezekiel while Neil marched purposefully into the bitter streets, searching for the Sealers. Street lights illuminated the empty midnight sidewalk in low orange tints as Amanda took hold of Ezekiel's hand and pulled him closer. "He's mean, and he screamed at me like a jerk, flat-out threatened me, and now we're chasing these guys out in the street…"

"Those were costly curtains," Aurora moaned under her plastic cow mask, "I get it, but it's been a long day, and I have to wash my hair tomorrow, so let's just get this over with."

"N-no offense," Ezekiel interrupted as he adjusted his eagle mask uncomfortably, "I don't mean to be rude, but there is just a lot going on right now. I just want to go home."

Neil's hasty step led him half a block before the rest of his teammates as they reluctantly followed his pursuit. Amanda's lips curved with frustration, "He's totally insane;

not like Lyssah Rhamiel crazy either, at least she has a cute owl!"

Neil stopped on the edge of a sidewalk, closed his eyes, and clenched his fist. He centered himself and focused on locating the demons. When his mind stretched out beyond his body, it extended in an invisible mental web. Supernaturally charged brain waves homed in on the creatures, and he opened his eyes in anxious anticipation.

"Found them," he announced. "Let's go put the fear of God in these mofos."

Frozen grass cracked beneath them while they crept through the empty black park. Shadowed in the dawn—every bush seemed menacing, and every tree served a sinister smile. The very breeze held an echo of wickedness, and Amanda pulled Ezekiel incredibly tight to her body. Static burst through the air as the street lamps in the park shattered. Amanda jumped to Aurora's side and nervously clawed her fingers into her arm. The park was silent, but the air was heavy and sizzled in their lungs.

A golden chain sliced through the darkness and struck Ezekiel with such force it sent him tumbling. Amanda rushed after him, and Aurora armed herself with her pistol. Without hesitation, the chain whipped around Neil, constricted him and lifted him off the ground.

Aurora evoked her power, but before she could freeze time, a glimmer caught her attention. The skinless Sealer reflected moonlight off his golden mirror and into the angel's face from the shadows. Though his head remained in a constant and erratic motion, he hypnotized her with the daunting weapon.

Immediately she fell to her knees as destructive memories ran through her brain. One after another, visions of the past took control of her physical being.

"Aurora!" Her mother was a tall, ebony woman laced in expensive purple cloth and hair pulled tightly in a bun. "We're going to pick out your wedding dress today, so don't you DARE lie to me. I don't want to hear anything bad about Biff. He comes from a good, well-off family! Your grades aren't exactly where they need to be for you to get into law school, so you marry Biff, and his father can write a damn excellent recommendation letter. You're obviously not gifted enough to handle your own life, so you'll marry Biff, go to law school just for show, and have kids. Our family name won't be tarnished because you're a lazy good for nothing! You're going to keep up the respect of this family, Aurora! You're lucky you're a pretty girl; otherwise, we'd be completely shamed... But with my way, you can use what you have to keep morale..."

Amanda's tiny nose wrinkled as she threw forth her energy and wiggled her fingers at the approaching Sealer. However, he was too powerful for her to manipulate his form. The demon venomously spun toward her as she reached for a log beneath a tree. She held the softwood and waved it weakly in the air in an attempt to protect herself.

What could she do?

She needed to defend herself, but this branch wasn't going to do the trick. She reminded herself of her studies with Lyssah Rhamiel.

Steel.

That was... iron mixed with carbon... right? What was carbon again? How much carbon needed to be mixed? Amanda frantically recalled her sessions. She imagined carbon and iron as though they were in her hands, the weight, grade, stiffness.

Instantly, the branch transfixed into a thick metal baseball bat. She swung but missed and stumbled to the ground. The fiend splashed her with the mysterious liquid in his chalice. It aggressively seeped through her pores, and she collapsed in a sickly green tone. Nausea painfully bubbled up inside of her, and she yelped out in agony.

Ezekiel released a carefully aimed death wave. The Sealer winced, and the life-sucking power drained him, but he fought through the pain then splashed Ezekiel as well.

Golden light singed Neil's skin, and the chain slammed him around like a dirty rug. Then it tied around a tree and bounded Neil to it. He was battered and broken and could not move his arms. The chain held him tight as the Sealer inched toward him. Without his arms, Neil struggled to use his powers.

He could see the others, and they were all immobilized. While Amanda and Ezekiel were incapacitated, the Sealer dipped his hand into his vessel and revealed a full-shining, golden sword.

The second Sealer unhinged the base of his mirror and also released a long golden sword. He ran the blade across Aurora's frozen face, cut her cheek, and drew blood. Then the final Sealer unfastened the tassel of his chain's end and mystically pulled a long sword from the small space.

"No!" Neil called as he watched the Sealers prepare to murder his team. Faithfully, he tried to maneuver through the chains, but his legs had lost feeling.

He drifted in and out of consciousness and half expected death. Sticky blood covered half of Neil's face. His senses felt numb. How could he let this happen? Was this really how this was going to end?

No.

There must be more to life.

The second Sealer sensed Neil and finally stopped spinning his head. He shoved his sword through Aurora's stomach with such vigor he lifted her into the air with one arm. Aurora fell from her hypnotic trance while gravity pulled her frame down the weapon.

Utterly impaled, and she could not breathe.

"No!" Neil called to Aurora as he gritted his teeth in vexation. He refused to give in to the excruciating pain of a dislocated arm and took over his body.

The shackles instantly burst.

Psionic energy blanketed the park. His wounded body staggered, and anger boiled up inside of him. Hot frustration steamed out his mouth in a ferocious roar. All the pain he felt, he released in his animalistic howl. Dirt shook off the ground, and pebbles feverishly bounced like popping corn. Air currents charged, and the trees bent under his power.

Blood poured from Aurora's gut, down her twitching fingers, and dripped to the grass. Her mind was blank, and she had lost focus as life fell from her with every drop of liquid. Just as she prepared for death, energy sparked within her.

Power from an unknown depth was emitted in waves. Her dripping blood slowed till it became stagnant. Then steadily, it crawled back. She opened her red eyes while her body slid up the sword. In a daze, the Sealer repeated his exact actions, only in reverse. His sword lowered and exited her torso. Her wound completely closed up as time rewound itself around this small area.

Unknowingly, the Sealer repeated his actions. This time, however, with her newfound knowledge of the immediate future, Aurora easily dodged the attack. She rolled under a bench, then nervously tugged her hair, and tried to take in her near-death experience and her new time rewinding ability.

"No!" Neil felt his heart drop in his chest. Aurora. What just happened? Was she just killed?

Immersed in rage, Neil bellowed as his wounds stung, and he managed to stand. The environment around him began to blur and shake under his might. He vibrated hysterically as mental energy ran from his body. Neil's focus made his flesh tense, and his hands formed fists. With one final burst of everything Neil had within him, the Sealers shredded in explosions of blood and fire.

Ezekiel tried to recuperate then gathered Aurora and Amanda. They were wounded but alive, grateful, and able. Ezekiel joined arms with the girls, and they stumbled onto the quaking tar path in the center of the park. Neil floated off the surging earth with black oval eyes.

Amanda removed her Harley Quinn mask to get a better look at her levitating teammate.

"Dear God," she murmured as her jaw fell open in awe.

Chapter 22: Dear God

"And the enemy who sows them is the devil. The harvest is the end of the age, and the harvesters are angels."
Matthew 13:39

"Aurora!" Mental energy steamed from Neil like heat from boiling water. The hatred and enmity used to destroy the Sealers grew with an aimless and extraordinary life. Emotions crashed in one after another. Suddenly Neil was overwhelmed. He instantly missed his son and the old life that was robbed from him. His body was tired and in pain. He was lonely. His ex was overbearing. He missed his parents. His mind listed his resentments continuously until they erupted in an untamed tantrum.

Neil's powers took control of his body and, without a particular target, reached out and snatched their surroundings. The land quivered under Neil's mental strength. Bark burst off trees, and dirt swirled off the terrain then floated around him in a cyclone. Rocks, branches, twigs, and small shrubs ripped from their dwellings in whirlwinds around the tornado Neil's power formed. The earth cracked, and pieces of concrete and hardened tar flew into his gravitational pull. Neil's lion mask ripped from him and his chestnut brown hair whipped wildly across his face as the other angels retreated.

Amanda's teeth chattered with trepidation, "Guys, I don't know if Neil is completely evil or if he's having a bad day because it looks like he is..."

Stones trembled under Ezekiel's feet, and he could feel the gravitational tug. He shielded his eyes from the pieces of flying dirt and asked, "Do you think he's possessed? Look at his eyes; they're black!"

Neil hovered within the storming rubble. Dark blue beams with stunning gray and gold lights flickered from his back in inconsistent pulses. Resembling glowing ink in water, the light glistened like the aurora borealis but moved with the flow and grace of soaring wings.

Aurora reverently watched Neil flap his holographic appendages as the ground ruptured to ruins. Neil was having a psychological breakdown. The stress was overwhelming, and he needed her, just like he did last time.

Aurora removed her mask and headed forward through the rift.

"Aurora!" Amanda screamed at the top of her lungs, her voice barely cutting through the wind's loud howling. "Stop! You're going to get yourself hurt!"

Aurora braced herself as she inched closer to the fissure. She held steady against the clinging gravitation; her pupils turned crimson. Aurora stopped time and rushed through the stationary debris. However, the thunderous twister quickly unfroze and crashed brutally around her.

Neil was too keen on her. Aurora squinted her eyes to guard them against the smaller pieces of wreckage but was swept off her feet into the damp air.

"Aurora, get back here!" Amanda screamed and reached out, but Ezekiel fearfully anchored her.

Neil's lips curled back to show his grinding teeth. He never felt so entirely out of control. His flesh was just a tool his powers wielded. His mind was broken, incapable of thought or emotion, and he gave into an energy way higher than he knew.

Aurora whipped around in the tornado, and fragments of broken rock dashed across her body. In circles around Neil, she spun, but she was close enough. She grabbed his arm as an anchor. She was momentarily safe, but still helplessly dangled in the way of the flow.

"Neil!" Aurora shouted. "Neil, listen to me!" she screamed as loud as possible while she swung through space. "Take my hand!" She reached towards him, but the tornado pulled at her, "Take it!"

Though they batted around like twigs, Neil locked eyes with Aurora. Her grip was loosening. He wanted to grab her hand so badly but was out of touch with himself. Neil finally moved his arched fingers and laced them with hers.

The two flew horizontally through the air attached by their fingers. Adrenaline surged through Aurora, but she knew she was protected. Dirt and dust attacked her mouth and nostrils as she shouted, "Neil, you have to control yourself; I know you can! You owe me! Remember when I cleaned your apartment?"

It took every muscle in her body, but Aurora pulled herself into him. His onyx-colored eyes gradually faded as she placed her head on Neil's chest. Her heart wrenched; she was scared to death but surmounted the fear with her belief in him. She never knew a man like him before. He was so powerful yet depended on her. She needed her to survive. To save him... Again. No one ever needed her for anything before. She was important.

She felt safe and warm in his embrace, as though they could always keep each other from harm. Aurora trusted Neil, she now understood, with her body, with her life, and with her soul.

She lifted her hand, clenched in Neil's, and rested it on his chest beside her face. "Neil..." she whispered weakly in his ear, "if anyone can do this. I know you can. I know you, you're stronger than this. I know you can control it. Please try."

Her cocoa butter aroma weaved through his nose hairs. Boulders and tree trunks dropped to the earth with a thud. The trembling turf simmered to stillness. Slowly, the dust settled as Neil curled himself around Aurora. The blazing kaleidoscope of gold, black and purple rays flapped from Neil's back and folded around them while they landed. Within moments, the pulsating lights gradually faded.

"Not that I'm not grateful," Ezekiel swallowed a rock in his throat, "but I don't think I can deal with this crap anymore." He grabbed his heart as it beat in his chest and stuttered, "I-I gotta get home."

Chapter 23: Flutter

> "An angel of the Lord went up from Gilgal to Bochim and said, 'It was I who brought you up from Egypt and led you into the land which I promised on oath to your fathers. I said that I would never break my covenant with you.'"
> **Judges 2:1**

Aurora stepped from Neil's shower and got dressed in his t-shirt and jeans. They looked enormous on her as he was at least six inches taller. She glared down at her dirty clothes and pulled her wet hair behind her ears. Even in a foggy bathroom mirror, Aurora's purple gash was visible on her face. She frantically smeared an embarrassingly generous amount of concealer on her injury. This was her Tuesday night. Her life immediately and drastically changed. Again. How long could she keep this up? She opened Neil's cabinet and fished a few cotton balls from a jar.

The angel held them in front of herself and dropped them. She concentrated and activated her new ability. All her thoughts and emotions were shoved out of her mind. Time reversed around the cotton balls, and they flew back into her hand. She explored her limits at the expense of her energy.

Time could only shift within her proximity and in short increments, much like her other powers.

Exhausted, Aurora walked out of the bathroom and into Neil's hallway.

"I got another noise complaint shoved under my door. Wanna scare away the rest of my neighbors?" Neil laughed as he approached her. "Sylvia Goldenblatt, apparently she's a judge, and she's threatening to sue." Aurora was silent, and he noted, "Is everything alright?"

She turned to see Neil standing in the hall, "Nope."

"Not even with your new powers? The ability to rewrite history could be handy," he acknowledged, folded his arms, and leaned on the wall. Aurora rolled her eyes, and he continued, "I wanted to thank you for calming me down... again..."

Aurora shrugged away from him and placed a hand casually over her makeup-covered bruise before she responded, "I couldn't just let you freak out like that in public. When you hang out with me, you have to keep it cute at all times. You should just… add me to the payroll."

He blushed.

"And my new powers? What about Hurricane Neil?"

"I never want to lose control like that again." Neil reflected momentarily, "It was like I was opening the door to something ancient and strong. Stronger than me, and it controlled me..."

"Whatever it was," Aurora sighed, "it wasn't cute."

"I'm sorry I put you through that," he apologized. "Is there something wrong?" Neil asked. "Look, if it was about what happened earlier today."

"No, it's not," said Aurora.

"Then what?" Neil inquired as her small hand covered half her makeup-caked face. "Aurora, why did you put on makeup if you're just going to go home and to bed?"

"I'm not wearing makeup!" Aurora shouted. "I just broke a really expensive pair of heels today, fighting those monsters, and I can't afford a new pair."

"And you're wearing makeup." Neil stared at her more closely. "You can take that off with a spoon!"

"Very funny," Aurora snorted and turned from him. "I put it on because that freak cut me."

"It's just a mark; it's not really a big deal." Neil shrugged. "Especially here, there's no reason to hide battle wounds from me. Are you afraid I'm going to judge you or something?"

Aurora rushed away from him and protested, "No, I just don't want to run around with a hideous mark on my face!"

Neil leaped in front of her and reassured her, "You could never be hideous."

He gently wiped Aurora's cheek with his sleeve. Her brown blush shimmered away as Neil revealed her bloody wound. Although he second-guessed himself, he continued, "You're the most amazing woman I know. Some of the things that I've seen you do. You're brave, sharp, you think on your feet, you're a great person, with your scar or not."

Aurora folded her arms. She looked to Neil for a moment, then lifted her sleeve and wiped off the remaining makeup. Reluctantly she submitted, "There. Are you happy now?"

Chapter 24: Weird Things

"Make them like chaff before the wind, with the angel of the Lord driving them on. Make their way slippery and dark, with the angel of the Lord pursuing them."
Psalms 35:5-6

Amanda's will outshone the bright mid-afternoon sun. March brought on slightly warmer weather, and this day she coaxed Olive into taking a daytime stroll. Amanda's persistent talking could be heard all over the park as she cheered and explained the details of her soon-to-be-wedding. After they crossed the grass, they found an open area with benches. Amanda sat and squealed with joy, "So! We set a date for late September! That's when my parents got married! I would love to have Purrson there… but because he's a mutant now, I don't think it's an excellent idea." Amanda exhaled loudly, "It's not that he's evil exactly…"

"I know!" Olive interrupted.

A cluster of pigeons pecked about in a frenzy while Amanda broke her green bread and threw it into the pile of hungry birds. Olive and Amanda routinely took trips to the park and fed the pigeons with their molded leftovers. Olive shook her head slowly and retorted, "Dude, you and the fam tradition... It's totally bizarre. But like... we all come from somewhere, you know?"

As bits of bread were thrown into the bunch, the birds quickly became anxious. Each squawk grew exceedingly desperate. Within seconds the gathering of birds boiled into a primeval pecking war. Violently they tore into each other with utter disregard. Blood and feathers were viciously tossed across the black pavement. Birds ripped eyeballs and vital organs from their kin without hesitation or fear.

"Oh my gawd," Amanda shouted as she ran into the heart of the battle. Pigeon after pigeon zoomed past her, clouding her eyes and deafening her ears. "Stop!" Amanda yelled. "Stop the madness!"

No sooner than those words were spoken, everything became still. She stood in the center of a miniature avian genocide—pigeon after pigeon slaughtered at the beaks of their kin. Feathers fluttered to the ground in gentle and mild movements. The battle was over, and the smell of blood was in the air.

"Dude... I'm tripping balls," Olive declared and stumbled hazily through the chaos. "What ever happened to love being like the ultimate power and some junk because those birds... were pissed."

Neil wiped the beads of sweat from his forehead. He had been in the gym for hours. Sweaty and wet, he entered his apartment then studied until his eyes were red. Neil's place was a mess, and he had to throw most of his furniture out because he had destroyed it. There were books placed randomly around the living room. In the kitchen, there were printed Internet pages stapled and thrown around in a disorganized fashion. He closed a thick book covered in leather and dropped it onto the pile of volumes.

He poured himself a glass of water when his body tensed. He knew that something was about to happen. The glass smashed in the sink. Even that failed to interrupt his heightened sensory experience. The doorbell rang. He sensed her before she arrived. He was reminded of her cocoa bean fragrance and could smell it even before he opened the door.

Aurora was wearing a lacy purple blouse beneath a short-cut leather coat with white wool at its edges and jeans. He watched her for a moment as she clenched her pocketbook closer to her shoulder. She threw her neck back and snapped, "Are you going to be rude and just stand there, or are you going to invite me in?"

Neil leaned on the edge of his door and shook his head slowly before he objected, "Look, Aurora, I'm busy."

"Or," Aurora cut him off, "option three, I push past you and let myself in like I always do anyway." And she did so with a lifted brow. "I tried calling you all day. I tried your job; then, I tried your cell."

He shook his head and closed the door behind her, "You can lose that number. I quit that job."

"What?" Aurora asked. "But your job was so important to you. Why? How are you going to make money?"

"I quit so I can focus more time on the important things," Neil announced as he pressed upon his countertop. "And don't worry about me getting money. I saved five percent of every check I've ever gotten since I was seventeen."

"Wow," Aurora gasped, "Well, em, I wish I was that resourceful.'" She stammered a bit as she took in the disorder around her. She always knew him to be neat. She skimmed the titles of books and their various demonic engravings before she questioned further, "Why didn't you answer your cellphone?"

"Because," Neil answered shortly, "I was at the gym most of the day."

Aurora placed a hand on her hip and scolded, "I don't care. Neil, what the hell happened in here? I never knew you to be this messy? And when's the last time you took a shower? When did you turn into Lyssah Rhamiel?" Aurora pointed to a dirty bowl filled with stale cereal and spoiled milk and advised, "I think you need to calm down. Just relax a little bit before you quit your job!"

"Don't tell me to relax! Aurora, I'm sick and tired of being the only one who cares about the little thing called the 'Apocalypse.' Demons keep coming to my home! I'm afraid to bring my son here! People are being killed! You were almost killed every other day. How can I relax when everything is clearly dying?" He jerked away from Aurora violently and confessed, "I can't just relax a little bit; I can't just calm down because if I do, someone could get hurt. I can't let that happen to anyone else, not you, not my son, not Ezekiel or Amanda, not even to some stranger on the street. Do you realize that this is all my responsibility?"

"Our responsibility," Aurora replied. "You are a mighty man, Neil, you're the strongest of all of us, but that doesn't mean that you have to bear this all yourself. We've all been through things. You can't be everywhere at every time, and you can't save everybody. You are still one man."

"I can save you guys," Neil corrected, "I've killed demons alone before."

"We are part of a team," Aurora countered. "This isn't the Alpha Neil. We each play our part in this... Please, go take a nap. You're running yourself into the ground." Aurora touched Neil's shoulder as he turned from her again. Her voice suddenly became stern, "You're scaring me. Do you really think you can save the world all worn-out and dreary?"

Neil knew she was right. He walked into his bedroom and closed the door behind him. Aurora lowered her head in disappointment. She looked to the messy living room with a grimace. He was sick and needed her to take care of him. She stacked the books on the glass table.

He awoke a few hours later. Neil walked into the living room and was taken aback. All of his disorganized papers, all of his disarray had been packed away neatly on the coffee table. There beside the table was a box of pizza with a note on it. Neil took it between his fingers and read it to himself.

Please get some rest and then eat up. Yes, once again, I cleaned your house, and now you owe me double. Fine jewelry or something in Prada wouldn't be the wrong place to start. When you're feeling better, please give me a call. ~ Aurora

The White Horsemen faced the horizon and admired the emptiness. Acid rained onto the outskirts of Manhattan Beach from the crackling sky as the water washed up on shore and soaked his white robe. The Horsemen had collected twelve Bishops and strewn them about the beach in a curved horseshoe line. "Let us hurry, the rains will be over soon."

Marcus awoke to painful sores from the chemical rain. The Bishop saw the Horsemen arranged in a circle behind him, near the water. He struggled to crawl across the sand, but his elbows sunk. "Our Father," he recited, "who art in heaven, Hallowed be thy name." A dark presence shadowed him: he gazed up at the Horseman in yellow.

"Hallowed be whose name?" the Horsemen of Death asked.

The Bishop yelped and struggled to maneuver away, but his wounds prevented him, "Thy kingdom come. Thy will be done."

Death took hold of the man's right hand. Then the demon broke the man's index finger and repeated his question through the man's screams, "Hallowed be whose name?"

The Bishop didn't answer, and the Yellow Horseman pulled the man closer to him. Death retrieved a clean steel scythe from his robes and brought it to the clergyman's cheek. The mortal's lips could only form pleas and cries of trepidation. Without saying a word, Death pressed the scythe into Marcus's left eye. He carved out the man's eye and sent it into the sand.

"Quiet," Death whispered, and he prepared his weapon again. He swiped the man's right eye from its socket. Disgusted, he tossed the screaming man by his collar into place, creating a symbol in the sand.

"Let us begin."

The Four Horsemen gathered to close the semi-circle.

"Seiza jai n'hast engai," the White Horsemen recited. "Semsa nahl eresh a'lahm. Geth na haroth castellum tol. Seiza jai n'hast engai. The holy order, marked in twelve. Their lives of nothingness shall now have meaning. With their blood, I bid thee eyes rule. They were ever watching and ever seeing, most beautiful of angels. Seiza jai n'hast engai. Semsa nahl, alahm. Geth na haroth castellum tol. Seiza jai n'hast engai."

At the end of the chant, the Four Horsemen ran off in different directions within the circle. One by one, they slaughtered the fallen Bishops. The blood drew into the thirsty sand and painted it red.

As the sky thundered again, the Horsemen watched with crooked smiles. Like mixing watercolors, the red sky diffused across the hemisphere from a single point. The shadow of the moon became a black stone in a puddle of blood. Upon completion, the demons fled the gruesome scene. "Come!" Pestilence shouted before they shimmered away.

Chapter 25: Solace

> "That night the angel of the Lord went forth and struck down one hundred and eighty-five thousand men in the Assyrian camp. Early the next morning, there they were, all the corpses of the dead."
> **Kings I19:35**

Ezekiel sunk deeper into the soft couch and nervously examined his luxurious apartment. Most of the familiar rundown furniture was replaced by new and expensive works of art. His living room looked like a perfect picture of an elegant magazine. He hated it. From his seat, he could see the scarlet sky, and it curdled his stomach. The angel rubbed his belly and sighed uncomfortably. Ezekiel watched television for hours while he sketched dragons and winged horses.

Jackie Adams organized her notes on Ezekiel's television screen before looking into the camera at all of America. With a cocky grin, she reported, "It seems that our downpour of acid rain not only left us with several thousand dollars in property damage but a reddish tint in the sky. It looks as though a ruby-colored fog blanketed not only this city but most of the coast. Due to pollution and the levels of humidity, it is said that our sky should be returning to normal in a matter of days. I, for one, am not really looking forward to the change. I think the red sky and black sun and moon are, well, I think it's kind of pretty." Jackie chuckled a bit, "Back to you, Charles."

Ezekiel ripped small holes in the new couch with his pencil. "Jackass."

Charles's smile filled the screen as he took over, "Not me, Jackie, it kind of freaks me out. Now, in addition to the unsettling news of the twelve slain clergymen (no leads there yet), we've gotten word of numerous animal suicides. According to what we've received from the Bronx Zoo and several zoos in the New York area and even some family pets cases in this area, random animals have participated in self-mutilation. In these cases, the animals would actually tear at themselves until their untimely death. Experts say that they have no idea what could cause this vicious and peculiar behavior in animals but suspect there is an environmental cause. Perhaps the contaminated water."

Ezekiel's apartment was eerily quiet after his birth father died. His parents usually argued at home, but recently the condo was always empty. The living room looked the best it ever did, but his mother always preferred to be out with Fred. The fact continued to perplex him. His mother seemed happier with a demon than she ever did with her true husband. She was joyful and carefree for the first time in years. It was like a disturbing dream come true. The shrieking of his cellphone broke Ezekiel's concentration.

"Hello?" he paused. "Yeah, I'm her son... What happened?"

The night was chilly, and the line was entirely too long, but Neil waited on the cold streets to enter the secret underground club. Annoyed, he pressed 'silent' on his black cellphone and ignored Victoria's fourteenth phone call for the night. She wanted him to take Zachary for the weekend, but Neil refused, not while he had demons trashing about his home. He loved his son, but Zachary was unsafe around him. He needed to work out his problems before he could be a great father to his boy.

He needed to save the world.

Neil breathed anxiously and looked through the massive glass doors leading into a hallway. Fourth in line, he stood behind some drunk teenagers. His skin shivered. He knew there was something unnatural about this club. He sensed a dark bitterness. Club Solace reeked of drugs, sex, and violence. It was like an alarm in his mind and wasps in his mouth. He sensed something demonic was rising here, and he needed to investigate. He took another step forward and sheltered his cold hands inside of his brown leather coat.

The bouncer had the body of a pro wrestler and the face of a twelve-year-old. He wrinkled his brow and scanned Neil for a moment.

His eyes squinted, and Neil read his mind: *This guy has so much power,* the man thought as he looked Neil up and down; *I-I shouldn't let him in. I can't even tell where his power is coming from! He's like no demon I've ever sensed!*

Neil was sure of it now; this guy wasn't a human. This meant that the club inside was full of demons just like him. He knew he was right all along.

"That's because I'm not a demon; I'm something far worse!" Neil boasted as he telekinetically sent the man through the air and across the street into the hard pavement.

Not paying him a second notice, Neil entered the vast dark room. The lights in Solace flickered with blinding intensity, and a foggy mist blew through the air. The music blasted loudly, light patterns flashed on the walls, and the crowd boogied on the dance floor and stages. Dancers openly shoved needles in their arms while the bartenders popped pills and swallowed tons of liquor with their guests. Others, too drunk to be ashamed, pressed against the walls in public intercourse. The thick smell of sweet honey sugar entered his nostrils and almost made him sick.

There were no rules here.

Neil had never seen anything like it. The loud techno music pounded in his eardrums as he looked across the bar where bottles of numerous alcohols were stacked decoratively and shot glasses and mugs were passed around. Neil examined the back of the club, where a vast glass window covered dancing strippers. He sensed the evil in this club. They were demons dressed as humans; he could feel it, taste it in his mouth.

The hairs on the back of his neck stood straight as he turned to see a woman in the corner: she had a man atop her, his face buried in her throat, and blood pooled beneath her. On her ankle was a Wither. The small naked troll sunk his teeth into her leg, invisible to mortal eyes. They were both feedings off her. Neil could feel the Wither whisper in her mind: *You've been a bad girl. You deserve this—every bit of pain. You are worthless…*

He put on his lion's mask. Neil needed no more proof; he sent out a mental attack, lashing out at humans and demons alike. The entire club fell to their knees. Screams drowned out the sound of the pumping music when everyone there was overcome with severe migraines that squeezed their brains tighter than the music ever could.

    Neil threw a fist into the air and mentally shattered the immense window before the strippers. The glass shards flew quickly through the air and created a tornado, and Neil telekinetically guided them as though he were conducting an orchestra. He bursts the shot glasses and bottles of liquor at the bar while the red and blue laser lights bounced off the glittering orbit of dangerous fragments.

    In the center of a sparkling cyclone, Neil thrust his hand forward and launched the glasses' shards. One by one, the demons were flattened as sharp chips of assorted shapes and sizes plummeted into their chests and faces.

    Billions of shimmering crystals whipped through the air like a rainbow blizzard. A man struggled through the slivers of glass. Unsure of his intent and unable to break his psychic flow, Neil cautiously allowed him to approach.

    When the man was close, his eyes grew huge and black. Two-foot-long dark horns sprouted from his hairy skull. In seconds its entire head became a frightening demonic goat mutation. Without hesitation, the demon raised a claw and sent a ball of light through the air towards Neil.

    The angel telekinetically returned the glowing sphere. Like all the demons in the room, he dissolved into bubbling acid. Neil knelt closer to the ground as he telekinetically forced the slivers of glass through those demons that were strong enough to be still alive.

Minutes later, Neil left Solace with a limp. His mask was stained but still intact as he placed it back into his jacket. Out of breath, he cleaned his bloody lip with his sleeves and stumbled, exhausted. He had murdered every demon there without leaving a single fingerprint. He saved about fifteen unconscious humans inside. And he did it alone. Proud, he hobbled down the street as fast as he could.

Chapter 26: Rhapsody

"'Your fine lie has cost you your head,' said Daniel, "'for the angel of God shall receive the sentence from him and split you in two.'"
Daniel 13:55

"Oh my word," Giselle fussed as she slammed her hands into her pink polka-dot apron, "these stains are so difficult!" The fallen angel shoved her rubber gloves into the bucket and wrung out a large yellow sponge into the red water. Giselle's sparkling blue eyes blinked flirtatiously as she hummed a tune and vigorously scrubbed the white tile kitchen floor.

"Hello Lilith," Nathaniel announced as he entered the modern kitchen in a solid black suit and a red tie. The kitchen table was covered with entrails and dripped a metallic smelling fluid that made his stomach growl. So solemnly, he asked, "What are you doing?"

"You scared me!" she gasped. She jumped, and her blonde curls bounced as she covered her small cherry, painted lips and greeted, "You're early! I was just cleaning up! We had a big lunch. If I knew you were coming so soon, I would have saved you a plate."

Nathaniel pulled out a chair from under the white kitchen table and took a seat before noting, "You're a thousand-year-old demon queen. What do you know about cleaning?"

"For the toughest stains," Giselle tittered, winked, and held up her small plastic bottle of cleaning product, "Dr. Scrub-Bubble works for my family and me!"

"You are a strange one, aren't you?" he chuckled loudly. "Ready to begin?"

She stood and snapped off her rubber gloves and accepted, "Sure! Legnanu is asleep. We just have to get Typhon from his study. He... likes to be involved."

Daintily, she escorted Nathaniel through the contemporary apartment, "I've been worried about him lately. He's usually such a sweetheart, but I think his blindness is getting to him. He hardly gets out, but he does enjoy watching...."

A small brown dog with a wet red mouth dashed across the hallway holding viscera with his teeth and dripped blood across the immaculate hardwood floor.

"Cerberus..." Giselle sighed, and she opened the door to Typhon's study. A rush of cold air burst into the hallway as the two entered, closing the door behind them. At first glance, the room appeared normal: Upper class with large full bookshelves, a glass bar, an overpriced dark oak desk, and expensive armchairs. The study was beautiful, classic, and homey but covered in human bodies.

It was a freezer, reaching an unbearable cold with frost blanketing everything. Six carcasses were ice sculptures frozen in agony. Typhon threw his long dark hair back then knelt on the soil-covered ground. He giggled and skipped closer to Jessica, a seventh victim who still clung to life. Her flesh was red and blue with cold, and she was running out of tears.

"Please," the freezing woman whispered as the bitter ice winds ate at her skin through her pink jogging suit, "I have children!"

Nearly frostbitten solid, she clawed and pulled at the icy rug beneath her. Typhon perched near and snickered uncontrollably through a broad oozing grin. He kneeled closer to her as she turned away in horror, "Tell me how much you love them."

The day had begun so routinely for Jessica. She got up, took a shower, made breakfast for the kids, then was off for a quick jog. She stopped for a short breath, and Jessica Meyers checked her watch, beaming with a sense of accomplishment. 10:30 was the earliest she had been out for her jog.

Her youngest, Nicholas, was a healthy five-year-old who loved sunny-side-up eggs with extra maple syrup and cheese every morning. However, today felt like oatmeal and fresh fruit morning to Jessica, and though Nicholas put up a fierce fight, she needed to put her foot down in the name of nutrition. He was fed, and the clean-up was quicker than expected. Jessica was in her mid-thirties and felt as though she was finally getting the hang of being a strong mother of four. She loved her kids but often felt very young, as though she had so much more of the world to experience.

"Ruf!"

Jessica threw her long brown ponytail aside, and a small Pomeranian sat across from her. The tiny brown puppy tilted its head and barked loudly. Girlishly she simpered, Jessica loved dogs, and this puppy was so cute! He was alone and looked lost. Jumping over to her, he licked her leg. Jessica couldn't resist. Picking up the puppy, his collar read: Cerberus, 129 Bergen Ave Apt 2B. Instantly she thought of her son and how heartbroken he would be if he had lost Charles, his stuffed dog.

"Well, Cerberus," she tapped him on the nose and reassured him, "I guess I have to take you home."

If only I had let that damn dog be, she thought as Giselle approached them.

"Honey," Giselle cheered, "Nathaniel is here."

"I know," Typhon confirmed while the temperature in the room subsided. "I could feel the weight of him from miles away. Feel the air around him. He's been eating well."

Nathaniel rested a hand on his stomach and agreed, "Why yes, I have. The great thing about political power is that there's always someone little around to eat." He adjusted his suit and criticized, "Anyway, this agreement is between your wife, her cursed womb, and I. I don't see why you have to be here."

"And I don't see why you're still talking," Typhon muttered as the soil on the ground shot about like water from a lawn sprinkler.

"You don't see at all," Nathaniel chuckled and watched the dirt swirl. "Ah, now, I understand. She did say you liked to watch."

The man turned to Giselle as she sat delicately in an armchair. She gazed deeply into a silver Victorian hand mirror with her name engraved on the back of it as she hummed to herself for a moment and then stood.

With her eyes focused on Nathaniel, she unbuttoned her white blouse. He nodded encouragingly as she continued to undress. Jessica took long breaths and clung to the icy carpet beneath them. Confused and panicked, every cell in her body urged her to escape. Unfortunately, her flesh was on the verge of giving out, and every movement was bone shatteringly painful. She trembled with both despair and frostbite. Jessica shed a tear with the specific knowledge that she will never see her children again.

Giselle bared her flawless body. Nathaniel grabbed a fist full of her Shirley Temple curls then viciously at her chest. She winced a bit with pain but couldn't keep her eyes from disconnecting with his.

"Well, I don't mind," Nathaniel blustered and unbuttoned his white shirt. "Someone's gotta screw your wife."

He shoved Giselle to the ground and violently kissed her. Without passion, they rammed over the freezing body of Jessica. Jessica screamed when the numbing cold turned to harsh pain. Nathaniel's eyes widened with a shock and glee that Jessica could only compare to her children opening a surprise gift they never knew they wanted.

"Ah!" he gasped and raised her by the throat as easily as he would a sack of produce. "Look at this. We have a live one."

Jessica sniffled. Her chest involuntarily convulsed in the air, "For God's sake... please don't do this."

Narrowing his dark eyes, he superciliously dropped her and admitted, "But you don't understand, it is precisely for the sake of God that we are doing this!"

Jessica tried to inch away, but her muscles stung with every movement. "But don't feel bad," Nathaniel cooed while he stomped on her knee and broke her frigid patella bone. "I'm sure at first glance this probably looks like the mere folly of demons, but what we do is not a sport. You need to appreciate your importance in all of this..."

"You, like every other living thing, are an artful work of God," he talked over her piercing screams and forcefully removed her frosted pink jogging pants. "Humans, being the most ravishing of these creations, were given souls... A choice. A power... free will... as you were made in his image, you were given a piece of the divine himself." He ran his fingers up her milky white thigh and tore off her baby blue floral underwear.

"You are the most beautiful production in the universe."

He unbuckled his pants and crammed himself into her. Jessica cried out in torment. Her eyes shut in agony as he ravaged her. It felt like someone was gutting her alive with a broad and sharp sword. The numbing pain quickly led to warm blood that streamed over her icy body like a heated blanket. Jessica gasped for air as Nathaniel disarranged her insides, so brutally, she knew she would bleed to death. "But we have our own craft," he muttered.

"We are the Forsaken!" Soaked in blood, he pulled himself off her and barbarically gazed at Giselle. Excited and determined, he rushed over to her and commenced, "And as he art in Heaven, we art here on Earth!" Jessica was frightened and dying but reflected on breakfast that morning. Nathaniel sadistically took hold of Giselle's ivory and perky chest. He squeezed until blood cracked from them and poured out like yoke from the torn membrane of an egg. Jessica thought about her last day on Earth; perhaps she should have made the sunny-side-up eggs with extra maple syrup for her son.

The two savagely mated on top of her, and Giselle covered them in fistfuls of dirt. The fallen angel closed her eyes and repeatedly whispered, "I love you, Typhon. Kiss me, Typhon. Kiss me!"

Nathaniel flared his nostrils as he forced into her. He pounded his knuckles into her face until Giselle's lower lip split open, and blood covered her perfect white teeth. She repeated herself. Jessica screamed out in pain while he forcefully invaded her torn body with his index fingers. "You see, our art comes from defacing him. The more we disgrace his art, the more magnificent our work becomes..."

Nathaniel laughed loudly as Typhon shook his head in a moment of uncomfortable pleasure. His hands dropped lower, and he motioned sexually, his bare feet sunk themselves into the soil. Nathaniel raised his arms and bellowed, "This is where you come in! Your body, life, consciousness, blood, your spirit are all merely the paint in the masterpiece we create in God's offense!"

I'm the worst mom ever. Why couldn't I have just made Nicholas his damned eggs? Why was I such a bitch? Now that's all he's going to remember me as.... Jessica thought through whimpers. *I'm so sorry, baby...*

While he fornicated, the fallen angel Giselle, the demon grabbed Jessica by her neck and crushed her until her cranium popped off like the top of a volcano. Laughing, Nathaniel held Jessica's head in his left hand and her body in his right. He poured her still-hot blood all over himself as he released his demonic seed.

Giselle scrunched her face in pain and shoved Nathaniel off of her. Her stomach tied up in harrowing knots as it grew more significant by the second. Giselle was pregnant again and came to terms within moments. She screamed, then grabbed at her fleshly womb and threw her head back.

Her new child began crowning. A large full head of brown hair covered in black ooze pushed itself from her. She clawed at herself and pulled at the body that exited her own. Primitively, she tore at her flesh and ripped out her newborn. In moments, Giselle had managed to give birth to an adult brunette. Naked, the beefy broad-shouldered woman stood covered in sludge.

"Nice work Lilith," Nathaniel smiled. "This'll do."

Ezekiel slowly pulled his sleeves over his fingertips. His mother lay in the hospital bed with several machines hooked up to her. It was unnatural. She was immobile, voiceless, and breathed by machine. His heart palpitated forcefully inside his chest, and a bitter taste manifested in his mouth.

"You aren't going to cry, are you?" Fred pestered as he walked into the room.

Ezekiel sniffled a bit, "No."

"What was that?" Fred asked.

"No!" Ezekiel shouted, then folded his arms.

"Lower your voice!" Fred hissed through gritted teeth. "She's not dying. We're just going to have to fix that." The machines in the room activated and beeped alarmingly. The electric green light that zigzagged on the screen quickly flattened into a straight line. Ezekiel wasn't a doctor by any means, but he knew what this meant, and he knew that Fred was responsible.

Ezekiel turned to him and spat through his teeth, "Stop it."

Fred smiled, "Stop what? I didn't do anything to you or your mother. Besides, you know, get bored and let the Withers in... Oops."

Ezekiel hyperventilated. He could feel something within him rise and change. A dark and powerful force. Rage.

"Stop it!" Ezekiel shouted. He opened his fist and sent out invisible waves of death.

Fred fell back and slid across the ground like he was hit by a truck. He coughed loudly; it seemed the life-sucking blast was too weak to kill him. Ezekiel ran to his mother and threw off the thin white sheet that covered her. He scanned her body and readily located the tiny brown creature. A miniature man was face down on his mother's hip, its teeth sunk deep in her skin. The naked demon looked up at Ezekiel with large brown fearful eyes. Lividly, Ezekiel grabbed the

Wither. Fury flared up inside him, and his life-absorbing ability killed the parasite instantly. Ezekiel tossed the fizzing demon organs to the ground as they dissipated.

Fred hoisted himself upright and badgered, "You son of a!"

However, before Fred could finish his sentence, Ezekiel charged at him. He rammed him out of the hospital room and onto the arched marble desk on the fourth-floor lobby. "Bitch!" Ezekiel screamed.

Large guards appeared at both sides of Ezekiel and forced him off the impostor. He noticed the shock on Fred's face and swallowed a rock in his throat as he threatened, "I swear, I'll kill you."

"Then bring it," he accepted. With those words, Fred grabbed hold of the guards beside him. He held each in an arm then, with a twist, threw them effortlessly to opposite sides of the room. Fred laughed, "I said this was going to be good." His image blurred, and Fred had dashed out of the hospital before anyone could make a move in a gust of wind.

Ezekiel frowned wretchedly. It was as he feared. The inevitable. He had to kill his father... Again.

Chapter 27: Guises

> "Then, the angel of the Lord came and sat under the oak in Ophrah that belonged to Joash the Abiezrite. While his son Gideon was beating out wheat in the winepress to save it from the Midianites, the angel of the Lord appeared to him and said, 'The Lord is with you, O champion!'"
> **Judges 6:11-12**

Against the advice of the doctors, Ezekiel insisted on taking his mother home. He hoped that since the Wither died, she'd get better. There was no way he was going to let Fred double back and do anything to harm her. Lauren unlocked the front door, and Ezekiel gently pushed past her. He scanned the corners of the very small apartment. There was no one inside; he was sure of it because there was always a sick feeling that made his skin crawl when Fred was in the room. Ezekiel's flesh tensed into goosebumps; he just couldn't leave his mother in the hospital awaiting Fred's return.

She frowned and rushed to him, "Ez, what's wrong? Why are you acting like this? And where's Fred?"

Ezekiel turned to his mother, held her by the shoulders, and ordered, "Mom, get your stuff."

"What? Why?"

"Mom, please don't ask any questions," Ezekiel swallowed, "I need you to trust me right now. If you love me, you will get a few things and go to spend the night with Grandma."

"Ezekiel," Lauren looked at her son and shook her head slowly before asking, "Where's your father?"

"I don't know," he solemnly told her. "Mom, please just trust me."

"I'm not going anywhere," Lauren declined and folded her arms.

Ezekiel's lips thinned, and his nose arched in vengeance as he retorted. He found the strength that abandoned him long ago. He was almost surprised at himself as he ordered her, "Mom, you are going to pack your things and get over to Grandma's right now. Don't make me drag you kicking and screaming out of this house!"

Lauren gasped; the new might within Ezekiel gave her chills. She paused for a moment to stare the angel down. "I don't know why you're acting like this. But I'll get my stuff," she consented, then she turned away from him and headed out to her bedroom.

On the way to his room, Ezekiel stopped at a small note on the refrigerator. He tore the letter off the fridge, he held it in his hand and read:

"Hi, my loving family,
I went to go get some groceries at the bodega on Helm's Street. I'm gonna need help, though, so Ez, when you get back, please come over to the bodega; I'll be waiting on top. Love, Fredrick"

    Cold night blanketed Manhattan, and Ezekiel's hot breath left small clouds in the crisp air that floated toward the red sky. The bodega on Helm's Street was a rundown family-owned business in operation longer than he could remember. Ezekiel stood on the sidewalk before the store. Trash blew across the street and tumbled over his sneakers.

    Empty, the store was vacant, except for Clara Rodriquez, who occasionally ran the cash register. Fred was absent but close; Ezekiel could feel him. How could he allow the beast who snuck into his father's body to get him alone? He was astonished and ashamed that he let this creature masquerade as his father for so long. The demon made his mother so happy and his household slightly more bearable, but it had to stop. Eve told him, "Life wasn't a picture," and he had to face the truth.

    I notice Ezekiel is not stuttering in this section. Was that intentional?

The letter said to meet Fred on top, and this store was two stories tall, with an apartment tenement on top of it. Fred was there, on the roof. There was a tall lamp post next to the store casting light onto the lonely sidewalk. He grabbed hold of the pole and climbed up to the ceiling like a clumsy monkey.

Fred sat at the opposite edge of the roof, watching the cars drive by. Slowly, he turned towards Ezekiel and grinned, "Wasn't sure you'd show up."

A chilly wind blew through Ezekiel's long-sleeved tan sweater wrapped around his skin, then his hair. He shivered a bit and squinted under the force of the air. Fred stood there across from him, his eyes smiled, and his lips curled, exposing his teeth.

Ezekiel's legs felt weak, and his arms like string. His stomach boiled, and his chest wavered. Despite all of this, he was blinded by the hate he had for the demon inside of his father. It was nice living in a dream world for a while, but there was no going back from this. He slid his eagle mask over his face.

"Really? A cheap eagle mask? Lame." Fred licked his lips swiftly before cracking his knuckles one by one. "Better think twice before you start something you can't finish, E-z."

"What are you?" Ezekiel asked. Fred smiled, "Ezekiel...'I... am... your father!'"

Ezekiel's lips tightened, and he urged, "Tell me what you are. What kind of demon are you?"

He shrugged mockingly, "The... very best kind?"

"Damn it; I'm serious!" Ezekiel screamed.

"Are you?" Fred asked.

Ezekiel aimed his fists waist-high before he sprung his fingers open to release his power. A loud lion-like roar ensued when Fred was hit with the blast. His skin became torn, decayed, and rotted. His lips were black, and his eyes grew a solid ghostly yellow. In a second, he shook his head, and it recovered its human shape.

Fred studied Ezekiel and grinned as he exclaimed, "My name is Corricr!"

"What kind of demon are you?"

"We don't like to be stereotyped. My kind has no names. We have no type, no form," Fred finally answered.

"I want you to leave," Ezekiel instructed.

Fred pouted, "And I want a son who isn't such a pussy. We don't always get what we want, do we?"

Ezekiel pointed his hands again, but before he could attack, he was thrown to the ground. Fred moved like gunshots from an automatic machine gun. Ezekiel arched his back from the floor and raised a palm. He looked around, but Fred was gone. Seconds seemed like hours as Ezekiel's eyes scanned the rooftop.

Before Ezekiel could think, long thin metal pins appeared flying toward his neck. Fred attacked with the large nails that ejected from his fingertips. Within seconds he pushed towards him and forced the angel backward. Fred was keen, but Ezekiel was able to divert Fred's thrust over and into the ground.

As Fred's metal spike clashed against the stones, Ezekiel's body fell lifeless underneath him. Ezekiel's astral form appeared behind Fred, with a broomstick that he found leaning across the air vent in his ghostly hands. With a single fearsome blow, Ezekiel knocked Fred backward and away from his fallen body.

Quickly, Fred retaliated and swiped at Ezekiel's gut. Ezekiel trembled and became intangible, allowing the spikes to fly right through him. Hastily, he lowered his incorporeal head, and his otherworldly body faded in dimming gray light.

Ezekiel opened his physical eyes and stood ready, but a crack of supernaturally strong wind burst onto the rooftop and threw him onto an air vent.

"Ezekiel," Fred yelled, "it's a damn shame. I can't believe you not only hit your father, but think you can beat him."

Ezekiel's forehead dripped blood onto his sweater, and he managed to counter, "But you're not my father."

"Aren't I?" Fred asked as the winds continued to blow. "I talk like him, walk like him, have sex with your mother like him. Embody every cell, every fiber. E-z, I am him. What he couldn't be and so much more. And I'm not going away."

Ezekiel pressed his palms on the stones of the rooftop and pushed his body upright. "You're a liar," he shouted.

"No," Fred shook his head and countered, "I never lied. About anything." He began to pace the rooftop while the wind continued to beat against Ezekiel's flesh.

"When I first met you, I could taste it, the darkness within you, the untold boldness. They were serious when they said that you angels would be the greatest power the world has ever seen. But I just recently found out that it's only when you're together when you all form that holy bond or whatever. But what happens when you break the bond? At first, I thought nothing... but... that's not true, is it?" Fred huffed.

"I wasn't going to kill you," he shrugged then suggested, "I thought the others would come after me. Now I know that if one of you dies, the bond is broken, and the Alpha Omega, oh so Sacred Angels are no more. It's funny the way things work out." Fred sighed. "You're so weak alone. You always have been—the soft, quiet, level-headed, responsible Ezekiel. Always letting someone else solve his problems for him. So since you're too weak to kill yourself, I'll do it for you!"

Ezekiel forced himself to stand again, though the winds beat down on him. Ezekiel granted, "I don't know which Fred is worse..." Ezekiel directed an opened palm at Fred and unleashed his poisonous ability. "At least my real father could throw a decent punch! Which... I guess... that wasn't such a good thing."

Fred growled and rapidly grasped Ezekiel by the throat, then bent his back over the air vent.

"You're nothing but a piece of trash," Fred whispered as he struggled to hold Ezekiel in place and fought against the angel's powerful death waves. Fred pushed the metal spike through Ezekiel's gut. He screamed out in pain as Fred buried it more profoundly.

Ezekiel bit his lip and unleashed his death strike full force. Fred's grasp weakened on Ezekiel's throat, and he stumbled back a few steps. Tadpole-like spirits faded in and out of thin air. Ezekiel peered down at Fred; his hand held his pierced gut, catching blood as it dripped through.

The angel's eyes squinted in pain as they filled with water. Ezekiel released his life-sucking ability, and Fred fell backward. Ezekiel attacked again. Fred fell back a little bit further.

Ezekiel lifted himself from the air vent and sent out his death ripple. A wide-open gash suddenly appeared on the demon's face. Repeatedly, Ezekiel opened his fist and released his power. Fred's face was cut up in wounds.

Veins on Fred's face grew irritated as his skin began to redden and thin. He reached the edge of the roof, and his hand brushed against the border. Fred was dying. His skin split and grew red then blacker by the moment. He struggled but managed to press two fingers onto his lips and blow a kiss as he hurled himself off the bodega's roof.

Chapter 28: Hospitalized

"Meanwhile, the angel of the Lord said to Elijah the Tishbite: 'Go, intercept the messengers of Samaria's king, and ask them, "Is it because there is no God in Israel that you are going to inquire of Baalzebub, the god of Ekron?"'
Kings 1:3

Rhion apprehensively scratched at his five-o'clock shadow and coughed into his fist. He was a detective for many years but never witnessed a scene so gruesome. An entire convent lay slaughtered and naked across the steps of their church. His jaw gaped inquiringly. Crime had not only soared in the last few months but also curved into the satanically immoral. He shook his head in disbelief.

Rhion attended the First United Methodist Church all his life. He was baptized here, and he brought his children here every Sunday. The holy women he knew by name were naked, defiled, and sprawled across the church steps in provocative poses. Photographers took pictures, and police blocked off the crime scene. He sipped his coffee to distract his tears before his partner came towards him.

"Glenn Marco," Rhion grumbled as the scene before him shook him to the core. "He's a hellish son of a bitch. After he was finished here, he tried to rob a liquor store. We shot him dead hours ago. Now we're stuck here cleaning up the devilish mess he made. We figured he's part of that Blood Wolf Gang. If not, the department is probably going to blame it on them anyway."

"I know you feel connected because this is your church," Detective Martin consoled him as he fixed his tie, "but you have to keep your head in this. We need you now more than ever."

He finished his coffee and gulped hard, "I'm ready. It's just all the strange things that are happening. The sky is changing color. Animals are committing suicide. Acid rains, disease, crime, drugs, bishops on the beach, and now this... What the hell is going on?"

Martin puckered a dark brow as he shoved half a deli sandwich into his mouth and spoke, "It's not like everything's all bad. We just shot the asshole that did this. And we did get a lead on what happened to that park. You're probably wrong. He's probably just one of those Blood Wolf punks."

Rhion huffed, "Neil Qin. Yeah, he has a clean record. But I can tell you right now that guy is into some really sick shit. You saw the mess in the park. No way vandalism like that was caused by just four people... Neil. Somehow he managed to evade me before I even questioned him."

"He didn't evade you." Martin finished his sandwich and stained his shirt in the process when he mentioned, "I told you, we all did. You really don't remember? You came out and told us to let them go. That they were innocent."

"I don't care what you say; I never said that," Rhion barked. "Something strange is going down; I can feel it."

"Okay, okay," he conceded and finished tossing his sandwich wrapper aside. "What are you trying to say?"

Rhion exhaled and threw his coffee cup in the trash, "I don't know. I-I feel. Maybe something supernatural is going on."

"Supernatural?" Martin choked on his last piece of bread, "Like what? Boogeyman type bull crap?"

"Like Book of Revelation type bull crap," Rhion jeered.

"Come on," Martin started as Rhion trudged away. "Let's not get all X- files…"

"Sure thing," Rhion shifted uncomfortably then got up from his desk. "I'm gonna head home. No way, just four people caused that much damage. I'll talk to you tomorrow."

The green-eyed officer returned home after a long night's work, removed his shoes, then crept slowly by family portraits and over misplaced toys. He snuck through the dark, cluttered living room filled with papier-mâché school art projects and into the kitchen without making a sound. He opened the door to the smell of pork chops and shuddered. There he met his wife, Elisa. The brunette leaned over the countertop and pushed her chest over the brim of her blouse. She smiled over a pork chop dinner, "Hello, honey. Hungry?"

Rhion lovingly smashed into her. He pushed her against the stainless oak cabinets and knocked over the dishes. He grabbed under her skirt, then caressed her thigh and ventured onward. "I love you, babe," he admitted.

"I love you too!" Elisa giggled.

"Rrrrrrrrrraaaaaaaawwwwrrrrr!"

The couple jolted.

Rhion pushed Elisa's chocolate hair behind her ears as he recognized the sound, "It's Ginger. You think she's ready?"

Elisa rushed into the living room and turned on the light. Ginger, the inflated striped orange feline, yowled with pain and curved uncomfortably in her bed. Elisa took Rhion's hand and beamed nervously, "Oh my god. I think she's ready to give birth!"

For several minutes the cat screeched. She woke the children and stole their attention. Haile Galloway walked her two little brothers carefully down the stairs. She puckered an adolescent lip as her cat quivered in pain.

"What's wrong with Gingie?" the twelve-year-old exclaimed and held the hands of her twin toddler brothers.

"I think she's finally having her kittens, Haile!" Elisa beamed, taking her children in her arms.

As the family huddled together, they hopefully scrutinized Ginger while she motioned uneasily within her sheets. Angrily, the cat wailed, then threw her legs out, and finally was ready.

The womb of the feline cracked open. Tiny hairy legs feverishly poked through. Within seconds, blood-drenched tarantulas instantaneously sprouted from the cat. Dozens of erratic spiders escaped from Ginger's stomach and sped throughout the house. They crawled over the walls, rushed through the baby blue curtains, climbed the furniture, and up the chimney, leaving red footprints behind.

"Run!" Rhion ordered while Elisa shrieked in horror and struggled to lift all three of her children up the wooden staircase.

Rhion wielded his designer leather shoe like a hammer and smashed a fuzzy tarantula. One by one, he crushed the giant spiders and smeared their organs across the fixtures. He found himself in a hysteric rage. He murdered the creatures soaked in cat blood. He ignored his cellphone when it rang then continued to voicemail.

"Rhion," Martin's voicemail had recorded, "I'm sure you heard there was a mass murder at club Solace the other night... Total disgusting mess, some really sick shit. An unknown number of John Does, but over fifteen surviving eye-witnesses. You were right. Live, accounts of your boy, Neil Qin in some sort of cat mask… identified as the only living person leaving the crime scene... Call me back when you get this."

"Do we know how bad this is?" Amanda asked as the three rushed into the hospital. "Ezekiel, I mean." She stared around at Aurora's and Neil's blank faces as she placed a stuffed puppy, a box of chocolates, and balloons into a large brown paper bag. "Do we even know if it's d-e-m-o-n related or just the flu?" Amanda continued, "Because I heard the flu was bad this time of year."

"Everyone who is not an idiot can spell demon," Aurora blurted out. "Well, you can spell it, so I guess some are lucky."

"That was so funny I forgot to laugh," Amanda countered. "Want some vegan butter for your corny joke?"

"It was no flu," Neil added coldly. "They said that Ezekiel was stabbed and beaten severely."

"Oh, my Lord," Amanda commented. "Let's not be pessimistic. Maybe he was in a gang fight? I mean, I know that's not exactly positive, but it is better than..."

"I'd say Ezekiel could handle himself in a gang fight," Neil snapped.

"Oh! He can because you say he can? Oh, Neil, the boss of everyone! Sure Ezekiel can handle himself in a fight! And sure, I can't tell the love of my life who I really am! Whatever you say, dude. I said I wasn't talking to you, and I've eaten an entire cheesecake in anger! That's four thousand calories! Now me and my gut, and my stretch marks hate you more than ever!" Amanda ranted, shook her fist then turned to Aurora desolately. "Ezekiel never really gets a break, huh? I mean, he certainly got the short straw with everything."

Aurora cranked the metal handle of the white door and slowly pushed it open. Ezekiel rested between white sheets, and his eyes opened slowly when they entered. "Hi, guys. How's everyone? Cool?" Ezekiel spoke weakly.

"'Hi, guys'?" Aurora quoted. "Are you kidding me?"

"Not unless there's something I don't know." Ezekiel was distracted. He wrinkled his brow and thought of the billions of demons that exist. "Which there better not be because I'm a little preoccupied at the moment."

"What she means to say is: How are you?" Amanda corrected and took a step forward, "We were all worried."

"Me?" Ezekiel asked. "It seems like my insurance, or lack thereof, means that I get treated like crap... But I get to live." He nodded sarcastically. "Not at all like I just got hit with a truck or anything because that didn't happen."

Amanda presented her gifts. "We're here to make you feel much better and presents! Let me show you what you have won," Amanda announced her offerings. "We got the 'Get Well Soon' balloons; those are standard. We got a very sad puppy dog, and even though he is crying, he is still adorable! And we got chocolate!"

"How'd you all know I'm a chocolate-loving friend?" Ezekiel admitted and narrowed his eyes. "I've tried to keep that problem a secret for years. I've been to group therapy and everything. Give me some chocolate!"

Amanda leaned over and passed the small rectangular box to Ezekiel, who readily opened it and munched on the candies.

Neil stood with his lips thinning. He shook his head slowly. "You don't have to amuse us, Ezekiel. It's okay to be hurt; we're not Gods." Ezekiel looked up to Neil but said nothing. "Who did this to you? Was it the Horsemen?"

Ezekiel shrugged it off and denied, "No, some random demon."

"Did this demon have a name?" Neil asked. "How did he look?"

Ezekiel recalled the recent memory of his battle with Corrier. He saw himself being stabbed, hit, then Corrier plummeting off the roof. He remembered how he killed his actual father. Ezekiel shifted in his bed uncomfortably and softly inquired, "Do we have to talk about that now?"

"Yeah, we do," Neil urged.

For a moment, Ezekiel paused, "His name was Corrier." He exhaled and wet a dry spot in his throat, "And he looked kinda like my father."

"Your dad?" Amanda took a step forward and gasped.

"What?" Aurora asked. "How did that happen?"

"I didn't really tell the truth..." Ezekiel's eyes softened a bit. "When I," he hesitated, "when I got my powers, I didn't know what I could do. My father and I got into an argument, and… I killed him. I tried to bring him back, but something else entered his body. Something dark and evil. It had me so flustered that I let it live in my house, trick my mother. I've been living a lie for a while now." Ezekiel's eyes fell into his lap, and he confessed, "I couldn't take it anymore."

"Did you kill him?" Aurora requested.

Ezekiel shook his head slowly and answered, "I don't know. I-I fought him, and he fell off a roof. I don't know if his body deteriorated or if he got away."

"You definitely should have told us earlier," Neil said dryly.

"I enjoyed living a lie for a while," Ezekiel moaned. "ven though it was killing me. You m-mad?"

Neil shook his head and declared, "No, I'm not mad. Just concerned. He could have killed you."

Aurora fought off an oncoming headache and questioned, "When are they going to let you out?"

"I don't know."

Neil lowered his head before stating, "Then I guess we're going to be here for a while. Focusing on healing you."

Neil's words echoed through the room and lingered there. It was the only words that were spoken for a long time. The room was silent and dead. Amanda pressed her back against the wall; she could feel the resurfaced tension between Neil and Aurora. Her eyes dashed over towards

Neil, who stood with his arms folded and his eyes closed. Amanda refused to say anything to Neil since he refused to let her tell her fiancé their secret. What was the problem? She was a good person. She loved her husband; she loved everyone! She absolutely loved Neil, but she also utterly hated him at the moment.

Neil shifted his shoulders nervously; there are many things that he didn't understand about Aurora. Why didn't she like him? Was she sending him signals? Or is it only that he was misreading them? It was a while since Neil had been in a relationship; the last (and only) one was with Victoria, and look how that turned out. He sighed and dropped his shoulders. Why was he allowing himself to experience these worthless feelings again? In the end, they didn't matter. He was unsure what mattered at this point and wondered: Is this all there is?

Aurora recalled when Neil tried to kiss her. She knew that he was not the type of person to hurt her, but the speculation that he might have haunted her. Neil was a good man. He was strong, a good worker, a good father, good-looking, obviously the most potent angel out of the bunch, but she could never truly trust him.

Aurora was so caught up in her own issues of doubt and suspicion that she hadn't thought of the possibility that she might love him. She did like him and enjoyed spending time with him. He made her feel safe, liked... But that isn't enough because eventually, one day, it would end horribly.

All men were the same, even if they were angels.

An eminent sensation grabbed the base of her spine and traveled up to her eyes. The visions were different now: warm, painless, and traveling through her system with ease.

Lyssah Rhamiel knelt before an altar full of candles, and her body shook and vibrated wildly. She was screaming in tongues. Amid a ritual, she pulled back the shirt on her body to reveal the messages scarred onto her and found a space. With a knife, Lyssah Rhamiel started to carve a new set of symbols while she chanted.

Aurora reached into her pocketbook and revealed red lipstick. She began tracing the symbols onto a pillowcase while Lyssah Rhamiel carved them into herself. This vision was more comfortable. She could move and control her body.

Shaking off the chills from her back, the other angels watched her intensely; she pulled her hair to one side of her head and presented the drawing on the pillowcase. It was a vision of the past, and she was almost shocked by how smoothly it went. As the others watched her in confusion, she held up her artwork and announced, "I just had a vision. A few hours ago, Lyssah Rhamiel carved these symbols into her side..."

Lyssah Rhamiel sat in her library, a tall room filled top to bottom with hundreds of fat texts. Before her on the table was a series of thick foreign volumes all opened and a half-read. She studied her busy table and her scrambled books placed on it. Her old lips quivered as she translated the ancient language into the vernacular.

Slowly, she carved the symbols into her skin. The translation read:

"When the battle of all worlds begins, the Four Horsemen and the Alpha Omega shall war with each other, and through the ashes of the battle, the Four Horsemen shall rise."

Chapter 29: Ornery

> "Bless the Lord, all you angels, mighty in strength and attentive, obedient to every command."
> **Psalms 103:20**

"I knew you would come," Lyssah Rhamiel perched at her usual spot with the angels around her living room. She held a can of apple juice in her boney hands. Before her were several open ancient books and scrolls curled up at the edge of their yellowing pages. She placed her can in her lap, and announced, "Here lie the books that I have hoarded over the years. I've spent time translating and reading them. The Book of Revelation tells of seven seals that need to be broken before the world ends. I just got word they are approaching the sixth seal. It is an act that will cause a terrible earthquake; thousands will die."

Lyssah Rhamiel took a sip of her drink and then continued, "A Noble named John the Evangelist was first to vision the Descended, four angels blessed with souls that exalt them with powers over creation, the mind, destiny, and death." Lyssah Rhamiel presented a pictograph and handed it to Neil.

The picture held four angels. To the farthest right was a brown-skinned man with silver and blue angel wings. His hair was pulled back, and although the image was abstract, it was a decent description of Ezekiel. He wore a white robe with a single silver stripe that ran diagonally down the torso. Beside him was a woman with shoulder-length blonde hair and huge blue eyes. She was dressed in a tan-colored Roman robe with bright yellow wings protruding from her back. Then stood another man with long black hair down to his shoulders, and a Roman black-and-white gown reached down to his toes. He held a long sword in his hand, from his back obtruded enormous black-and-white wings. Last in line stood a woman with dark locks and skin, dressed in a burgundy robe with ruby wings extended from her back.

"Look, that's us!" Amanda excitedly pointed at the blonde one. She lined the sun-colored wings that were on her back. "This is so cute! Can I keep this?"

Aurora located herself but was slightly afraid of how they got that information. Quizzically she asked, "How did this John know?"

"I would think you would know the best. He had visions of all of us." Neil winked.

"I don't know, Neil," Ezekiel said, pointing to one of the figures that he could not distinguish. "That doesn't really look like you." Ezekiel ran his finger around the wings of the characters and explained, "Look, the wings are black and white. Yours are just solid black... maybe a little gold or purple... And the hair is darker... and the sword..."

Neil nodded his head and agreed, "Yeah, I noticed that too. All psychics can't be right."

Lyssah Rhamiel solemnly continued, "The Alpha Omega would be born human, and their powers only be divulged when the war has begun, shaking both Heaven and Hell. As the Horsemen fight to end the earth, the Sacred Angels will fight to salvage it and keep it under the many allied Heavens' rule. Before the full moon, the eight will fall into battle, and only four will arise. I've been told that the Four Horsemen will be the ones to live. This is what Aurora saw me write on my side,"

"Oh my god," Aurora spoke, gasping through breaths. "That thing says we're going to die?"

"Wait, let me finish!" Lyssah Rhamiel interrupted her. "This battle will be the first of many. The outcome of the war, however, is decided by those who fight in it... Stolas and I have been watching you, and you have all made us proud. This is why I am giving you this information. I have devised a way to kill the Horsemen. Call them to four different arenas with this prayer I have written. I recommend summoning them to a place where you are the most powerful—a special place in your heart. Follow your winds, North, East, South, and West. You must pierce them with their weapons."

"Okay, not that that's not great and everything," Aurora started. "But I'm more concerned about the part where you said that we were going to die!"

"I never said that," Lyssah Rhamiel tried to assure her. "I only read that the Four Horsemen would live."

"Which means what?" Aurora's voice elevated, "That we're going to die!"

"How do we know what you read is right?" Neil inquired as his heart sped, "How do we know those bastards didn't change the text just to screw with us?"

Lyssah Rhamiel stood and finished her drink, then concluded, "These are sacred texts that are told to me through divine messages. No demon can get hold of them." Lyssah Rhamiel paused for a moment and lowered her head, then finished, "That's what I have called you here to say. I suggest you attack quickly. Stay here tonight; there are two extra rooms upstairs, and we will prepare in the morning."

"I'm not going tomorrow," Aurora spat lividly and watched Neil, knowing he would disagree. "I'm not going to sign my own funeral papers..."

"Existence is a test. When we first began this journey, I told you not to let the psychological ramifications keep you from your goals! Greatness begins by conquering your fears. You must be brave. Repent! My sick patients, you must abide by my prescriptions!" Lyssah Rhamiel warned.

Aurora protested angrily, "You're crazy as hell!"

Lyssah Rhamiel countered and jumped from her seat, "I am not crazy! I am special! Paranoid Schizophrenic! Dysthymia! Existentialist! Bi-polar! I am crazy! I am chosen! I can handle it! We are special! No one can hurt us but ourselves! We are special! Repent!" She repeated this while she exited the room in a hysteric fury. "There was never meant to be only one."

Neil fumbled with his fingers then looked up to meet Aurora's glare. He tried to convince her, "We have to. If we don't, thousands die."

"If we go, the world ends!" Aurora exploded.

"She didn't say that," Neil revised.

"She didn't say we win either," Amanda added.

Aurora's stare was cold, dead set on Neil when she spoke, "She said we die, Neil. Which means the Horsemen win, which means the world goes to Hell!"

"She said, 'The outcome of the war is decided by those who fight it,'" Neil defended himself.

Aurora shook her head violently and amended, "Not feeling cryptic right now! Do you not understand, or are you just stupid? We're going to lose tomorrow, and the whole world will go to Hell because of us!" Aurora crossed her arms.

"I'm not stupid, and I think we can beat the Horsemen..." Neil continued harshly. "I've been thinking if the Horsemen were so powerful, why haven't they killed us already? Why haven't they even tried? When we first met them, we were at our weakest, and rather than kill us right away; they tried to get us to join them. They keep sending bounty hunters after us. Why? Because they're afraid to face us themselves!"

"Yeah, that's a pretty interesting theory Neil," Aurora sarcastically snapped. "But I'm not gonna base my life on it."

Neil closed his eyes; he couldn't accept what Lyssah Rhamiel had read. He had fought so hard, trained so vigorously, and yet he was destined to die in the end? No. There must be some way around it. Even if he did die, would the world be saved because of it? The scroll was wrong. Neil stood and picked up the scroll. He crumpled the ancient paper into a ball without hesitation and threw it against the wall behind him. Neil addressed his team, "She's wrong, just like that scroll was wrong when they drew the picture of me... When this began, we all signed up for it."

"We didn't have a choice," Ezekiel woefully interrupted.

"You could have run away!" Neil shouted, then repeated his sermon from the beginning. "When this all began, we all signed up for it, knowing the risks and peril that we might be put through. We signed up and knew that this cause is more important than our own lives. We knew that we very well could lose them in the process. Tomorrow is what we signed up for."

"I didn't sign up for death," Aurora quipped.

Neil shot her a disheartened look and attempted to convince her, "Whether we die tomorrow or not is up to us. All I know is that before I do, I'm ripping the head off one of those sons of bitches and taking it with me. I'm doing it for my son, for all of you, and for the rest of the world. That should be everyone's attitude, and if it's not, it better be by tomorrow. Find your motivation! Like Lyssah Rhamiel, I've seen you three grow, and we're ready. We are all going, and that is final."

Amanda shook her head aggressively. How could he say that? she thought. Emotions mixed inside of her body. Terror. Grief. Fury. She couldn't take it anymore. When everything flowed to its boiling point, she stood up and yelled, "Don't tell me that at twenty-six years old, I'm going to die!"

Neil remained silent, and Amanda stormed out of the room.

"Try to get some sleep," he muttered, "if you can. First thing tomorrow, we're going in. We should eat something too."

"I'm not eating anything," Aurora retorted.

"Goodnight then," Neil countered as Aurora got up out of her chair and followed Amanda out of the room.

"What do you want to eat?" Ezekiel miserably asked Neil. He folded his fingers under his nose and rested his elbows on his knees. "I'm not that great a cook, but I can make something."

"Let's go see," Neil said, and he led the way into the kitchen.

Though the size of the house was great, the kitchen was tiny. It had barely enough room to fit the necessities and a small square table. The walls in the kitchen were made of white tile and paint. As the rest of the house did, this room had an antique style to it. Neil and Ezekiel rummaged through the cabinets for something edible.

Ezekiel opened the refrigerator and mumbled, "I guess Lyssah Rhamiel doesn't entertain guests much. I can fry up some canned ham."

Neil turned from the empty cabinet. "Canned ham?" he asked disgustedly with a smile spread across his face.

"Come on; canned ham's not so bad. I've been eating it for years. What about if I sweeten the deal and add cheese?" Ezekiel asked. "I can make canned cheese and Spam, and after we can have this can of fruit cocktail!"

Aurora walked into the bedroom to meet Amanda curled up on the bed with a pillow to her torso. Amanda's eyes welled as she bit the fabric of the pillow. She growled and wept at once. Aurora sat beside her and stroked her hair. "It's okay..." Aurora spoke in the most relaxing voice she could muster. "If you die tomorrow, I'd pretend to miss you... Would you pretend to miss me?"

"That's not funny," Amanda exclaimed.

"You're right. I wouldn't pretend. Haha."

Amanda wiped her eyes and vented, "Neil's a real jerk. I can't leave my fiancé, my family, Olive, Purrson, my kitty... it's not that he's evil exactly but he's just been upset since he has eight legs... He's gonna be so sad..."

With those words, the reality hit Aurora. She wouldn't have anyone to say goodbye to. She had dropped out of college to pursue her dream against her family's wishes. She moved far from them and hadn't even spoken to them for months. If she died tomorrow, they would never know, would never care. Aurora recalled the horror of her very first vision, and though she wanted to live, she needed to stop that from happening. "He's right, though," she whispered softly, and she continued to brush Amanda's hair.

"I know," Amanda replied.

"My power is to change destiny," Aurora admitted, continuing to stroke. "Maybe I can change ours."

"Or maybe that thing is wrong!" Amanda declared. "That picture messed up on Neil's wings... they could have messed up on this too."

"That's right," Aurora agreed, "it would be like any other battle we fought, and we're going to win."

"We are!" Amanda said, exploding with positive energy. She looked at Aurora and wiped the rest of the tears out of her eyes. "What now?"

"The best girl's night like ever..." Aurora smiled. "If we're going to die, we might as well die happy. Think a nun would have ice cream? I have some nail polish in my bag; I think you need it."

With a splat, the canned ham fell on the frying pan. Ezekiel slouched and moved the solid cube of meat around the sizzling pan with a spatula. He didn't want to ask, but the question was burning inside of him, "Neil... are you scared?"

Neil swallowed hard, "Why should I be? Are you?"

Ezekiel broke the meat up in the pan. "No, I'm not scared..." he lied, snarling a bit. He turned to Neil as he flipped the cube to the other side, then admitted, "Okay, of course, I am. What happens if we do lose?"

"We'll be dead."

"But what happens after that? We need some kind of backup plan," Ezekiel muttered.

"If we die, then the world is done," Neil answered confidently, only to shake off the shiver down his spine. "So we can't lose. No pressure. Right?"

Ezekiel nodded miserably. "Riiight."

"Just beautiful..." Aurora muttered as she rummaged through her belongings. Holding a bottle of nail polish between her fingers, she shook the only bottle of polish she had, "I only brought the clear."

"But..." Amanda shook her head, contemptuously. "You have me." Amanda folded her legs Indian style.

"Oh, that's right," Aurora laughed and pointed to her. "What color do you want?"

"Pinkish red," she retorted and Amanda took the bottle from Aurora's hands and gave it a small shake, as the bottle of clear liquid slowly transformed its color into a rosy red. "Hungry?"

Aurora nodded, suddenly feeling her stomach grumble. Without hesitation she decided, "I'll go see what she has." She got off the bed and headed to the kitchen while a strange sense splashed over her. She couldn't help but feel it—guilt mixed with shame—and the utter feeling that she was lying to herself.

She refused to acknowledge the men in the kitchen and searched through the bare cabinets. She got bowls and spoons and took out the large can of fruit.

"You better not eat that whole thing," Ezekiel warned. "We want some too!"

"Fine," she spat wearily as she left the room.

Aurora entered the bedroom then placed the bowls on the bed. "And we have fruit cocktail..." she said, folding her feet on the bed. "They said that we could eat the whole thing!"

Chapter 30: Gone

"But to which of the angels has he ever said: 'Sit at my right hand until I make your enemies your footstool?'"
Hebrews 1:13

Neil took a deep breath of fresh air, and his chestnut eyes examined his dark surroundings. Trees crowded his vision, but he knew that the White Horseman was close. There was a ruffling in the bushes nearby. Awaiting a surprise attack, Neil arched his fingers at his side. A lone arrow shot through the air and was headed right at him. Neil swiped his hand and re-directed it into a tree trunk. He tried to speak, but something held his voice.

Fear tickled his skin, but Neil walked in the direction the arrow came from.

Another arrow flew at him. He was barely fast enough to send it off target. Neil forced his power through the bush but there was no reaction. There wasn't anything there. He turned around to meet the devil who stood behind him with an arrow pointed at his head. The demon pulled back on the string of the bow, then let the bolt loose.

Neil awoke with a start, the blankets that covered him flew into the air and parachuted to the ground, as sweat trickled down his face. His eyes darted around the room. It was only a dream.

Restless, Neil staggered into the dark kitchen when a notion transpired within him. It refused to shake off. He could lose that fight tomorrow. They all could, and if they did... He grimaced with the very thought. Didn't want to think about it.

His bare feet touched the icy tiles of the kitchen floor, and as he moved towards the refrigerator he noticed Aurora. She leaned on the counter with a glass of water in her hand. The former model took a sip as she watched him. His body shook while he opened the refrigerator. He quivered with rage then slammed the door shut.

Sensitive to the tension, Aurora approached Neil. Though it was dark, her vision was keen enough to catch the forlorn expression on his face. Gently, she spoke to him. "What the hell is going on?"

"Nothing," he said almost as grimly as Ezekiel would. He turned to leave the room. She smoothly pushed Neil onto the counter.

"What's wrong?" she asked again more compassionately. "Did something happen?"

Neil forced the words through his lips, "Tomorrow."

"What, are you afraid we won't win?" she inquired and moved closer.

Neil hesitated. One of the hardest things in his life was admitting to someone that he was wrong. He peered into Aurora's eyes; they welled with stress. Suddenly, he was able to answer her. "Yes," he admitted as warm tears rushed down his cheeks.

"Neil," Aurora begged, "please don't cry..." She wiped a tear off his face, but another quickly followed. Her jaw trembled open; she never saw a man cry before, not in person. It was raw, honest. Neil looked so vulnerable. He was the most powerful man she knew, yet he was weeping right before her. She never felt so awkward in front of him and could not remember the last time she was ever speechless... Aurora leaned in and placed her lips on Neil's just for a second. It was an unexpected impulse that she instantly regretted.

Embarrassed, she teetered back and watched Neil return her wide-eyed stare. He stopped crying.

Her heartbeat was in her throat, and she could barely breathe when Neil lunged at her. He was like a wild storm that overpowered her. His lips were soft, but his grasp was authoritative and severe. Before she knew it, Aurora's back was on the wall. What was she doing? What was HE doing?

Adrenaline raced through her body when he started to kiss her neck, and the warm tears on his face smeared over her shoulder and chest. She could feel his desperation, and it untamed her body. It was a while since her last kiss, and her flesh ignored her mind's blatant warnings. She let her eyes roll into the back of her head, relaxed her mind in defeat, and gave into physical temptation.

Okay well... Tomorrow I could be dead, so at least it won't be awkward for long.

Without resistance, she returned his passion.

Neil carried her into a small prayer room nearby. Dozens of dim candles filled the area with the scent of wax. Neil looked tall on his knees as he watched Aurora's curious gaze as she lay on the ground. Suddenly, her pajama blouse unbuttoned and slid off her body as though it were alive. In nervous reaction to the spotlight, she clung to his undershirt till it tore at the seams and off his torso. Unsure, she fell back as he telekinetically removed her silk shorts. She winced. *What if he doesn't like my body? What if he's disgusted by the mole on my stomach?*

The cold, hardwood floor sent chills between her thighs. Her chest was hot and quivered under Neil's touch while he unfastened her bra. Her heart jolted as though she was entirely out of contact with her body.

She studied him hazily. Vulnerable and afraid, she unbuckled his heavy black jeans and threw them to the ground. Neil entered her body, and Aurora's eyes dilated. She had forgotten how much this had hurt. Her back arched, then she took a deep breath and trembled.

Aurora closed her eyes and dug her fingernails deep into his back and begged her body not to freeze up. His touch sent electric shocks through her, and she quivered under his power. Hot tears rushed down her cheeks, and she bit her lower lip to keep from screaming. She was the one who cried now.

Silently she bawled as he pushed into her.

She remembered her last physical encounter and couldn't help but compare. As an unloved object to her ex, she always feared intimacy. She felt like she was used for a single purpose, then placed back on the shelf. She soon believed her body was all she could offer. That each time she lay with Biff, he took away a piece of her. She was scared to continue with Neil, but she was sure this was what she wanted. He deserved a part of her, and she needed a piece of him.

With every thrust, she could feel his ambiance fill the room. His musky scent drove her wild as she tasted his soft, salty skin. Her body numbed with long lost pleasure. She felt like she was making love to something far more significant and influential than she saw before her.

Rising energy took control of the space as candles floated from their stands, and paintings lifted off the walls. The entire room was alive. Small plastic Virgin Marys, rosaries and tiny bottles of Holy water levitated in orbit above them. The walls vibrated when Neil curved his back and transparent black and gold wings sprouted from him. Large wet tears crawled down Aurora's cheeks while the large ghost-like wings made of light unfolded. They rose into the air—her body filled with excitement, arousal, and awe.

Levitated and free from the uncomfortable restrictions of the bare floor, Neil ventured deeper inside her while the room spiraled around them. She cooed as he threw his head back and climaxed, telekinetically shattering the orbiting objects on the wall. He moaned, and all at once, they fell to the ground with a thud. His body tingled with the exhilarating and uncontrolled sensation between pleasure and pain. They winced from the fall. She pressed a hand on Neil's shoulder and the other on his lower back then closed her eyes.

"We're not done yet," Aurora announced. She focused her power around his lower half and rewound time. Beyond his control, he repeated. Again, his face cringed with sexual release. It was as though all his energy exploded in sizzling sparks over his entire body.

Neil rested his head on her shoulder and whimsically admitted, "I... can't move..."

"Uh-huh..." Aurora wiped her eyes and ran her fingers through his hair. "Cry now, and we're gonna have a huge problem..."

The morning came quickly for the couple. They walked out of the small room and into the kitchen where Amanda and Ezekiel were already sitting at the table. Bathed and clothed, they ate canned peas and corn for breakfast.

"Where have you two been? It's eleven!" Amanda yelled and devoured a fork full of corn.

"Praying!" Aurora blurted out. Neil looked at her and smiled.

"Yeah, praying," Neil repeated right after her outburst.

"Oh," Amanda whispered understandingly, "well, that's okay then, excuse me."

"Yeah..." Ezekiel nodded suspiciously and cocked his eyebrow. Closing his eyes, he changed the subject, "So it happens today... Are we really going to fight them alone?"

Amanda started, "They're the most powerful together, but so are we...We can't fight them by ourselves."

"We're going to have to," Neil informed them. "We can't risk them coming together, and if we just summon one, the others will follow. We all killed demons on our own before; this won't be any different."

"And all we need to do is kill one of them, right?" Ezekiel asked. "Kill one, break the square, and they're done. If one of us can do that, the world's safe... besides the ones that would be dead..."

"You shouldn't let that negative thinking in," Neil scolded Ezekiel. "Where's the prayer?" Neil asked, and Amanda passed him the folded page in her pocket. "We're doing it,"

"Where?" Aurora asked.

"Places where we're most powerful," Neil answered. "A lot of space and in our assigned directions..."

"I guess the park." Aurora nodded. "There is a lot of room..."

"The mall... it's on the Westside, and Raphael is West," Amanda muttered. "It's closed down, and I know the place like the back of my hand. Plus, there are a lot of things I can morph into there..."

"East represents death... The graveyard," Ezekiel piped up. "It should be easiest there to summon spirits if I have to."

"Here is as good a place as any. Spiritual and in the North, Michael's element." Neil looked around the church and considered. Out of the drawer, he picked a pencil and pad of paper. He wrote down the spell and handed it out to the others in the room. "Angels doing spells," he mused. "Now I've seen everything."

"I think we should say goodbye to our families before we do this," Amanda lamented.

Neil looked at her sympathetically. "Of course," he said with compassion. "Finish eating and see your loved ones. We leave in two hours. We shouldn't go into a battle cold, so don't forget to get warmed up."

"I called you both here today because I love you guys so much, and you're my best friends!" Amanda exclaimed in a shrill sob. She squeezed the hands of Olive and Henry while they questioningly gazed around the apartment. Two large open boxes with their names scribbled with a marker on them were filled with stuffed animals and sat on the plastic living room table. Some soft toys were old and tattered with missing parts while others were new, made of expensive fabrics, and movable parts. "This is the stuffed animal collection I started the day I was born! And since I love you both most in the world... I wanna split it between you two... I even got a stuffed kitty for Purrson!"

Olive looked perplexed. She was dressed in a slender gray business suit. Her hair was pulled up in a bun, and she looked down pretentiously through thin black glasses. "I thought you insisted on being buried with that senseless collection."

"Well, that was my original plan," Amanda sniffled. "But I don't think that's gonna happen anymore."

Henry consoled Amanda while she blubbered. "Babe, why don't you think that's going to happen? Why are you giving this to us now?"

"And more crucially," Olive snarled down at the boxes. "Whatever shall we do with such frivolous trinkets?"

"B-because," Amanda wiped her nostrils and whimpered, "I don't know yet, but I might be g- going on a trip."

"When? Where?" Henry asked.

"Oh... Oops..." Amanda paused, then fell to uncontrollable tears as she struggled to answer, "I was so busy packing up these boxes I forgot to think of a place to tell you I was going!"

"Wait," Olive thoughtfully whispered to her friend. "This doesn't happen to pertain to uh... preternatural matters, does it?"

Amanda bit her lower lip, "Huh? I don't know who Peter Naturatters is!"

"Um, does this relate to affairs of a Heavenly sort?" Olive muttered more clearly.

"Heavenly sort?" Henry shouted impatiently as Amanda gave Olive a woeful nod.

"I just remembered," Olive supported Amanda standing while she bawled. "A great Aunt of mine has just passed. She and Amanda were particularly close, and it seems Amanda must go to Illinois for the wake."

"Illinois?" Henry moaned. "For how long?"

Olive locked eyes with Amanda. "Not too long, right?"

Amanda's knees buckled.

It was the middle of the day, and Victoria was at work. Neil placed his palm on her front door and sensed his son and the babysitter inside. In his mind's eye, he could see the brunette blast music while she screamed on the phone, and Zachary slept in the other room. Distressed, Neil placed a knock on the wooden door.

The door opened to a young girl. Just as he envisioned, Clara Rodriguez wore pigtails, multi-colored nail polish, and a Marilyn Manson t-shirt. She cocked her arms around her stomach and peevishly spat, "And you are?"

Neil charged into her mind: *"Could this be the plumber? Victoria did say someone would be here today. I guess he sort of looks like a plumber..."*

"I'm here to fix the toilet," Neil replied.

"Oh," the girl opened the door and, as Neil entered, demanded. "Hey! If you're a plumber, where are your tools?"

"They're in the car," Neil fibbed. "I just want to see what tools I need first."

Clara placed her cellphone to her ears and retreated into the living room. Neil opened Zachary's bedroom door. He only visited a few times, and the room looked different every occasion. There were new toys. New pictures graced the walls—new clothes hung in the closet. Zachary was living an entire life wholly estranged from his father.

Neil lifted Zachary as he slept. Were things truly better this way? He gently rocked him. His son was safe and protected in his distance, away from all the demons. But he was without his father. Neil was familiar with the loneliness of growing up. He hummed to his child. He held his son for possibly the last time and declared, "I'll die before I let anything harm you. You're a part of me. As long as you're safe, the demons can never hurt me."

"Um," Clara suspiciously uttered as she tapped an annoyed foot on the ground and followed Neil into Zachary's room. "What are you doing? Ay dios mio, the bathroom is actually over here dude."

Ezekiel was consumed with guilt. If he died tonight, she would be alone. Suddenly, he regretted all that he said to his mother as a child. All the worries he caused her. Ezekiel stood before his door. 4D.

"Why do I always do this?" he asked himself. He knocked, and his mother answered. Her surprise turned to irritation.

"You didn't come home last night," she scowled.

Ezekiel shook his head and skipped to the point, "Not really. I came to say goodbye."

"You going somewhere?" his mother asked him. Ezekiel closed his eyes and thought of an answer.

"Yeah. And I don't know if I'll be coming back." He pulled his sleeves over his fists.

His mother turned away. "Where are you going?" she pleaded.

"I'm going far away," he said and leaned over and held her in his arms. "I killed Dad," he said softly. Lauren pushed off him. Her eyes enlarged from sadness to shock and resentment.

Neil turned around to Aurora in the back seat of his Jeep. Her heart pounded in her chest, and her face twisted in uncertainty. Conflicting forces within her battled it out. One side told her to get out of this car and run down the street, never to return, and the other knew that she had to face off in a battle with the Horsemen.

"What's wrong?" Neil asked.

"With all my powers of destiny, I don't know what's going to happen. It's annoying. I have no one to say goodbye to" Aurora muttered. "There is no one that cares about me, and no one that I care about."

Amanda closed her eyes. "Always a good motto to have. What happened to the confident girl that painted my nails last night?"

"She got hit with reality," Aurora answered dryly then folded her arms neatly above her belly button.

Ezekiel opened the car door, and Amanda moved over a seat so he could fit. His eyes were red from crying. The blonde blinked and asked, "How'd it go?"

Ezekiel laughed, "I'll live." He blurted out the answer before he realized how ironic it sounded. "I hope." A nervous smile flickered across his face, and he forced it away. "I told her I killed him. My own mother kicked me out. Threatened to call the cops..." His eyebrows inclined in unison. "As if I wasn't leaving anyway..."

Ezekiel could feel his blood run a little quicker through his body. They approached the cemetery. A place that had long been closed for years due to the lack of space. The salty air filled his lungs as he drew closer to the beach. Neil and Amanda dolefully looked back at him. Ezekiel gazed out the window as the car parked on the sidewalk. The cemetery was vast, filled with bright green grass and tombstones that ran in orderly rows.

"This is my stop."

"Do you have the prayer?" Neil asked him and heaved out a handful of palms and passed them over. "I know you can do this. I have faith in you..."

Ezekiel took his hand awkwardly. They glared at each other then shared an unnerving hug. Neil patted Ezekiel's back until they parted.

Aurora was next in line. "Die, and I'll be really pissed, okay?" she muttered as she took her turn in an embrace.

Ezekiel looked up as the couple parted. "I won't," he promised her weakly. Aurora walked back into the car, and Amanda approached him. She held him tightly while the cool wind tossed her hair. "I have nothing interesting to say," she spoke laughingly. "Just go get 'em!"

"Don't start the spell until a half an hour after we leave," Neil instructed. "We have to summon the Horsemen all at the same time."

"Yeah..." Ezekiel agreed as he watched the graveyard, and a chill ran across his skin while his stomach tightened. Ezekiel placed nine black candles in a circle. He needed the dry palms in his hand to write the name of a Horseman on it. It only seemed natural that the Angel of Death would take on the Horseman of Death.

Much had changed since the last time Aurora had been at the park. The peace and tranquility were replaced with uproar and upheaval. She almost changed her mind about fighting here, but it was far too late now. She was reminded of Neil's psychic outcry in the park not too long ago and hoped that she could channel some of that energy. Aurora checked for her handgun, then took a deep breath.

"Wow," she sighed. This was the first time she had seen this particular park at night, it was scarier than she expected.

"Well, it uses to be a nice park," Amanda murmured.

"Just find a nice spot. I'm sure there's one somewhere," Neil combated her murmur with one of his own. He pulled out nine black candles and an auburn-colored palm leaf from the trunk of his car. He placed them into a large brown paper bag and handed it to her.

Aurora and Neil watched each other for a few seconds. She held the bag waist high and took a step closer to him. Amanda eavesdropped while Neil pushed some of Aurora's hair out of her face. He leaned closer to her ear and whispered something Amanda couldn't hear.

"Don't worry, you'll come back," he encouraged gently.

Aurora closed her eyes for a moment, concentrating on extinguishing the fear inside her.

"Remember before, when I said I didn't have anyone that I cared about enough to come back for." Neil nodded, and she continued. "I lied." Gently pressing her lips against his, she could feel her body charge with excitement. It was a mild distraction, but it was something to look forward to.

Amanda struggled to keep her jaw off the floor.

Aurora waved at Amanda. She closed her mouth then simply waved back. Amanda retreated into the parked car. Neil closely followed her, moving into the driver's seat. She twisted her head mockingly, and Neil started the car. "What was that back there? You and Aurora were looking kind of cozy..."

Chapter 31: The Beginning of the End

"And he said to me, 'These words are trustworthy and true, and the Lord, the God of prophetic spirits, sent his angel to show his servants what must happen soon.'"
Revelation 22:6

Neil stood in the center alley between the vacant church pews. He needed to do the spell at the right time to separate the Horsemen. It was all about to end. His fingers trembled anxiously, and he reminded himself of the past few months. He sacrificed precious and invaluable moments of his life for the greater good. It was a notion like a vague dream he struggled to remember. Whether he lived or died, it was over. Was it all worth it?

"Neil Qin," Rhion Galloway shouted as he stormed through the church doors, "I'm going to need you to come down to the station. I have a few questions that need answering."

Neil turned to him with a cocked eyebrow and sneered, "You're not serious."

"I'm very serious." His bright green eyes narrowed while he accused him with confidence. "You thought you were slick, but I knew you would slip up. Ever been to club Solace? Don't bother lying because I know you have. Running around in a lion mask? You think you're some sort of Batman villain?"

"You need to leave," Neil warned and started toward him, "right now, before it gets dangerous. I don't have time to explain anything to you, but you need just to trust me. I'm a good guy. So just go!"

"Or what?" Rhion took an approaching step and aggressively waved his hands while he scoffed. "There's a lot of strange shit going on in this city, unexplained shit, shit that gets people killed. And I think, wait... I don't think; I *know* that you are involved. Fifteen eyewitnesses place you at a major crime scene! I caught you myself at another! Both me and my boss had some kind of weird memory loss when your cases were involved! Something really fucked up is going on with you, and I'm going to figure it all out. Neil, you're getting in the back of my car."

"Detective," Neil snarled, "it's about to get a lot more dangerous for you unless you leave right now. You're not getting me to go anywhere. And if you think you can force me, you're dumber than you look. I promise I can explain everything later; you just have to leave now."

Rhion reached into his pocket and whispered, "I thought you might feel that way."

The green-eyed cop whipped out a taser and fired. With a twist of his wrist, Neil sent the weapon across the room. A stupefied look splashed across the cop's face. Stunned, he reached for his gun, but it flung through the double doors behind him.

His penetrating eyes blazed with rage. Weaponless, Rhion charged at Neil.

Neil instantly regretted it, but he hurled his arm at the cop. The room shook, and Rhion flew. The blast of energy knocked his frail body through the church's front doors; it carried him across the steps, then finally through the windshield of his parked car. Neil locked the doors behind him and took a deep breath. There was no time to think. He initiated the spell. He forced his grip to loosen on the palm leaf labeled The Horseman of Strife, Neil started to light the candles.

The candles were lit and in place. Her fingers nervously danced on her thigh. Indignant, Aurora huffed and scribbled the name The Horseman of War onto her dehydrated palm leaf. She held the dry palm near her chest. Aurora read the spell aloud: "Of the nine burning bright."

"I seek the one causing blight," Ezekiel spoke the second line of the spell. A cloud rolled through the cemetery and an icy blanket of air wrapped around him. He continued the hex, "Born..."

"...of evil summoned here," Amanda uttered quickly. She looked over the abandoned mall vestibule again nervously. No signs of risen evil yet. Her knees wobbled, and her thighs clenched. She had to pee... again. A glimmer of light shone through a skylight of the shopping mall through an immense glass chandelier that hung above her. She needed a plan and possibly new underwear. Wearily, Amanda continued the words of the spell. "To..."

"...a heart and place so bare," Neil spoke. His entire body stiffened with anxiety. From his pocket, he drew three shiny Shuriken throwing stars. He held the metal stars between his fingers, prepared. He continued the spell, "Beseeching thee..."

"...in the circle of fire," Aurora's throat was dry. "The Horseman of War," her heart beat on every syllable.

Ezekiel took a step backward. The name of his adversary escaped his mouth: "The Horseman of Death!" Ezekiel tossed the light palm leaf into the circle. The leaf floated towards the ground and lit on fire.

"The Horseman of Hunger!" Amanda yelled as the leaf took flight into the air. It glided on a gentle gust until it hit the floor and exploded in flames.

"The Horseman..." Neil's fingertips caressed the sharp edges of the stars. "...of Strife!"

The flames atop the candles curved as if blown by the wind and linked together to form a thin circle of fire. It took a moment, but Pestilence finally faded in like a white ghost in his massive cape and ivory crown. The greasy-haired Horman smiled as he looked around the church. "Do you know how long we've been searching for this church?"

Neil grimaced at sight and readied the tiny metal stars in his pocket. He had to admit, he was slightly excited for this encounter. Feverishly he spat, "Time to repent."

With a shriek, the model's curls flew behind her from the small explosion. War spun his sword wildly around in the air. Adrenaline pumped rapidly through her veins, and Aurora felt the power rush into her eyes. Her almond irises reverted to red. She cast a white light over the Red Horseman and held him in time. However, he was too strong and pushed through her power after only a few moments.

"Yee-haw!" War shouted as he charged at her. "Looks like we filletin' angel wings tonight!"

The ashes burned, and Ezekiel watched them float into the red sky. From out of the fire stepped the Pale Horseman, the lion skin rug he wore like a robe draped over his shoulders, and he rolled his eyes as he lit his cigarette. The Horseman of Death took a moment to study his surroundings. "Why have you summoned me?" he asked mindfully.

"Take a wild guess," Ezekiel snapped.

"You're trying to stop my ride," Death supposed. "The next seal will kill a lot of people. More than we did on that bridge. The earthquake is gonna happen one way or another."

"Or I could be here to kill you," Ezekiel shrugged.

"Kill the Horseman of Death?" He didn't allow Ezekiel a chance to respond. Death charged at him, a scythe at hand. Before the blade touched his gut, Ezekiel's spirit shimmered out of existence and appeared back in his own body, hidden in the cemetery.

Amanda tried to keep her eyes open in the bright flame show. The Horseman of Hunger's raspy voice echoed, "A quart of wheat for a day's wages, and three quarts of barley for a day's wages, and do not damage the oil and the wine." As the massive mound of flesh crawled out of the fire he threatened, "I can't wait to know what an angel tastes like..."

"What does that even mean?" Amanda muttered bluntly to herself. The overweight shirtless man held his hand forward and revealed his weapon: a white pearl and marble scale with golden dishes on both sides.

"Heads up," Amanda smirked. The thick iron chains that held the magnificent chandelier melted into water. The chandelier fell from the ceiling and crashed into his body. The spray of glass twinkled as it met the floor. Shards flew hard enough to scrape Amanda's face and fling her to the ground. Amanda's big blues took in the monstrous sight: a shimmering rain on a black mountain.

Hunger was unfazed by the assault. He trotted toward her, the glass crunched underneath his feet. She jumped into the air frightfully when the right side of the marble scales plummeted downward.

The tiles beneath her snapped like glass plates with such force that it bruised her hands and arms. An impulse forced Amanda to her feet while another pipe broke under her foot.

Amanda focused on the scales and tried to transfix the weapon to dust, but both the Horseman and his weapon were too powerful to affect directly. Amanda bit her lower lip; she needed to escape. Her skin began to tingle, and her body started to change.

Flapping her brown and gray wings, she took to the air. Adjusting to new animal bodies and senses always took a moment for her. But she needed to move swiftly and fought through the disorienting change in eyesight. She flew as fast as she could muster over the Horseman and onto the second level of the mall. She landed there and, in white light, reverted to her human shape. Sheepishly she teased, "Catch me if you can."

The scales in Hunger's meaty claws shifted and advanced on the opposite end. Like a lizard, he crawled across the wall with full power over balance and physics.

Neil struggled to catch his breath after he dodged yet another arrow. He ducked behind a wooden pew. Where was the Horseman? Hesitantly, he raised his head over the bench. Before he could see anything, an arrow landed into the wood, and he withdrew into his rabbit hole. Neil reached an arm over the pew and grabbed the shaft out of the wood.

A trap.

It was like he grabbed a bomb. A hot tornado flung Neil through the air and smashed him through the bench and across the church floor. He was exposed, and his spine felt fractured. The Horseman of Strife stood ahead of him, in the front of the stage.

With a smile on his pale white face, he pulled back the string of his bow past his ear. If Neil ever hoped to kill the White Horseman, he needed to hit him with his own arrows.

The angel forced himself to stand, and the entire church shook as he summoned his power. Bulbs flickered and burst. Even the walls vibrated with horrifying intensity. With his hands at his sides, Neil mentally ripped three concrete tiles from the ground.

Neil's head pounded incessantly. Pestilence fired another arrow. Neil could hear the dart cut through the wind even though it was a while away. He reached out with his mind. A static mental web built itself around the church. The arrow stopped in mid-air only a few inches from his head.

He was injured but had to move on. Neil propelled his right hand forward.

For that split second, Neil's fever heightened, and his headache pounded heavier. The arrow raced through the air and the three russet tiles followed. With deadened accuracy, the Horseman was struck.

Pestilence dropped, and blood leaked over his clean, white robe. He didn't scream, didn't make a sound except for the thud that erupted when he collided with the floor. Neil rested shortly and regained his strength.

The air was thick and electric when Aurora used her temporal shifting abilities. She knew her power's limits, and she needed to work promptly. The steel blade was only a few inches away from her neck. Though the white light rose from him like steam, War's hold on his sword was firmer than ever. When she summoned all her energy, she pulled the weapon from him. The electricity in her lungs weakened, and the air began to thin.

Aurora swiped the sword into War's gut, the white cover faded, and her time spell lifted. The Red Horseman pulled out his blade—his dirty smile had changed to a decayed snarl. Aurora's feet numbed, but she ran faster than she ever had. He swung his weapon down and cut into her back. The blow sent Aurora spinning into the air.

Her body fell to the ground with a thump. Blood oozed from her like water from a faucet and she was blinded with pain. She could feel warm inside [of her sweatshirt spread.]awk phrasing Aurora squirmed in agony, then threw herself to her side.

Before the Horseman got to her, she shut her eyes and Aurora rewound time. In slow motion, War moved backward. Disappointed in her inability to rewind to a point where she was healed, Aurora pulled two pistols from her jacket and opened fire.

Death found Ezekiel behind a tombstone and swiped his curved knife at him. Missed. The Horseman swiped again and aimed for his head. Ezekiel blocked him with his wrists resting on his forehead as the scythe cut into the backs of his arms. Ezekiel winced but tried to ignore the pain as he scrambled away from the warrior in the oversized yellow fur.

The angel turned to run when the right side of his body sizzled up in hives. He yelped as he tumbled to the soil as a dry burning rash covered his skin. Ezekiel lifted his shirt to see if he were on fire but revealed nothing but irritated, red boils. Confused, Ezekiel gasped as the Yellow Horseman laughed.

"Shingles," Death shrugged, and Ezekiel winced in pain. "Oh, you didn't think this was all I was equipped with, did you? It's a shame we couldn't work together. Our powers both revolving around death and all…"

"N-no," Ezekiel mustered through his teeth, "you're evil..."

"Evil is such a relative word… Most people run away from it," Death twirled his scythe in a circle as he explained. "But ever since I was a little boy I've always just thought, 'It's all just fun and games'. A little bleach in a water bottle, a cigarette in your puppy's eye who cares? Why does everyone have to be so sensitive? We're all going to die anyway."

Ezekiel released a clumsy death wave as the Yellow Horseman kicked him in the torso and continued, "Or perhaps, maybe, I'm just a really terrible person."

Death pointed his arched fingers at Ezekiel and threatened, "Now let's see what we can do about those hands. Ever try sickle cell disease?"

Hunger was thousands of years old, how could this young one escape him? He trod closer to a fountain in the heart of the mall. In the center of this fountain stood four statues; each was a woman dressed in a long gown. One held a string of yarn in her hands, two carried scissors, and the final figure grasped a large pot, letting water pour into the pool around them. Hunger cringed with annoyance. A scrap of pink clothing lay across the statue of the woman holding the yarn. Though he wasn't a hunter, he knew the apparent signs of a passing human being.

"Come out, come out wherever you are? I promise I only want one bite." Hunger waddled through the empty mall with his ivory scales at hand. He could not see Amanda, but he could undoubtedly smell her sweet, briny skin. Finding her was easy.

Hidden underneath the water fountain in the center of the room, Amanda's overalls were quickly soaked. When he approached, Amanda slapped the surface of the water. She gritted her teeth in deep concentration, and the water turned to ice. Her stomach tightened as the entire pool froze over and bound the heavyset demon.

Hunger giggled, and the scales tipped. The ice exploded beneath her like detonating mines under a frozen lake. Amanda's skin began to crawl. Her stomach muscles tensed. Organs moved. Bones adjusted. She was a duck again. She took flight, but the Black Horseman was too quick, he grabbed her thin leg right out of the air and slammed her onto the ice floor.

Amanda's body slowly changed. Her feathers turned to cloth, and her webbed feet morphed into toes. Her body felt numb as blood dripped from the back of her head. The scales tipped again. She felt her heartbeat slower. With every beat, she could feel her life slip until only remaining conscious became a battle for her.

Amanda was dying. She could feel it, taste it in her mouth. She trembled, but she had to live on. There was so much she still had to do, so much she desired. What about Henry? And her unborn children? Amanda fisted her hands. Hunger was not going to rip her future away from her.

The Black Horseman stood before her and waited for her to die. He felt her heart slowing and laughed. Amanda pulled so much power from her abdomen it felt as though she were being torn apart.

Hunger was set aflame.

She jumped upwards and distanced herself feet from the flaming Horseman. The marble scales fell to the ground with a thud. His scream was a blood cry as he swiped at his engulfed black pants.

Amanda slid across the ground and picked up the scales. They were more substantial than they looked. How do I use this thing? She asked herself, but she didn't have time to think or time to breathe before Hunger rushed at her.

Neil felt an arrow rip through the invisible web he formed. He turned and threw his hand, redirecting the arrow into the wall beside, causing it to explode upon impact. Pieces of concrete and plaster threw Neil off his feet and across the front pew.

Pestilence's aim was frighteningly accurate. Neil fell in and out of blindness. He was never this afraid, but there was no time for fear or thoughts. He retreated to a calm place deep in his mind and let intuition take over.

Another arrow flew. Neil deflected it into the floor this time. The floor burst, throwing him several feet back. The skin flapped off his forehead, and his clothes were soiled with debris.

Arrows flew at him. With one arm, Neil sent an arrow astray and felt the impact of the explosion. With the other arm, he averted a second arrow, but the final bolt struck him right in the chest. The collision tossed him through the air, then pinned him to the wall. Neil reached out in agony as if to reassure himself; he was still alive. His limbs throbbed in and out of numbness, and he tried to comprehend the moment. One by one, his senses escaped him. The unholy arrow elongated, and like a spear, it extended into the wall.

Neil was paralyzed.

All he could feel was the hot, sharp weapon in his chest. His skin was broken, his muscles were torn, his blood vessels were severed, and his lung was punctured. He could barely speak or breathe as blood seeped through the shirt and dripped onto the floor.

His dangling body quivered uncontrollably in pain. He has never been this close to death before. Sizzling tears collected with dirt and sweat as they raced down his cheeks. Finally, he could think again. He was about to die. After everything, he thought, This is all there is?

Pestilence walked out of the shadows, his bow and arrow lowered at his side, his white robe now partially red with blood. "You have to give yourself credit," he started. "No one ever made me bleed before."

Blood spilled from Neil's mouth.

"I'll make sure you get a nice place in Hell," the White Horseman added. "The question is, though, which Hell do I throw you in?"

Neil choked. He closed his lips and let the blood in his mouth fill; then, he spat it into the demon's face. Neil struggled to speak, "F-f-f" he paused for a beat then summoned the strength in his body, "Fuck you!"

Pestilence smirked slightly through his stained teeth. "I think the first thing I'm going to do is eat the soul of your mother. She's dead, right? You lost, Cherubim of the Church."

Neil felt his death now. He could hear the church bells ring in his head. Death was obligatory, but as he always did when he knew he was going to lose, he decided to go out with a bang.

    He mustered up power from every living cell in his system. Again his body trembled. Tiny ink spots appeared in his irises and expanded until his eyes resembled coals. Black-purple and gold rays of light burst from his back and twisted like paint splashing in water. Neil's eyebrows arched with rage as he released an ear-splitting roar. Intense invisible waves of energy radiated off him, and the White Horseman took an unnerved step back.

    The Horseman fired a desperate arrow.

    Neil wrinkled his brow in savage ferocity, and the weapon rushed back towards its owner and nailed Pestilence in the chest. Neil's massive light wings flapped with might then suddenly dimmed. He fell on the floor into a pool of his own blood.

    Aurora repeatedly released rounds into War. Riddled with bullets, he dropped. She trembled in uncertainty but knew she had no time to spare. Aurora stumbled to his fallen body as claps of thunder tumbled through the sky. It started to rain.

    She wiped the water from her eyes just as the demon sliced into her side. Red liquid dripped down her legs. She tensed every muscle in her body and summoned her power. War looked at her menacingly but frozen inside the white light.

His grip was firm, but she managed to get the sword from him again. Her wound bled openly, she struggled to lift the heavy blade above her head. It was now or never. Then like a lightning bolt, it struck her.

Blood caked the streets of Times Square, thick as mud. People ran the grounds like craven dogs, gnawing, and killing each other. Ferocious horned demons trapped them in metal cages, and burned them alive. Families were ripped apart and ran the streets in desolate horror. Children were used to feed demon dogs while others were desecrated.

Skyscrapers were demolished, and massive Egyptian pyramids stood in their places. Bloody chaos crashed through the streets as humans struggled. Naked and in barbed chains and auctioned off to a monstrous audience. Crowds of demons howled, cheered, and fought each other in drunken celebration. Harpies tore through the poisonous black clouds and shrieked. They fought over remains, hunted and grabbed anyone they could carry.

Aurora instantly recognized this vision; it was the first one she ever had. She never had a repeat of a vision before. She brought the sword down across the demon's neck in emotional defeat. Did this mean she had changed nothing? Was the End of Days still on its way?

Before Ezekiel reached the Horseman, he was slammed with the butt of a scythe. Death rushed up to Ezekiel before he fell, and grabbed his throat. His eyes were void of color and matched only the paleness of the skin on top of his forehead. Death's fingers clenched around Ezekiel's throat even tighter, slammed him against a mausoleum.

Ezekiel's fingers clawed at the stone wall behind him. Ghostly figures appeared around Ezekiel and swirled in an eddy of white transparent ectoplasm. Ezekiel's throat hurt like he had been screaming for hours, and he could feel his body begin to pass out. However, the Horseman wasn't dead yet, and Neil counted on him.

As the Horseman was distracted with the swirling spirits Ezekiel astral-projected from his body as it fell into the mud. He floated across the dirt and concentrated on grasping the scythe. His nervousness boiled up inside him, even as a ghost, but he eventually took hold of the heavy weapon. Ezekiel recklessly swung it. He ripped through the demon's yellow robe and hacked until the scythe was covered in red.

"Die, you bastard!" Ezekiel screamed, and his side ached with even more pain.

Amanda looked back at the charging Horseman and curled her fingers with precision and precise accuracy. This transformation was new to her, and she refused to mess it up. The extinguished fire steamed off him while ice froze him over in suspended animation.

Amanda blinked at the pair of marble scales. Unsure of how to use them as a weapon, she thrashed forward. With the butt of the scales, she cracked open Hunger's skull. Pieces of red ice resembled melting cherry snow cones as they showered the concrete. Was this enough to kill him? Did she use the weapon in the right way?

Amanda stood before a broken neck and body, fell to her knees. She closed her eyes but still, water fell from them. Slowly, she dropped the scales and heard the heavy clang on the floor.

Her throat hurt, and it was hard to swallow. It was a painful gulp, but reality rushed in like a river by the end of it.

"Ahhhh!" Amanda let out a prolonged and suppressed shriek. She was both physically and mentally drained. Her scream lasted longer than she realized, and her body was left shaking with an unknown emotion. All her negative pent up emotions released from her. Fear. Hatred. Disappointment. Loneliness. They all forced themselves out in an outrageous battle cry, "I win! I did it! I did it! I saved the world! Go me!"

The wounded angel struggled to dance through the pain and sing, "It's my birthday! Well, not really! But now it will be... in a couple of months! Cause the world's saved! And I could get married! And have a baby! Hoot!"

Cracking concrete sizzled through the air. Distracted from her celebration, Amanda glanced toward the Horseman's headless body, and it had turned stone. Even the red ice on the ground was now gray pebbles scattered across the floor.

The earth underneath her rumbled. Amanda looked toward the vibrating marble scales. She took a few steps backward as the ivory scales began to glow in yellow light. Hunger's stone body detonated. A thick black smoke erupted from the broken statue in two snake-like shapes. For a moment they danced harmlessly in the air.

Then the smog attacked.

As the short bow shone in its great black light, the White Horseman's stone body cracked. Through the small cracks, black smoke escaped. The pain had stopped, and Neil felt his last breath escaping as the smoke formed itself into two black tendrils. The gaseous serpents shot eagerly from Pestilence's wound and up into Neil's nose.

Aurora swiped at the black smoke as it entered her lungs, but the dark air continued its course into her body. She turned to run, but the smoke extended its reach from the Horseman's neck and followed. She scratched at her hands and arms. From her fingertips, black arcane writing ran up her skin. It was strange but somehow familiar. Boxy symbols made of sharp geometric shapes and alien lines covered her flesh in moving black tattoos. Her skin burned as the symbols moved around her body and she itched feverously. She was sure she saw this language before, carved into Lyssah Rhamiel. Was it Enochian?

Epilogue

> "It is I, John, who heard and saw these things, and when I heard and saw them, I fell down to worship at the feet of the angel who showed them to me."
> **Revelation 22:8**

Ezekiel was suffocating. The force of the smoke wouldn't allow air in. Entire scriptures of strange language ran up his skin to his head. Ezekiel screamed, and drops of rain entered his mouth. He thought he won, but Death was still attacking?

He knew he was too weak to take on a Horseman of the Apocalypse. Why did he let Neil convince him he was strong? Filled with regret, he clasped his burning neck. Despairingly the Angel of Death waited to die.

As he hyperventilated on the ground his senses started to wane, but over a rumbling utterance, he could hear someone singing. "'Who has seen a beautiful lady, being led by the dead?'" The Hallowed One appeared from the shadows. He was a frail man and used a long walking stick to balance himself as he approached the angel. He tipped his Amish hat and continued, "Did you hear, my Constantine, what the little birds have said? They are little birds; let them sing. There are little birds, prayers on wing.'"

"W-who are you?" Ezekiel muttered.

"Ah yes, this is our first meeting in this lifetime," the Hallowed One announced. "You see, you, Mors and I... we are very closely related, as Angels of Death, one might say we are connected. I've been called many names on Earth, commonly renowned as the Lord of the Underworld."

"Are you here to take me to Hell?" Ezekiel resisted, having already visited the dark place once.

"On the contrary my son," Hades explained. "You are about to embark on an incredible journey all four of you are. But you, you're different from your brothers and sisters. Angels of Death tend to be."

"So what do you want?" Ezekiel mustered.

"Insurance," the Hallowed One declared as he shoved the silver end of his cane into Ezekiel's open wound. "With the consecration I plant inside you a fail-safe. You can't trust everyone nowadays you know..."

Ezekiel heaved in pain but managed to ask, "F-f-fail-safe?"

"Surrender your flesh," he warned as the angel faded in and out of consciousness, "leave your body when the time is right and your brother shall be there to protect you, honor me, and rain down healthy vengeance on deceivers..."

Neil quivered on the wall of the church as the arrow slowly pushed itself out. Within seconds the injury around it completely healed. A gentle wind brushed across Neil's face; his body was lifted off the floor. He was blind for a moment. Confusion and disbelief rattled his bones. His body was a tool for something uncompromising.

When the blindness waned, he found himself floating in the center of the church.

So I am dead... Neil clenched his fist in fear but turned to see Aurora, Ezekiel, and Amanda hovering around him. Each of them looked confused and dismayed. The only time they floated this way was when they had become the Alpha Omega: Four angels born as men.

They were petrified then, yet underlying tranquility reminded them they were loved, a peaceful certainty of something benevolent. This time, however, something was drastically different. Chalky staleness boiled around their tongues. All at once, they were filled with an unyielding sorrow. They covered their faces and wept in overwhelming shame.

Each angel was empty—void of God's love and spirit.

The difference was both emotional and physical, like being torn apart from the inside: To be unloved. Unworthy. Ripped from the Holy light.

Their entire world felt as though it were imploding. All their worst fears and emotional pains surfaced at once, crashed in on their minds, and overpowered them. Shame and dishonor awakened long lost terrors and anxieties. Their stomachs ran up in knots, and nausea almost caused them to vomit.

Hopelessness.

They floated and desperately grabbed at their hair and clothes. Even their very skin itched until it burned with shame and self-hatred. An overload of emotions took over, and they sobbed hysterically as they struggled to process reality.

This is how it felt to fall from grace.

To be continued...

About the Author:

La'Von Gittens was born on May 7th, 1987 in Florida. He was raised in Brooklyn, New York, where he grew up with interest in writing. He wrote little illustrated novels throughout primary school, but his knack for fantasy literature followed him into high school, where he began to write his first novel, *Divine Apocalypse*.

Unable to get published and recognized because of his lack of experience and age, he honed his craft throughout college, where he created his own company, NoV'al Publishing. The goal of his company is to focus on and believe in new authors.

Divinely Apocalypse: The Beginning of the End is the first novel in a series and the first of many delights from this bright young author. Make sure to visit his website at www.novalpublishing.com for details.

Printed by Libri Plureos GmbH in Hamburg, Germany